M000222799

PRAISE FOR BOOKS BY LEO LITWAK

Nobody's Baby

Long after reading these stories, I find myself feeling for everybody—Lorrie, Paula, Shirley and Wesley, Alice and her son Emory, Heartless Willy. The people in Leo Litwak's fine stories make the reader laugh and cry. *Nobody's Baby* is at once fun and tragic. A most satisfying book.

MAXINE HONG KINGSTON, author of *The Fifth Book of Peace*

Leo Litwak has followed his great World War II memoir, *The Medic*, with an extraordinary collection of short stories. *Nobody's Baby* is the work of an artist of deep compassion and insight, equipped with an impeccable control of storytelling craft. With these resources he probes human behavior, values, and spirit in ways that bring his stories affectingly to life. This is important fiction, fiction of the first rank. The final tale, "Heartless Willie," can stand with the most moving short stories of our time.

LEONARD GARDNER, author of *Fat City*

His terse stories build to an explosive pressure point—and the characters escape, transform, or make a motion toward grace.

FRANCES MAYES, author of *Under the Tuscan Sun*

Nobody's Baby is full of what wakes you up in the night—life, not made-up monsters. Litwak says it himself: "With a point of view always on the bias toward irony," he is "possessed by the illusion that the issue of life is pleasure." The bad seed holes up with his mom in her retirement, Heartless Willy survives a pogrom, a patient tries to strangle his doctor and recovers. A deft writer and a wonderful read.

TERESE SVOBODA, author of *Trailer Girl and Other Stories*

Here are eight stories about "ecstatic, ferocious, incandescent, dangerous" characters, many of them frankly mad, who force their more ordinary fathers, mothers, daughters, and students into the difficult acceptance of love. Litwak writes with an intimate, commanding cadence that compels attention. These are stories you will not only read, but hear in your heart for years after.

MOLLY GILES, author of *Iron Shoes: A Novel*

Leo Litwak's stories are expert, funny, alive, full of quiet fury. *Nobody's Baby* reveals Litwak's talent for mourning the loss of feeling and affection in our own mad America, where philosophers live in palaces and waltz around with a bent back.

JEROME CHARYN, author of *Bronx Boy: A Memoir*

Leo Litwak's stories are sharp, subtle, surprising, and wonderfully true to life.

LYNN FREED, author of *The Curse of the Appropriate Man*

Leo Litwak's stories are painful, sometimes funny, and always affecting. They delineate wayward lives, inappropriate behavior, the impossible requirements of love. They will deftly, almost imperceptibly, hook you—and then they will not let you go.

KIM ADDONIZIO, author of *Tell Me* and *Little Beauties*

A master chronicler of domestic pain, Leo Litwak brings to his stories a kindly spirit and a mind that pierces every excuse we give for failing one another. In less gifted hands, some of his characters might seem monsters of self-absorption; in Litwak's they are tortured souls—awful, to be sure, but inescapably human, and with implacable claims. Those who find the claims compelling—sons, mothers, neighbors, husbands, wives—twist in their suffocating traps: can they flee or must they stay? And with spare, incisive prose Litwak makes us bleed for human anguish.

CELIA MORRIS, author of *Finding Celia's Place*

It was a pleasure to read open-ended, formally beautiful modern fictions with all the old pull of sheer story. Whereas many of us write the same narratives over and over and reuse ourselves disguised as different protagonists, each Litwak story requires the reader to get in touch with, and get on the inside of, new people in settings that are able to surprise. What these characters have heartbreakingly in common is their search for a consoling or redeeming love without which they will not be able to live out their own fates, fates that are worth being lived. We can give ourselves to these stories because they are trustworthy—don't reach for the purple, or special effects. The prose, like Kafka's, has an achieved plainness that puts one foot before the other on the march toward conclusions that are really appointments with the old beginnings. The stories had this reader in such thrall that I found myself wanting to believe, against my better knowledge, that these new acquaintances, these new neighbors of mine might have found new beginnings.

LORE SEGAL, author of *Other People's Houses*

Whether writing about an emotionally entangled sportswriter or spectators, artists or academics, therapy or theater, Upper Peninsula Michigan or downtown San Francisco, Leo Litwak inevitably explores love and the infinite yet specific way it always matters in shadow and light. Whatever the voice, whatever the catch, whatever the moment upon which a story turns, he bears dramatic witness. Delivering all the feeling, color and well-told detail any reader needs to jump from one body or one heart into another, his kinetic, prose-cinematic stories speak directly to the angel-and-demon resident in each of us.

AL YOUNG, author of *The Sound of Dreams Remembered*

Leo Litwak writes with wonderful grace, economy, and wit. His stories have a look of permanence and are a sheer pleasure to read.

BILL BARICH, author of *Carson Valley*

I've long admired Leo Litwak as a novelist and memoirist. This book demonstrates that he's also a master of the short story, tender, funny, and wise.

CYRA MCFADDEN, author of *The Serial*

Deeply serious in their engagement, Leo Litwak's stories paradoxically attain a high level of the best kind of wit, that is: precision, concision, an exact naming of reality. The struggle to go deep into the reality of our lives is rarely so engaging. Litwak is one of the best writers of our time.

HERBERT GOLD, author of *Daughter Mine*

Leo Litwak's admirable stories of love and desperation are exciting, intense, and troubling.

OAKLEY HALL, author of *Ambrose Bierce and the Tray of Pearls*

Leo Litwak, the author of the finest memoir of WWII combat I've read by an American, *The Medic,* again demonstrates his superb gift for narrative in this astonishing collection of short stories, *Nobody's Baby.* His insights into the complex motives of human behavior and the effects we have on each other feel utterly true. In these largely urban stories, Litwak presents us with a fascinating collection of characters, people largely under stress, people with the ordinary daily courage to endure because they must. He can be outrageously comic in stories that finally make you weep. The prose moves with that necessity we associate with true poetry. It is so rare to encounter such mastery and such humility in the same book.

> PHILLIP LEVINE, *Ploughshares*

The Medic

A Barnes and Noble Discover Book 2001
Los Angeles Times Books of the Year 2001
San Francisco Chronicle Books of the Year 2001

A book that should be given to every schoolboy in the country at the age of thirteen... *The Medic*, which teaches us so much, makes clear that sometimes the monsters in war are not only the enemy.

> GLORIA EMERSON, *Los Angeles Times*

Spare...strong and vivid.

> *The Denver Post*

Litwak's lively and compassionate sharing of his stories brings the reader right to his side on the battlefield, on leave in Paris, and through his extraordinary journey as he encounters a recently liberated slave labor camp.

Depictions of friends and comrades-in-arms are all vividly brought to life as we are given glimpses of the last days of the Reich in a small corner of Germany. *The Medic* is an honest and powerful rendering of a moment that reflected both the best—and the worst—of what encompasses and motivates the human spirit.

> ELENA SIMON, *The Barnes & Noble Review*

Litwak's tough-minded narrative portrays war's peculiar customs with compelling honesty and wry humor.

> *Publishers Weekly*

Litwak, who served as a medic in World War II, is a novelist, and he currently teaches English literature at San Francisco State University. ...this brutal and yet frequently uplifting saga of war has the ring of authenticity. There are no "good guys" or "bad guys" here, although the presence of both good and evil is constant. Instead, we witness ordinary men, most of them quite young, striving to survive a conflict that few of them understand. This is a disturbing, revealing, and very important glimpse of warfare at the most elementary level.

JAY FREEMAN, *Booklist*

A terse, vivid, occasionally funny, quietly ironic, often brutal narrative... An unflinching portrait of the times.

Kirkus Reviews

Litwak punctures easy pieties, and his brief but important book speaks to us with all the authority of letters from a father long gone.

DAVID KIPEN, *San Francisco Chronicle*

Waiting for the News
Winner of the Jewish Book Council Award 1970
Winner of the Edward Louis Wallant Award 1970

Leo Litwak has written a vigorous and arresting novel about lower-class people—both proletarian and *lumpen*—in Detroit during the 1930s and 1940s. He has broken into an area of life few American novelists even notice, and he has done this with sympathy, detachment, and force. His main character, Jake Gottlieb, is a rough-and-tumble, marvelously strong figure, a leader in the drive toward unionization, a Jew with fighting blood and also something of a charming braggart. He is a superb characterization, full of juice and energy—a rarity in modern fiction, a deeply credible man of goodness.

IRVING HOWE, *Harper's Magazine*

HOME FOR SALE

× × × × × × × × × × × ×

Leo Litwak

EL LEÓN LITERARY ARTS

Berkeley, California

Home for Sale is published by El León Literary Arts and
distributed by Small Press Distribution, Inc.

Previously published parts of this book:
"In the Mood, a Prologue and Finale," in *Mānoa: A Pacific
Journal of International Writing*

El León Literary Arts is a private foundation established to
extend the array of voices essential to a democracy's arts
and education.

Publisher: Thomas Farber
Managing editor: Kit Duane
Cover designer: Andrea Young
Book designer: Sara Glaser

For sales information contact:
Small Press Distribution
1341 Seventh Street
Berkeley, CA 94710
www.spdbooks.org

El León books are available on Amazon.com
El León website: www.elleonliteraryarts.org

ISBN 978-0-9833919-3-7
LCCN 2011937317

To Friends and Brothers:
Herbert Gold and Eugene Litwak

CONTENTS

In The Mood

Mom said to me, "Dad isn't feeling well. He didn't sleep last night."

I heard the pacing. The boards squeaked. He moved from bathroom to kitchen. He set off the dismal pipes that girdled our walls.

But he looked good to me in the morning. No evidence of hard nights.

Eyes wide open, even though shadowed. On his feet, talking. He'd already finished the newspaper. He celebrated his heroes—Ted Williams, finishing a big season; FDR, warning the Japanese not to push us in the Pacific; John L. Lewis, demanding a living wage for coal miners.

He should have been down opening the store, but he was having a great time releasing the voices that had raced in his head all night. He swayed back on his heels, his arms swinging free, his head pulled back for laughs, the big Adam's apple bobbing.

Mom said, "Time to open up. Delivery men due at seven, Eph."

He said to us, eyes glittering, the swarthy face illuminated, "I wait to be delivered," an explosion of laughter. "The day comes," he said, "when I shall be elevated to my station and its duties. Meanwhile,"—he bowed to Mom—"the grocery, my dear Ruth."

She warned me, "It's going to change. Don't be disappointed. Enjoy him while he's in the mood."

She called it "being in the mood." I knew what she meant and resented her not speaking plainly.

When I left for school he was outside on the walk, ushering customers into the store. Mom later came down to take over the register and check the orders. While in the mood, he was too exalted to tend to business and messed up the charge book and botched the orders.

At the same time he was full of joy and invention. He lit up, his mouth supple, his smile flowering, the extravagant beaked nose somehow appropriate to the spirit of the brimming eyes. He looked skinny but he had a powerful grip.

He claimed to be preparing a history of the Smiths. It was time, he said, we made ourselves known. We were a remarkable people. Ancient, he said. And then giving up his apparent seriousness, he worked out a genealogy that led to Homer and Ancient Greece. He derived Smith from Zeus, the "Z" speeding up and collapsing into "Sm" by a rule he called the "Smith sibilant," the "eu" losing its voice when the tongue slackened in grief at our fall and idled on the floor of the mouth, barely managing the almost mute "i" of Smith. He called that process the "Smith elision." He found permutations of our name in the lists of Trojans. He appeared again in the *Aeneid*. The joke was elaborated; it went on and on, and when it seemed as if he were stuck in the posture of a clown, he changed tone and there he was, again the true believer.

Mom insisted on straightening me out. We had no history. We were anonymous. There was no trace of us in any book. We had no one to mourn, nothing to recall. They were both born in Chicago. Her family was wiped out in the flu epidemic of 1918. His family had drifted out of sight. That was the true Smith elision.

She wanted to prepare me for the shift in mood when he was no longer a source of energy and pleasure. He would begin drawing everything back into himself, leaching the air of joy, sucking us into his abysmal suspicions.

When he finally peaked and was looking down, bound to his rock by a spiderweb conspiracy, he could trace any event to cosmic origins.

I knew these matters better than she did. She spoke her warnings to arm herself against vain hope. She received no profit from his exaltation.

At the end of summer he took me to Boston to see the Boston Red Sox and Ted Williams. We stood above the dugout after the ball game among the crowd greeting Williams, and Dad called out, "Mr. Williams! Congratulations, Sir! You have had a magnificent season! You have given us all great pleasure!" Williams was impressed by the regal tone and stretched over the dugout to shake Dad's hand. Dad said, "I brought my son from Syracuse, New York, to witness this memorable occasion." We were invited to the locker room. The rarely gracious Williams autographed a ball for me, confessed to Dad that this had been for him a magical season. Bat and ball and arm and heart and eye and the field were all linked, and almost every time at bat was a perfect realization. He confessed he'd never talked like this before. "You pushed my button, Ephraim. You've got a way with words."

Dad heard the news of Pearl Harbor on our Philco. The next day he put on his doughboy outfit. I hadn't known he'd been a soldier.

1917 to 1919.

He meant to enlist on the spot.

Mom asked, "Who'll take care of the store?"

"It's war, Ruth!"

She appealed to his fatherly obligations, but he couldn't be stopped. She told me to go along. I found him in the Ford, ready to take off.

"There'll be time later for goodbyes, son." It was a tremendous opportunity for him. He would make his way through Officer Candidate School and rise to the top. We would be stationed in California, quartered near the ocean. Friday night dances at the Officers' Club, partying in Hollywood. It was a joke and not a joke, and I couldn't decipher what was serious in his understanding.

I joined Mom upstairs.

"He'd leave me with the store if he could. It's not fair."

It wasn't fair. She looked older than Dad, though he had a ten-year advantage. While he was in the mood, she was aged by anxiety, scrambling to be ahead of him or behind, wherever the obstacle might appear, clearing the path, trying to prolong his season of joy—her season of grief—knowing any event might be the trigger for his transformation. She was the keeper—so she supposed—of the monster—so she imagined him. His bleak time was better for her. Once he was down, she knew where to find him—hiding behind a newspaper in the store, sitting for hours at the kitchen table. She didn't have to fear cunning stories, extravagant orders, wrong entries, offended customers.

He was rejected out of hand by the army and he returned home subdued.

Mom insisted that we close the store and take a drive into the countryside while it was still light. We passed denuded apple orchards, cornfields with dead stalks skewed by weather, grazing animals, wonderful barns, groves of willow that traced streams.

"What kind of cows are they, Eph?"

"Guernsey." Perhaps they were.

In our '39 Ford, springs bouncing at a steady forty miles an hour clip, we were together and yet parted. He was off on a journey we couldn't share. Mom prodded him to answer her questions. He answered grudgingly. Then we passed an enormous oak. Blackbirds had settled on every twig. Dad said—it came from nowhere—"*Les oiseaux du bois.*"

Mom asked, "What?"

"Birds of the wood."

"But what did you say?"

He'd picked up French during the war.

I asked him if he'd seen men die. He told me in a documentary voice, not his flamboyant "in the mood" manner, that he'd been at Chateau Thierry and Belleau Woods. He was an engineer. He dug trenches. He crept on his belly through no-man's land. He laid pipesful of dynamite beneath coils of barbed wire and wiggled away fast while the fuse burned. I recall his experience as vividly as if it were an old movie I'd seen.

Mom was surprised that he could speak French. He'd never spoken French to her. She was puzzled by the sober tone of his revelations. Where had he learned French?

From a nurse in a Paris hospital named Katya.

What was he doing in a Paris hospital? Her questioning was sharp now.

"You know. When I was gassed. Chlorine in the lungs," he explained to me.

"What kind of name is Katya?"

"She was a Russian. Her people were chased out by the Bolsheviks."

"Oh, come on!" She tried to egg him into his ordinary flamboyance so she could deny his invention.

"She worked for a princess."

"Eph, she was telling you a story."

"Maybe. It was a long time ago." She asked him to speak more French and he spoke the words of a song.

"A quoi bon entendre
les oiseaux du bois?
L' oiseau la plus tendre
Chante dans ton voix."

"Why listen to the birds of the wood? The sweetest bird sings in your voice."

Was she pretty?

Who remembered?

Was she young?

Who wasn't?

"Well, I can see," she said, "that you're not in the mood."

The army had rejected him because of his age. He was forty-five years old.

"War's for the young, Eph."

"I had to tell them I was in a crazy house."

She said that was more than twenty years ago.

"Nothing's changed."

Well, she said. Their loss was our gain. Maybe he wasn't indispensable to the war effort, but the Smiths sure needed him.

She told me later that he had never belonged in an asylum. "It was after the war. He was gassed. It was the first time he got in the mood. His folks didn't know what was happening. They sent him to the Michigan State Asylum in Pontiac, called Eloise. He was there for a few weeks and then he came out of it like you know he does. We were going together and I told him it didn't bother me he was at Eloise. High or low, he was my man, and they had no right to send him to Eloise. What you and I know," she said to me, as conspiratorial for a moment as he had ever been, "is that your dad is someone special. He is not your ordinary grocer. And we Smiths," she said, "are not ordinary people." When it came down to the final judgment, crazy man or eccentric genius, she chose the second alternative. "It was a tragedy they sent him to Eloise."

He didn't at first seem disturbed by the rebuff. He started out joking. These were army doctors. Peacetime medics. Professional army cadre. Did I know what that meant? Incompetents who couldn't make a go of it in civilian life. Butchers. Literally headshrinkers. Recruited from the Amazon to establish an armed service that would preserve their incompetence. Willing to go to any length to disguise their appalling lack of skill. The old boy network. The issue wasn't for them to defeat the Nips or the Krauts. In fact, they were closer to their confreres overseas than they were to the Americans. We really didn't need a League of Nations. We already had working a coherent international network of military establishments totally indifferent to political ideologies, more alien to civilian traditions than to their commonly shared outpost experience. British, French, Russian, German, Japanese, American, it made no difference. Officers' rations, officers' quarters, officers' prerogatives—they would choose whatever armies were necessary to guarantee these. And that was the reason, he said, for the judgment against age and uniqueness—against any eccentricity that might jeopardize the docile acceptance of their authority. It was people like that who had shoved him into Eloise.

"Yes, Dad."

Mom hoped she could stop him now while there was still a trace of humor in his invention.

"You're right, Eph," she said. "But I'm sure they mean well. It's not deliberate."

"Ah," he said. "My own Pollyanna. She sees no evil. Wonderful woman. Great hearted. Perfectly suited to a corner grocery in Syracuse, New York. The very center of the world. A marvelous vantage point for deciphering the code of the universe."

The change had happened. He wouldn't sleep, he wouldn't eat. He began to feed on himself. He was tireless, the eyes huge. His inventions were embellished, the narrative became richer every day. He was caught in the flow of it. It invented him and us and the world. His narrative absorbed creation and advanced forward to ultimate judgment and redemption. Himself growing in divinity, food unnecessary, his excitement enormous. It was too much for Mom. She was overwhelmed by the assault on her own point of view. Her own loosely strung disconnected narrative was undermined. She struggled against the tyranny of his story. If she found holes, he immediately filled them. His premises were powerful and fecund and generated the world, and he was as excited as Newton or Einstein on the trail of universal law.

The army doctors were part of an international cabal. He dispensed with the multiplicity of parties in favor of one—a ruling party that created all others, and either ruthlessly eliminated any independent observer who might decipher the true order or else co-opted him into the fraternity.

Did she fear she'd have a fight on her hands keeping him out of the crazy house? She bought his story at a deeper level than I imagined, as though she agreed there was an all-powerful authority that scanned the universe for inassimilable points of view. What grieved her wasn't merely Dad's outrageous story, but that he exposed himself and she had to assume the burden of defending him. Each day when I returned from school, he had me listen while he enlarged his narrative.

Once, while he was in the john, she whispered fast. Did I believe him? He had everything tied together. But things weren't together. I understood that, didn't I? She whispered, "No one had it in for him. He's too old for the army. Eloise is a fact. The army doctors aren't in league to oppress him. Do you know that?"

I told her not to worry.

Dad came out of the john and asked why we'd been whispering. She denied we'd been whispering.

He said, "Don't you know I hear everything, Ruth? Before you speak I hear what you say. I can hear the noisy machinery of your brain trying to turn the boy against me."

She denied it. It wasn't fair. She was his closest friend. How could he refuse to trust her? Couldn't she even speak to her own son without risking his suspicions?

He was triumphant. "Then you WERE whispering!"

I said to him, "Mom thinks you're tying things together that don't belong."

He told her, "That's what you should have admitted."

I told him that Mom was tired.

"Of course she's tired. She wears herself out fighting me."

The next day when I came home from school the store was closed. They were upstairs and he was in his doughboy outfit, a rifle in his lap. Mom, just about cracked, said I had to stop him. "He's going to the Armory!" He sat calmly in the armchair, working the bolt of the Springfield .30 caliber rifle, a spilled box of cartridges in his lap.

I told him, "That rifle is pitiful, Dad. They got tanks and airplanes. They got a million soldiers in New York and New Jersey."

"It doesn't matter. I want to go out like a man."

I asked if he wanted me to go out with him. I could get a knife.

"All right. Get your knife."

I went into the kitchen and returned with a ridiculous bread knife, trying to stall him, hoping his mood would collapse.

The uniform smelled of camphor. The jacket strained at his chest.

I offered to carry the gun.

"Not on your life."

She followed us downstairs to the car and begged him not to go. "So what if they don't want you in the army? What would you be fighting for anyway?"

"Better to go like this, snatching for glory, than to smother in the dead air of a dying grocery."

"What glory?"

"The glory of being a man." He climbed into the driver's seat, put the rifle on the floor. I climbed in alongside.

"I'll call the police!"

"I don't care whether it's the police or the army, Ruth. It's too late."

I asked him what we were dying for.

"I named you," he said, "after Eugene Victor Debs, who was a martyr of the working class. He opposed war. He was a man of peace. I, too, was a man of peace. I wanted to organize the workers. I believed in a new Eden."

I asked what new Eden.

"The New Eden here." He struck his chest. "Here," he pointed to his head. "Here," he touched his genitals. "Not a goddamn grocery store." There was a better world than this one. This world was hopelessly fragmented into two billion parts and could never be made one. Who was ready to give up his minute sovereignty? "Only Ephraim Smith. I give up."

When we reached the Armory I tried to alert the guard at the door. He wore khaki and leggings and white gloves and a pistol belt and a holstered pistol. He stood at ease. He looked at Dad's uniform and rifle and stared at us but we walked past him into the vast room where troops were drilling. Recruiters sat at a table near the entryway, a marine in blue, a sailor in white, a soldier in khaki. It was a couple of weeks after Pearl Harbor and recruits massed around the table. They made way for us, assuming, I suppose, that Dad in his World War I outfit was part of the recruitment.

"My father's here," I said, "to volunteer his weapon."

The army sergeant looked at the vintage rifle and the ancient uniform. "You got the wrong war, Dad. This is 1941."

I gripped the rifle. "Give it." I tugged and he let go. I laid the rifle on the table.

"What am I supposed to do with this?"

"We're enlisting this Springfield rifle in the war effort."

I took Dad by the hand and let him out of the Armory.

"There were too many of them, Dad."

He shook so hard I had to open the car door and help him in. I reached into his pocket for the keys. I'd watched him drive, and had practiced shifting, and I drove home in first gear and parked three feet from the curb.

We led him to bed and undressed him. He asked me to stay. I sat in a chair by his bed while the spirit subsided. He looked frail. The shadows around his eyes were dark as bruises. He looked so mournful I wanted to hold him in my arms and tell him I loved him. The room darkened. His eyes remained open. Mom peeped in the door. I shook my head. I smelled coffee, dinner cooking, saw light under the door. It must have been close to midnight when he finally sighed, a deep letting go, and then groans, murmurs I couldn't decipher, lip smacking. I waited until his breath was deep. Afterward I joined Mom in the kitchen. "It's okay. He's out." The two-week episode had used up years of her life.

By Christmas vacation he had entered what she called his "dark time," withdrawing like a hibernating animal for a long sleep. He sat in the rear of the store, hiding behind a newspaper, not reading. It took him long seconds to respond to customers. Mom shouted at him as if he were deaf or far away. Thieves could have emptied the store with a hand truck and he would have been indifferent. His spirit had vanished. The premises were vacated. The occupant was out to lunch. Mom kept him moving. She prodded him to eat when he stopped with his fork in the air. A child could have authored his actions. The touch of a hand set him in motion. She gave him a broom and he swept. The newspaper kept him hidden.

"Mrs. Alfieri says, 'Hello,' Eph."

He said hello to Mrs. Alfieri.

Home from school, I asked, "How are you feeling, Dad?"

Blank consideration of the question, then finally, "Okay," puzzling what had been said to him and what he had uttered.

We took the train to New York before New Year's Day and saw the Rockettes at Radio City. There was a movie with Betty Grable and Harry James. Mom enjoyed it for the three of us. Million-dollar legs, she said. The legs were something special. The face, though— thick lips, plump nose—wasn't a million-dollar face. "Do you think so, Eph? I bet you're crazy about her. She's your type, I know."

"She's not his type," I said. "He's not crazy about her."

"Oh, Sonny. We don't have to be so serious."

I felt the disrespect and was offended. I was so close to being him that I could look into his eyes and locate the very deep place to which he had declined. The blankness was only apparent. The upper stories of the house were vacant but what happened in the deep interior was far more intense than anything the grocer had ever experienced.

We walked into Central Park at night and came to the pond with the skaters. We lost track of dad. "Ephraim!" she yelled. "Eph!" I called, "Dad!" We asked people if they had seen a big-nosed skinny man with earmuffs, a gray felt fedora, a plaid scarf, and a dark blue coat. Then we spotted him on the ice. He had rented or borrowed skates. We watched him skim over the ice, his hands clasped in back, somber and joyless. He skated with perfect grace, the fedora square on his head, the scarf tucked into his coat, his huge beak red and dripping. He swooped among other skaters.

Mom was shocked. "Is it over already?"

He said to me afterwards when I complimented him on his skating, "It doesn't change anything, Son," warning me against imagining that the season had turned.

He came back to us in the spring. Again the change was abrupt. Once more the spirit shone in his eyes. He checked everything out—my school, my clothes, the store. He was courtly and tender to Mom. She was as shy as if a stranger had entered the house. And for a time the feeling was so generous that none of us had the heart to anticipate what lay ahead. The days started indolently. She wasn't anxious about opening precisely at seven. She urged him to linger at the breakfast table.

He suggested a summer vacation. Pack up the whole show, he said, take it on the road. Maybe head home.

Home? Not even the word was familiar to her. Where could that be but Syracuse?

He meant Chicago. Back to origins. Find the key to Ephraim Smith and unlock the door. He was serious and lucid. Free the imprisoned soul. He again tiptoed on the razor's edge between clownishness and something deeply meant. A voice had told him to go back home and uncover the design of his life. The words "voice" and "design" scared her.

"There's no one left. Everyone's gone, Eph."

How about the Lake Michigan island where they'd honeymooned?

She remembered that time as the most beautiful of her life. But who would watch the store?

"We'll advertise. We've got almost three months."

She wanted to go. She checked with him the next day and the next. "You're sure about this vacation?"

"Absolutely. July One, as soon as Gene is out of school, we leave."

She offered the full profit for someone to tend the store. She interviewed candidates, checked their references, decided on an earnest young man recommended by a Methodist minister.

Dad said the trip would change our lives. "We're going to a new world."

A week before the trip I caught him by surprise. Someone else appeared in the guise of my father.

Dad usually opened the store at seven in the morning. Mom didn't come down until nine. She got me ready for school, then straightened out the apartment. This morning there was no bread for my lunch and she sent me downstairs. Dad wasn't in the store.

I went to the stockroom, a ten-by-twelve windowless space, lined with shelves from floor to ceiling. Staples were on the lower shelves. I recall the Grape Nuts and rolled oats and corn flakes, the cases of Campbell soups spilled on the floor. And spilled Jello boxes and jars of Postum, the shelves trembling as my father pressed into Mrs. Alfieri in the midst of fallen inventory.

At first I didn't understand that there were two people there. I saw his back, the skirt of his apron, arms around his back, her face looking at me, his head nowhere to be seen, her mouth open to release deep hoarse, "Ahs!" She saw me and they lurched apart. It was Mrs. Alfieri, burly, with enormous breasts, her nipples at the bull's eye with coffee-colored rims. When he turned toward me the face was not my father's face. The eyes were dreadful, the mouth wide open as though he meant to kill by biting. I picked up a bread, left the room, and said nothing to Mom.

His eyes were stretched wide. The lids had vanished. The pupils filled the space in the sockets. Her breasts—the target of his eyes— summoned up from deep caves a demonic, predatory spirit utterly unfamiliar to me.

I read my father and Mrs. Alfieri as clearly as if their impulses had a text. Her eyes were dragged into his, thick wormy lips pulled back, crooked teeth exposed, jet-black hair, a trace of mustache. Fertile and available. She gathered in her breasts, swooped them into her brassiere, tucked them in as if they were not herself but something she wore.

I see a demon father offered the sacrifice of breasts and he bends to feed.

Mrs. Alfieri, a hoarse-voiced customer, was usually accompanied by a meager, sullen boy, but not this time.

When I returned home that afternoon, I saw my familiar father, innocent and exuberant. He'd bought a tent and air mattresses and canvas folding cots. Could I have invented the scene in the stockroom? I didn't want to see what I had seen and submitted to his enthusiasm.

On a July morning we loaded the Ford. A nest was hollowed in back for me. I was wedged in against the door, surrounded by pillows and blankets and air mattresses. Dad lashed the tent to the roof of the Ford. Mom climbed in with thermos and picnic hamper. Dad turned the ignition, yelled, "Okay! All you demons and gremlins who want to hold us back, out of the way! We're driving right over you!" and we were off.

He talked until he exhausted us, and finally he, too, ran out of gas and was silent. There were no superhighways then. Much of the trip was on two-lane rural roads that broadened at the thresholds of towns and cities. The only sound I heard was the rush of air, the squeak of the Ford, the slap of the tires crossing asphalt seams. Dad didn't want to stop. He told Mom we would stop when the car needed gas.

He was silent and smiling, dreaming probably of Mrs. Alfieri in the stockroom. He bent down to her breasts. She stretched up with her offering.

Mom's silence didn't hide erotic visions. Her dreams simply extended her ordinary experience to include a more stable grocer, a more grateful child, a kitchen with butcher-block counters and overhead cabinets and a coffin-sized refrigerator-freezer and a copper hood fitting over a gas range like the mouth of an enormous tuba.

We drove with only two quick stops and by dawn had reached the outskirts of Detroit. It was barely dawn. I was half asleep, couldn't make out where we were. In hell, perhaps. Billowing flames from an open-hearth furnace reddened the sky. Outside, a hiss like the sound of an enormous steam iron. I saw the chimneys of the Ford River Rouge plant in Dearborn. The land hissed and breathed fire.

Dad tensed and I saw what he saw, something enormous in the shadows far down the road, perhaps a billboard or a silo, vague, yet ominous with its threat of motion, edging on the road, unstable—as if it would fall or leap—a silo that could topple or a billboard that was alive. The shadowy light bred illusions.

"Oh, lordy," Dad said.

Mom asked, "What is it?"

"Oh, lordy."

He slowed down but kept going even after the shape was defined. I could dismiss it as possibly a hoax meant to flimflam tourists, two-headed buffaloes or one-hundred-foot anacondas. It resembled something from the Saurian age, armor plated, on its haunches, with claws spread chest high.

We all saw something. Mom asked, "What is that?" irritated by the malice of those who had placed it there to alarm us. I came from sleep and there were fires all around, and the huge stacks, specters everywhere in that dawn light, and what I saw was at first a silo backlit by the open hearth and then—perhaps for an instant—this serpent, and I heard deep steamy respiration. It was Dad, turning to me, his eyes swallowed by the pupils as they were with Mrs. Alfieri, saying, "Didn't I tell you! Isn't it so?" who fixed that object clearly in all its details—vivid, unmistakable—and I saw that enormous reptile and its armor and outstretched claws, fire in its mouth. "Isn't it so!"—exultant, as though this were final proof. Of what? That they'd never had a right to stick him in Eloise? That his visions were true? Because now for the first time I saw the world he saw. And it moved. When we reached its shadow—*it moved*. Did Mom scream because she also saw what we saw? Or because she knew that she was dying of it? He wrenched the wheel; he stepped on the gas; he shouted and lost control and we soared past unblinking, glistening reptilian eyes, black slit pupils the size of fists within green irises. The head turned to follow our flight. I saw a morning sky bare of complications. The sky tumbled; Dearborn wheeled into view, long chimneys plugged into the slate sky. There was a hiss like my father's sigh amplified a thousand times. I sailed through air, the Superman of my dreams. I ended beside the road, watching the Ford settle in a nimbus of dust and smoke, rocking on its back, wheels spinning, a frantic bug that suddenly took fire. Brakes screeched, people ran toward us. There was no sign of the reptile.

Later, I saw Mom and Dad in white linen. The doctors carved up my dreamer and forced him to acknowledge the real world. He was briefly alive, already doomed, his brain shut off too long, everything erased. I had for a moment an awareness cutting like a knife that this man was myself, not merely a mad, ineffectual grocer, but someone whose roots went underground and emerged to become me. There were tubes up his cock, into his veins, his nose.

She was wrapped like a mummy. I could spot the blistered skin around her bruised eyes. There would be no last word forgiving the son, who, instead of unraveling her cocoon, sewed her up tight.

I waited in a white lounge. I hadn't slept in thirty hours. Nothing seemed remarkable or dreadful. I sat on a black sofa. The lounge was so white I lost sight of its edges. Somewhere a generator throbbed and the room pulsed like a heart. Intermittently a mechanical voice—unflappable despite the urgency of its summons—called Dr. Shapiro—pronounced with an "ai" as if the name contained a wail—and Dr. Klein.

There I sat—and from this late view I can see that boy's future. He's not yet ancient, nonetheless at ten already permanent and unalterable—waiting on the couch, wearing a felt beanie, a black T-shirt, corduroys, tennies, weary, weary, weary, not offering any prayers for the dying, even wanting death to come so that he could be released from the couch, the white room, the nagging persistence of that raspy call for Klein and Shapiro.

Finally the red light above the operating room door blinked on and off, a whorehouse beckoning, and the doctors emerged, wearing green surgical gowns and masks and caps. Klein delivered the news, too blasted after six hours of surgery to be solicitous.

"Be brave, Sonny. We did our best."

No tears. No sign of panic. Someone said, "Brave young man." An older nurse, with a solid stance, accepting every enormity, even death, as natural, waited to console me. "Do you want to see your dad?" I didn't say yes but she assumed yes and took my arm, ostensibly to support me, but directing me toward what I dreaded to see. She didn't offer me a sight of Mom and that was more terrible. Into a room off the corridor, on an examination table beneath a sheet. I shook beneath her hand. She tightened her grip—to support me? to compel me? I closed my eyes, opened them to the dread thing. And it wasn't Dad. "It's not him!" He was gone. Vanished. Left that facsimile of himself behind, colorless, spiritless, eyes closed, mouth slackened, gray teeth showing. The gleeful, demonic man had vanished. Gone! She shook me to stop the laughing. "Gone!" He'd said, "Isn't it so?" as if he offered proof of the conspiracy that had sent him to a crazy house.

There had been a reptile. I was close enough to see myself mirrored in its eyes. It left no tracks. No one else noticed. It seemed to have no more substance than the smoke from the Ford chimneys. But then neither did he leave any tracks.

One moment it had been a drab industrial outskirt of Detroit. We were among those Dearborn chimneys which, like exclamation marks, stressed the boundaries of what we were enjoined to accept. A ravaged landscape, silos, flame in the background, the stench of metal, slag heaps, parking lots. A sullen Detroit dawn—no people, no traffic. Then he said, "Behold!" and all that dislocated stuff crystallized into something so vivid, so palpable, I could even smell the acid, seared-flesh odor of its gaping stone mouth. All my senses affirmed the green-scaled reptile, claws held in brutal prayer, surveying my flight with lidless indifferent eyes. It was a vision that for an instant linked me to my vanishing father.

I yelled, "Take me to the crazy house!" and didn't stop laughing until she raised me off my feet and commanded, "Stop it! Enough!" and shook me into grief.

I never forgave him that glimpse into his crazy world. I had meant it never to be mine. I kept my eyes on the ground under my feet and hoped for walls that could house me.

ONE

Asylum

I was ten years old when Mom and Dad died. We were on our way from our home in Syracuse to Lake Michigan where we were to spend the summer months. Outside Detroit the Ford flipped over and caught fire. I was thrown out and bruised. Mom and Dad didn't survive the day.

They left almost no trace of themselves.

We had a grocery in Syracuse but he was no humble grocer. He had periods of great exuberance and when in the mood he was inventive and brilliant and full of joy.

He was a doughboy in France and cracked up after the war. He was sent to the Eloise Asylum outside Detroit. He was there a few months but was never again hospitalized. Mom wouldn't let it happen. She lived for his good times and sheltered him when times were bad.

We'd been driving all night. The accident happened at dawn

near the Ford River Rouge plant. He saw something on the road, twisted the wheel, and we flew apart.

I couldn't believe in their death.

I was taken to an orphanage, the Margaret Tessler Home, in Northwest Detroit.

The only photo I have of them was found in their Bible. We were not religious—we never went to church—and I didn't know there was a Bible until it was delivered to me after their death. It had his name in front, Ephraim Smith, the letters deeply slanted as though they bucked stormy winds. The photo marked a place in Judges. It was probably taken during their honeymoon. They are in a woods. They stand in front of a tent. Beyond the trees I see the glitter of a lake. She leans on his arm. He looks at her and smiles. He is a lanky young man with close-cropped hair. He wears a white shirt, the sleeves rolled, displaying muscular arms. I imagine they have just gotten up. She's still in her robe and her hair is down. I recognize her mouth and eyes but she's not otherwise familiar in this different time and place. She is buxom, petite, very lovely. She looks directly at the camera. They're not grocers yet. He's back from the war. He has by then sojourned at Eloise Asylum. She presents herself to the camera with no doubt that it will be a sympathetic reflection.

I was interviewed by Miss Wyman at the Margaret Tessler Home. She tried to find where we Smiths were connected. I told her there were no connections. She thought this very odd. No neighbors? No close friends? No congregation? No relatives?

We came from Chicago, but we were not Chicagoans. We moved to Cleveland when I was five but we weren't Clevelanders. We moved to Toledo when I was in the second grade but we weren't Toledoans. We moved to Syracuse and I had just started the fifth grade when we took that last trip. Miss Wyman had my school records. It was evident, she said, that I was very bright. She was impressed by my coolness and maturity.

She asked about Dad and I told her he was at one time or another a schoolteacher, a shoe salesman, a buyer for the cigar concession at Sam's Cut Rate in Detroit. Even in the depths of the Depression he found jobs. He didn't hold any very long. He ended as a grocer only because Mom decided Syracuse would be our last move and her folks were grocers so she knew the trade.

"And her folks, Eugene?"

"They died in 1918 of the flu."

Her maiden name?

Ruth Atwood.

No aunts? No uncles? Wasn't I named after a relative? Eugene Victor didn't sound like a name chosen out of the blue.

My father had named me for the martyr of the working classes, Eugene Victor Debs. In his early years Dad had been a member of the Socialist Party.

A long pause before her pen again lowered. "Well," she said, "that's not your ordinary politics, is it? Who are some of his party comrades? Perhaps they can help us."

It was long ago. There were other political affiliations, none of them held very long. Finally he was a party of one, Ephraim Smith, who sought the new Eden in his own heart.

"What new Eden?"

A place where there was no mine or thine, no war, no oppression.

"I don't know about 'no mine or thine,' but no war or oppression would be just lovely, wouldn't it, Eugene? Didn't they have close friends?"

No friends, I told her.

She put down the pen. "Eugene, I want you to think of Margaret Tessler as your new home."

I told her I had a home.

"Eugene, dear—" she took my hand, "—you've suffered a terrible loss. I know you're not finished grieving but we've learned that the best policy—and it's *so* hard, Eugene—is to get right into the Margaret Tessler routine. Do you think you can try?"

I had a home in Syracuse, an apartment above the store. The wallpaper of my bedroom was patterned in a smudged fleur de lys whose endless regularity afflicted my sight until I stopped seeing it. There was a large photo above my bed of a sunset over a lake in a pine forest. There was a photo of me on a Shetland pony, both of us sulking. I still belonged to that room.

I thanked her, but I wasn't ready for another family. I was still with my old one on that interrupted trip to Lake Michigan.

She led me to a third floor dormitory among the older boys. She introduced me by my full name, Eugene Victor Smith. There were thirty in that dorm. "I want you boys to make Eugene feel he's at home here."

Lenny Lucca was in the cot next to mine, bony and tall with thick lips and a wisp of mustache.

Where was I from?

Syracuse.

Where was that?

New York State.

Did Syracuse have a ball team?

I didn't know.

What did I think of the Tigers?

Who were the Tigers?

Who were the Tigers! Syracuse must be on Mars.

I slipped out before dinner. It was a balmy evening, still light.
I passed through the gate, walked to the end of the block, down
Six Mile Road. I stopped at a service station and asked for a map
of Detroit. They had no maps.

I passed an Italian restaurant. Families waited outside for tables.
The natural order in Detroit, as in Syracuse, was father and mother
and children. Somehow I had fractured the natural order and I no
longer had a place.

Miss Wyman led me into her office, the beginning of many
trips there. "You have no excuse for leaving the grounds. Everyone
here has lost his parents. I expect every boy to obey the rules."

She wanted to plant me in Michigan history, which she taught
in the morning period after calisthenics. She expected us to know
the exact dates of the early explorers and missionaries—Father
Marquette, the Chevalier de Cadillac, the founding of the Hudson
Bay Trading Company. First, she said, there were the Indians. We
learned what the Pottawatomies and the Ottawas ate, their sacra-
ments, their system of kinship. She wanted us to know our begin-

nings. Since my origins were forgotten, she wanted me to latch onto whatever was available, rehearsing me—as a spy about to enter alien ground would be rehearsed—in all the coordinates of my location.

She prodded me to be alert—testing me constantly—Who was the father of Henry Ford? William. Where did the family come from? Ireland. Where was Henry born? Dearborn. Why did he develop the internal combustion engine? To free man from menial labor. What was the greatest boon to American workers? Henry Ford's offer of an eight-hour workday, five dollars a day.

Plainspoken Henry scorned the fuzzy-minded academic breed. He said, "History is bunk." We went to the Greenfield Village Museum he established and saw the memorabilia of his childhood and his young manhood. I asked Miss Wyman, why, if Ford thought history was bunk, did he save all his used street streetcar tokens and his watch repair tools and his early motors, and take photos of every apartment and house he lived in, and carefully lay a trail which would inevitably conclude in the glorification of himself? She said, "Men lie. Old engines and street car tokens don't."

What lies did men tell?

Lies when they slandered Ford. She wanted to restore me to real time. The true history of Michigan was the first step.

We were up at six. An hour for cleanup and inspection and breakfast. Then Miss Wyman led us in calisthenics.

She put me in the front row to prevent malingering. Hopping up and down, she yelled, "HUP, HUP, HUP TWO, HUP TWO—GET WITH IT, EUGENE! ON YOUR TOES!" She came up behind me during study period and flicked my ear. It was humiliating rather than painful. "No nodding off! Stay awake!"

"I wasn't asleep."

"Your head was on the table."

"I was thinking."

"I want that book open. I want to see you writing in that note pad." She bent close to me. "Don't get smart with me, Eugene." She spoke in an intense whisper. She meant the others to hear. "I know every trick in the book and there's nothing I can't handle."

Michigan wasn't my state. Margaret Tessler wasn't my home. She wasn't my mother. These orphans weren't my family. I still hadn't concluded that trip to the Lake Michigan island.

Mr. Atkins reported that I was unteachable in shop. My soldering joints wouldn't hold. I ruined the threads when I uncoupled the plumbing. I couldn't get a level on a block of wood. When I spliced wires, invariably the circuit was shorted.

"Why?" she asked. "Why?" I had to know the machinery of the world. I could rely on no hands but my own. If my hands failed me, then what? What, Eugene? She asked me to consider Henry Ford whom she revered as the culmination of Michigan history. As more. A farm boy in a small village, hardly accessible to the civilized center of the world. The State of Michigan was itself an orphan until Ford. It had to make do with Michigan produce and Michigan factories and the know-how of Michigan farmers. Henry Ford liberated the farmer from the control of reins and put hundreds of horses at his fingertips. Presto! Roads opened to the world. No longer orphaned in the hinterland. An orphan's vision founded the River Rouge plant. Complete self-sufficiency. The Ford plantations and mines produced the raw material that was refined and molded at River Rouge. The Tin Lizzie was produced at the Highland Park plant. The triumph of the Lizzie. Miss Wyman had the figures. Millions had come off the line into the holding lots. The assembly absorbed the raw material and extruded it with the proficiency of a queen ant dropping eggs into the maw of the nation. He located us, she said. He put us on the map. The city of Detroit, still focused around its frontier legends, swelled into a giant. Number five in the U.S. The auto hub of the universe. River Rouge the largest plant in the world. And on and on with the figures that were proof we were no longer alienated.

Ford dreamed this greater Detroit at the center of the universe; himself, then, something like a god.

She wanted to inspire me with the life of Ford. I could be saved if my spirit would descend from some unfathomable but suspect region of the mind into my hands. A gift? Nonsense! Hard work, Eugene! Apply yourself. She said I had no choice. What would become of me? No family, no connections. Who would give me work? If I didn't enter the life of Detroit, what life could I have?

I returned from dreams of exotic landscapes to a steaming classroom, hearing a barely literate orphan painfully reciting Miss Wyman's favorite bard. "Tell me not in mournful numbers life is but an empty dream, for the soul is dead that slumbers, and things are not what they seem."

She stopped the class. "One moment, William. We'll continue when Eugene Victor arrives from his travels. He's off in Cloud Cuckooland."

I, too, had dreams of self-sufficiency. I invented an island. It was ruled by myself but in another incarnation. I was then reading the

Iliad and named this version of myself Prince Hector. We were stranded and isolated. We were loving and familial. We had no connections to the outer world. We cut our own lumber, built our own homes. Our fishing boats, at anchor in the harbor, were crafted by our own shipwrights. We were masters of a simple technology. We grew our own flax, spun our own thread, sewed our own sails, mounted our own masts, cast our own nets. We dined in communal lodges. We married. We bred. We thrived. Between ourselves and the world there were barriers of ocean and mountain and forest and we required no commerce.

This invention of mine became detailed and elaborate. I carried a notebook. I worked out a curriculum for Hector so that he would be an educated ruler. I made him a philosopher, architect, builder, engineer, general, sailor, poet. I called my island Arcadia.

Behind Margaret Tessler there was a potting shed and a garage and a thicket of forsythia along a chain-link fence. One day, penetrating the forsythia, I found a perfect spot of rich, soft turf, hidden from the playground by the forsythia and from the street by a row of elms. Exploring the potting shed, I found a shovel and pick mattock and a stack of quarter-inch plywood sheets and I decided to go underground.

I dug a trench two feet deep, two feet wide, perhaps six feet long, no larger than a grave. I covered it with plywood. I spread dirt and leaves over the plywood and left a small opening.

I was careful about entering my cave. I approached it from different directions and entered when no one was looking. Nonetheless I was found out by one of the younger boys. Zeke was waiting for me when I climbed out. I swore him to secrecy and told him the story of Arcadia and made him an Arcadian. Our land was safe so long as the barbarians didn't find us.

We dug a connecting trench for Zeke and covered it with plywood and soil and leaves. He was a fine audience and I inducted two of his friends, Mark and Billy, into our nation. Our four trenches met in a large hall. We crawled through an opening and crouched together in the central chamber. We brought candles from the refectory. We had meals underground and acted out Arcadian dreams. We exhausted the air, came up for breath, plunged down again.

Mr. Wilson, the gardener, saw the bulge in the earth. He stepped on the central chamber and fell through and sprained his ankle. They found a drawing Zeke had made, a diagram of miles of tunnels. The proud author had signed his name. The little fellow told all. She confiscated my notebook. The next day she shook her bell in refectory, commanded silence. She told of the garden vandalism and the secret confabs, not using my name, but everyone knew I was the culprit.

She told me in her office that what I'd done was very serious. Mr. Wilson might have broken his leg. The earth could have caved in while we were underground and we'd have smothered. She didn't make rules simply to annoy us. The rules were necessary for the safety and well-being of Margaret Tessler.

This was no doubt true. But safety aside, she would not allow us any secret places. She forced us to go public.

Her censure was a signal to the older boys. "He plays with the kiddies. He's a kiddy himself." I was short-sheeted, my trousers knotted, my bed messed up. When I climbed into bed and was abruptly halted by a doubled-over sheet, everyone snickered. I pulled back the blanket, unfolded the sheet, tucked it in, climbed back into bed.

Lenny Lucca yelled, "Hey, Smith! They made your legs too long."

I was, from the time I arrived, Miss Wyman's special irritation. Did I crystallize her own worst dread of being orphaned? She was an orphan with us. Margaret Tessler was as self-sufficient as she could make it. A four-story red brick building on five acres of lawn, girdled by a wrought-iron fence, towers at each corner peaked with witches' hats, a steep pitched slate roof. We had a greenhouse, a truck garden. A gym and pool in the basement along with wood and metal shops. Auditorium and kitchen and refectory on the first floor. Study halls and classrooms on the second. Dormitories on the third and fourth floors. There were about a hundred of us. We ranged in age from six to eighteen.

Miss Wyman tried to place all her boys. When we were ready to leave she would send us to the friends of Margaret Tessler with a summary of our talents.

"Where will I place you, Eugene?"

I was losing time. She herself was always on schedule. You could hardly forget the time at Margaret Tessler. Bells sounded at the hour and then ten minutes after. We were free for a couple of hours on the playground and before lights out. The rest of the time was hers. She didn't want any evasions. She meant to imprint the Margaret Tessler schedule inside our skins so that we ran by her clock.

We had a library. The Krause Room. Founded by a Detroit dentist. We could be there only if one of the staff was present. That didn't often happen. Still, I found Homer and Ovid and Plutarch. I read *Ivanhoe* and *Green Acres* and *She*. I read *Macbeth* and *Julius Caesar*. And Altsheler's frontier novels and Zane Grey.

There wasn't even privacy in the latrine. The toilets were not partitioned. The only chance for solitude was to get a bathroom excuse from class and go to the latrine when it was empty. Or perhaps shower at night just before bed check. Or under the covers. Or give up the need for solitude, as they all finally did, and expose their private acts in the latrine or under the blankets, fabricating women with every part eroticized. Most of the boys released powerful feelings and didn't stay dreamy. Our shop teacher, Mr. Atkins, had no complaint about them. They were on schedule. Miss Wyman's boys graduated to service stations and repair shops. One or two went to Lawrence Tech. Some had their own businesses. Solid citizens, and yet their desires each limited by the woman they invented and ridiculed and abused in the latrine of Margaret Tessler. Hunted for her perhaps the rest of their lives. She was bigger than life, endlessly available. Avid. Whatever they settled for, I'm sure, was less.

I tried to avoid their frenzy, but later—I was perhaps eleven or twelve—the vision of Woman would overwhelm me. I dreamed of Miss Wyman. I plucked her from her schedules and her time and her bells and attributed my frenzy to her and she wrenched off her clothes and mine and instructed me—commanded me—forced me to do what nothing had ever so pleased me to do. But done with—quickly—and afterwards I was unfit for other dreams.

The frenzy over, there was nothing left. A story whose conclusion was so final had no further implication. I could go on and on, stringing out my story of Arcadia. It was endless, richer than life. She could fill in my tunnels, take away my notebook. She couldn't thwart my vision of Arcadia. Sex ended in terrific and final release. There was no further consequence to that tremendous feeling I thought could explode me from my body—was my body a burden to me?—and leave me ecstatic and enlightened.

The others made light of it and so lightened themselves. Heads cleared. Ready now for real life. No visions of women in real life. But of machines—the pistons pump, the moving gears engage the fixed gears on the shaft. Every particular is there—the oil sheen on the pistons, the tarry deposits on the engine head, the wobble of the faulty flywheel. I could not manage machines and yet I imagined them perfectly. I could visualize every detail of a machine. The drive shaft turns, the wheels spin, the brakes grip, and though I can't give an account of the force that drives the machine, in dreams I have it all.

Miss Wyman placed her boys on the Ford assembly line or at Al Green's service station or at Clamage's Radio Emporium. She said to me, You won't be here forever.

The other boys thought I held myself apart.

This she told me in her office. "You're too smart to keep on sulking. You don't have any friends because you won't make the effort."

There was an intimate hour before lights were out. It was a time when private thoughts were spoken, but not mine. Detroit Tigers, '34 and '35, the greatest team ever, Right? Right! A litany of names—Charley Gehringer, Billy Rogell, Pete Fox, Schoolboy Rowe, Tommy Bridges, Hank Greenberg, Mickey Cochrane, Goose Goslin, General Alvin Crowder, Elden Auker, on and on until even I could recite the roster of the '35 Tigers. Rating the fighters. None better now than Joe Louis, the Brown Bomber. But Dempsey would have flattened him. The Manassa Mauler. Rating autos. One said, no better car than the Buick Roadmaster. There were Chrysler fans and Lincoln advocates. They immediately put me through a catechism.

"How about you? What kind of car?"

"An Argos," I said.

"What kind of car is that?"

"Greek."

"Who are you, smart guy? What country are you from?"

"Arcadia."

"Where is that?"

"An island off the coast of Michigan."

They felt put down and what right did I have, the youngest and smallest in that third floor dormitory, to put them down? How come I didn't know who was shortstop on the '34 Tigers? Why did I avoid their rituals? Why wouldn't I say CUNT?

"Say 'CUNT!'" they commanded. "The nice boy won't say 'cunt.' What a good boy. He won't even let 'cunt' out of his mouth."

I said "MYTHOLOGY," which they took to be a euphemism though I didn't know any euphemisms for "cunt."

"The nice boy won't say 'cunt.' Say 'CUNTLAPPER'."

"Metaphysics," I said.

"COCKSUCKER."

"Ovulate," I said.

"FUCK."

I said, "Copulation."

"NICE BOY. MISS WYMAN'S PET."

They messed up the books on my shelf.

My contest was not with them but with her. She meant to make me a Margaret Tessler boy. She wanted me to turn away from Mom and Dad, and I wouldn't do it.

They insisted that I speak their language. Did they read contempt in my holding back? Perhaps there was, but why should that threaten them? I suppose they were so tentatively located in the time and place she arranged for them that they couldn't afford a dissonant voice. They wanted a unified language. We clung to each other out of a shared fear of life after Margaret Tessler. Real Life. As the poet writes in Miss Wyman's favorite verse, "Life is real! Life is earnest! / And the grave is not its goal; / Dust thou are, to dust returnest, / Was not spoken of the soul."

That was confusion. If "life is real"—if life is what the blacksmith does beneath the spreading chestnut tree, if real life is defined by Henry Ford—then the grave is its goal and returning to dust is exactly the destiny of the soul. And we all knew—Miss Wyman, Mr. Atkins, and my fellow orphans—that exposing our most private, most intense, most soulful moment to public spectacle, undertaking to degrade that ecstatic vision of Woman, reducing her to Pussy and Cunt, was to affirm the body as machine and deny the agony of the soul.

Deep feelings trivialized? Fine with Miss Wyman. Get down to necessary business—that is, enter a time and place from which we had been excluded. Henry Ford was her exemplar. The Machine was affirmed. We were machines, sex was in our hands.

Harold Mitchell had replaced Lenny Lucca in the cot next to mine.

No dreams in Harold. He hit the sack and was asleep. He stood in front of the mirror in the latrine, combing thick brown hair, a steady eye on himself, not disturbed by ambiguity. Another kid impatient for the mirror tried to elbow him aside. "Okay, pretty boy, let someone else take a look." A swift turn, a solid whack, the other boy staggering, clutching his face, pulling away a bloody palm, bawling at the sight. Harold back to the mirror, indifferent to his victim, no pain in his fist, no rancor, no regret, no reconciliation—on to breakfast.

He joined us from another orphanage, in transit, already a man in appearance. He didn't have his full height, but he was heavy chested and needed a shave. He didn't jerk off; he didn't say FUCK, he didn't say CUNT; he was uninterested in the Detroit Tigers. In our intimate hour before lights out he lay on his cot reading *Doc Savage* and *The Shadow* and Big Little Books. He had status as Mr. Atkins' shop assistant. He had only to release his hands and he performed welds and levels and made perfect cylinders on the lathe and did elegant scrollwork on the jigsaw.

Did Miss Wyman deliberately assign him to the cot next to mine? We never spoke. He had few words for anyone.

Everything about him was powerful—his reticence, his physical grace, his aloofness. He wasn't her boy. He didn't go with the crowd. He didn't participate in the hazing. I even forgave him his infantile reading. He had a taste for romance. He only needed instruction to become aware of his possibilities. I could be his instructor. You see, I'd tell him, we didn't wish to conquer anyone. We had an idyllic life. They invaded our island. We had a citizen army, ready to set aside plows for swords. We knew every trail, every hillside, every ambush. We spotted intruders while they were still on the other side of the mountains, in the plain below. We let them infiltrate our labyrinth. We divided them. Small groups were cornered in dead ends. Our object was to transform the barbarian prisoners. We let them experience a harmonious life. We awakened them to tender feeling. They returned home as our advocates.

I dreamed of instructing Harold, who continued to flip the pages of a Mickey Mouse Big Little Book adventure in the bed next to mine. Without peace, I would tell him, there could be no industry, no commerce, no cultivation, no books, no libraries, no grace of existence. (Had I pitched my argument to the level of his understanding I would have added, no Mickey Mouse.)

The delusion that I could be his mentor caused the trouble between us.

Miss Wyman didn't nag Harold, though his shortcomings as a student were obvious. What good would it have done? It would have led to quarrels she couldn't win. He was only asked simple-minded questions. He was incorrigible because he was perfect, already the master of machines.

One afternoon we were doing American literature, reading aloud, easy poems of Riley and Longfellow, going down the aisle, row by row, and it was Harold's bad luck that we had reached Bryant's "Thanatopsis" when it came his turn. Miss Wyman perhaps wasn't attending. She let him get started, and then couldn't rescue him without embarrassing him. So she let him go on. He didn't get far. He was mired in the verse, struggling with it so fiercely no one dared get in his way. Sentences collapsed around him and sucked him under. He wrenched at syllables. None of it made sense to him. The class didn't dare snicker. Miss Wyman was, for the moment, unable to relieve his thrashing. "Earth," he said, "earth—earth—earth—that . . ." reluctantly approaching the impasse ahead—"Earth that . . ." so helpless I couldn't bear it and I said aloud, "NOURISHED. Earth that nourished thee..." He saw me for the first time. He returned to the passage and immediately plowed into "resolved" and was stopped in his tracks. He tried it as "solved," broke the word into "Res" and "Olved," glared around the room as I said aloud, "resolved to earth again. RESOLVED." He slammed the book shut and sat down. Miss Wyman said, "All right, Eugene, since you're so eager to read, why don't you finish the passage?"

"Earth that nourished thee shall claim thy growth to be resolved to earth again. And lost each human trace..." and so on, desperate to get through.

That night he sat on his cot, torso heavy as a man's, staring at me.

"I only wanted to help. Sorry," I said.

"Who asked you?"

I went into the latrine after lights out and wrote him a letter. I didn't finish till early morning. I told him about the island. I wanted him to join our crowd and enter our fantasy. It was totally mistaken. It is a letter I am embarrassed to recall. It ended in an almost rhapsodic confession of admiration. By morning I offered him "the gift of my kingdom."

We shared a shelf above our cots. He placed a lovely model of a three-masted ship on his side. I'd watched the ship in the making. He sawed ovals of wood, glued them together, each oval smaller than the one above. He planed the ovals into a sleek hull. He worked for a month on that ship. He would remove the hull from wood clamps, turn it, study it, then resume sanding. He applied enamel coats to the completed deck and hull, sanding down one coat, applying another, working the finish into a jewel-like sheen. The completed ship was placed on a wood stand on our shelf.

I put my letter on the deck of his ship.

When he woke up and stretched, yawned, looked up at the shelf, I knew I'd made a mistake. He picked up the letter, turned it over. He didn't open it. That night, returning from the john before climbing into bed, he held up the letter. "Did you write this shit?"

He tore it in two. Then he tore it in quarters. He ripped it again. He held the pieces over my head and let them rain down.

"Asshole," he said.

And I said, breathlessly, barely a whisper, not sure I meant him to hear, "You fool."

He jumped me, smothered me in the vise of his arm. When my breath was shut off and he heard me gagging, he released me and returned to his bed. I was stained by a machine odor his body exuded. Everyone saw what happened. No one said a word.

I had done him an unimaginable offense with that letter. He seethed. The next night he said, "Fairy asshole."

I pulled the blanket around my ears. "Sissy punk," he said, and I said again, "Fool," meaning more than he could have understood.

Fool to have rejected my admiration. Fool not to have allowed me to introduce him to his own power. Fool to be so unwittingly Miss Wyman's instrument. She encased him in wood and metal and reduced him to a machine.

It was no trick overwhelming me. I was a skinny promise of a man and he was almost entirely arrived. Ground against a tuft of sandy hair into the smell of machine. He squeezed till I couldn't breathe, applied more pressure. I scratched at his back and he wrenched until I blacked out.

I was illuminated in the dark of his arm, embedded in his flesh. The muscled arm rolled against my temples like an avid boa. He excreted his fury in little grunts—uh-uh. In that ripe earthy nest—smelling of old labor and new—I learned—uh-uh—there was no dreamland—uh-uh—there was no magic vanishing, reappearing father—uh-uh—no interrupted journeys—uh-uh —only Real Life in the stink of an armpit. Real Life, earnest and undreamy. But it was not my wisdom. I wouldn't submit to the apostle of Real Life.

No harm was done. My ears were bruised. My nose scraped. My lip cut. I went into the latrine so they wouldn't see me shaking.

No more hazing. I was ignored as if my humiliation might degrade them.

Harold bumped me while making his bed. He turned and shoved and sent me sprawling. He put his foot on my bed, tying his boot. He edged his things over onto my side of the shelf—his magazines and ship leaving little room for my Bible, my Homer, my library copies of Altsheler and Zane Grey.

To affirm himself, he tried to reduce me to nothing. He lay on his back, Joe Palooka on his chest, flipping pages, a beautiful serene face that you might find on a Michelangelo. I went over the same line in Homer again and again, hearing the dumb steady pace of his reading, the noisy flip of infantile literature. I was more than forgotten. Erased. And I couldn't accept it.

I spoke into the silence of the dorm, the calm voice of a pedant, "Earth that NOURISHED thee. NOURISHED!"

He turned over my bed and flopped on me. He was pried loose by Miss Wyman and the other boys. She stood between us and ordered him, "Back! Back! Control yourself, Mitchell!" I wasn't his age. Wasn't his size. What was he thinking of? Had he lost all control? "Back!" she warned. "Back!" And when he persisted in struggling for me she stepped forward and cracked his face, a shocking slap, and in her sergeant's voice, "THAT WILL BE ENOUGH!" He hugged his arms to keep from hitting her and lowered his head. She led me into her office with its American flag and tinted photo of the President and portrait of young Margaret Tessler and the bubbling fish tank.

"All right, Eugene. What happened?"

I opened my mouth and couldn't speak.

"Speak up!"

I started shaking. I shook as if I had been wired and the juice turned on. She came around the desk. "Okay. All right." She took me in her arms. She soothed me. "Hush," she said. "All right. Okay, my darling." Then, murmuring, her lips on my cheek, "Don't you know you're very special? I worry about you. I expect great things from you."

Her wonderful odor, the simple smell of someone who was what she appeared to be, our Mother who gave us history and placed us in time and would never abandon us until we were located. "You'll wake up; you'll get on the ball. You're going to amount to something. Do you know that, Eugene? Do you know that you're going to amount to something?"

I made myself stiff. She let me go to arm length and looked me in the eyes. "No more foolishness, right?" She moved me to the other side of the dorm, away from Harold. After lights out, he came to my bed.

Someone whispered, "Leave him alone, Mitchell. Please."

He asked, "Are you crazy?" He meant the question seriously, weighing his action in the light of my answer.

"Yes," I said. "Take me to Eloise."

"You're nuts," he concluded, a surly voice, already thickening toward a bass baritone rumble. "What are you trying to prove?"

I told him my father ruled a mountain kingdom. These were my wander years. I experienced the world until it was time for me to assume the throne.

He'd been squeezing a crazy kid. To what purpose? A lunatic could give no offense. Was that the effect I wanted? Trying to save my skin by pretending to be loony? Yet squeezed into his side I had never been closer to another human being. No one had ever touched me so intimately. I wanted him to be charmed by my Arcadia. I wanted to pass beyond the barrier of his inarticulateness and touch his spirit and release him from his bondage to machines.

This is how Prince Hector became master of the world. He knew the only safeguard for his kingdom was to conquer the barbarians. But they were too many, his forces too few. So he encouraged invasion. The invaders, defeated, became his disciples.

He sent them out as emissaries of his vision. His kingdom was extended to the mainland. He established sovereignty everywhere and finally there was one world at peace, no mine, no thine. That was the conclusion of my Arcadian fantasy.

Harold was with us only a few months longer. We never spoke again. He stayed away from me. He was placed at Clamage's Radio, which he left to establish his own repair shop where he employed other graduates of Margaret Tessler. I understand he has a family, all the children an orphan could desire, and doesn't lack for a place in the cosmos.

I was the one who troubled Miss Wyman. She feared what would happen when I was no longer under her protection.

"Wake up, Eugene!" It was a plea.

TWO

Giving Breath

Miss Wyman instructed us in first aid. When she demonstrated the new method of resuscitation, she used Lenny Lucca as a model. He lay on his belly and she knelt astride his back, turned his head sideways onto his hand, cleared his mouth and checked his tongue with her hanky. Then, braced on her hands, she leaned forward and pumped to the rhythm of her breath, a few strokes of demonstration before she dismounted. Her skirt rode up the back of her legs and she was bare to her thighs. She explained that somehow the breathless body would learn its own living rhythm through this act of sympathy.

She was in charge and no one snickered. Afterwards in the dorm Lenny said, "If I died and Miss Wyman tried pumping me back—boy!—I'd come alive!—you bet your ass!—and I'd buck her off!"

I hated that image of himself and Miss Wyman. She astride him? The everted lips with a wisp of mustache, clumps of hair on his chin, receiving the sympathy of her breath? I hated the notion.

We weren't eager to do such service to the dying. To link our own breath with someone corrupted—by god knows what disease, what foulness—would poison our souls. We speculated about other possibilities. If it were a breathless Hedy Lamarr or Lana Turner whom we were lucky enough to straddle we might take from their honeyed vitality the power to transform ourselves from toads to something princely.

The demonstration ended in these jokey speculations. Then, a few weeks later, as if a model had been provided by the fates, our janitor, Mr. Harkness, collapsed while hauling in the flag. He staggered under billowing Stars and Stripes. We watched his comic dance as he batted at the flag and then sank beneath it. We tentatively giggled. But he was no clown. He was a dour, simple man who insisted on respect for the flag. He would fold the flag in precise triangles, concluding in a tight package he devoutly carried to its place in the office. He was a churlish man, easy to provoke. The boys were annoyed by his way with the flag. We knew almost nothing about Mr. Harkness except that he'd been a doughboy and had served in France and remained a patriot. The shabby old man in dirty overalls assumed a proud ceremonial attitude as he lowered the flag. He pressed one of the younger boys into service while he folded. It was someone like Mr. Harkness whom we imagined when we thought of the indignity of rescuing the dead.

Miss Wyman rushed to him when he collapsed. She knelt among the billows, spread aside the flag, pried into his mouth with a handkerchief. She waved us off. "Give him air!" Then arranged him on his belly, lowered herself, pumped breath into him. She only gave up when the firemen arrived. They attached oxygen; his chest was convulsed by forced air. He was covered with a Margaret Tessler blanket. His feet protruded. Miss Wyman hustled us back on schedule. It was time to clean up. It was a subdued dinner. When we were done Miss Wyman clinked her glass and announced that our janitor had died of a heart attack. She asked us to lower our heads. He'd had no family of his own. We were his family. He considered us to be his children. She wanted us to think of all the orphaned people of the world who didn't have anyone with whom to share their lives. She asked us to thank god that we at Margaret Tessler had each other.

I thanked god, but not that we had each other. Only through her did we have each other. She was what we had in common. She was with us every day of the week. She was only gone from Margaret Tessler on an occasional weekend night. The night she would go out she showed up on her rounds wearing a tweed suit rather than her customary skirt and smock. Her dense reddish hair was down to her shoulders instead of in a bun. She'd stand at the threshold of the dorm room checking us out and we'd be comforted by that sturdy military posture she encouraged us to assume. She seemed to me so firmly grounded nothing could unbalance her, not even Mr. Harkness dying between her thighs. When she arose from his dying she was as clear and unaffected as if she'd pumped away death and remained uncorrupted.

There were more than a hundred of us. She knew all our griefs and enthusiasms and bent ways. She meant to straighten us while we were in her hands. On those nights when she was gone, Margaret Tessler didn't feel secure. It didn't matter who else was in charge—Mr. Atkins or Mrs. Hempleman or Miss Sample—it was only a holding action until the commander returned. Miss Wyman did the planning. We lived by her schedule. She introduced what novelty there was—the Christmas visit to the Ford Rotunda, the showing of "Fantasia" in the refectory, the free trips to Briggs Stadium and the Barnum & Bailey Circus, the performance of *Alice in Wonderland* by a troupe from Wayne University.

When I left the orphanage she had been there for twenty years, director for seven. In that time, she must have released more than two hundred of us to Detroit. She made sure we were settled before she let go the tether. Interviews began during our last year, which was for some as early as age sixteen, and for a few, like myself, as late as eighteen.

I didn't want to give her trouble, but it wasn't easy releasing me. She couldn't get me pegged. I could type. I was good at math. I knew how to keep books. I had no mechanical skills. I was too young for the kind of jobs that might have used my talents. I refused to work at the fountain of George V's pharmacy. I turned down a job as stock boy at A&P. I wouldn't accept a scholarship to the Ford vocational trade school. I told her I was too old and would never learn.

"If you don't try, Eugene, how do you know what you can do?"

She was increasingly annoyed. I caused her as much trouble as any boy she could remember.

"You're not going to be president at the start. You have to begin somewhere."

I wanted to go to Wayne University. I had read the bulletin and it promised me Troy, Athens, Rome, Renaissance Florence.

"That's fine," she said. "But what are you going to do about a place to live? How are you going to eat?" She found me an opening in the shoe department of Sam's Cut Rate.

I refused to work in a store. My father and mother had been grocers in Syracuse.

It was my heart's desire to please Miss Wyman but I couldn't accept her notion of a safe place. She found a position she thought perfect, a bookkeeper at Clamage's Radio Emporium on Livernois Avenue. Clamage, himself a Margaret Tessler graduate, was a chunky crew-cut man. He wore spectacles secured by a thong. He wore white overalls. His name was in red yarn over his pocket. He had been in Miss Wyman's first classes. She had begun as the gym teacher and history instructor twenty years before. He told me he considered Margaret Tessler to be his first home. He wanted to return a little of what had been given to him so he hired orphans. He showed me the cubicle where I would work. It contained a battered metal desk and an ancient adding machine set among what seemed to be a ruin of radio parts—speakers, coils, tubes, cabinets. There were piles of withered manuals and circuit diagrams.

He offered me the job. "Kate says you can do it and her word's good enough for me."

I told him I'd call and let him know.

"What do you mean you'll call? Don't you want the job?"

I went back to Margaret Tessler and told Miss Wyman I couldn't work at Clamage's.

She said I was a snob. What right did I have to look down on people like Al Clamage? He was a wonderful man, loyal to the Home. There were three Margaret Tessler graduates now in his employ. "You don't have to stay forever. Start there and when you get a better offer move on."

I told her I couldn't do it.

"You can do it. You will do it. There's nothing else."

I feared such a start would be my finish. I'd never get out of that cubicle. I'd be buried in the smell of grease, the absence of daylight, the sputtering fluorescence. The other workers were more kin to pliers and screwdrivers than to orphans.

She said, "All right, Eugene. You're on your own. I've got nothing else for you."

On my last day she told me that the offer was still open and again I refused. I had twenty-five dollars. Everything I owned was in a cardboard suitcase. I wore a suit that, though new to me, was someone's cast-off, and too heavy for the summer weather. She accompanied me to the outer gate. We embraced, then she took my hand, and squeezed.

"Don't be your own worst enemy, Eugene. You're very talented. You're very bright. You have it in your power to make something of yourself. I expect great things from you. Don't disappoint me."

And then she let me go. Once beyond the threshold of Margaret Tessler's I was on my own. It was sink or swim and if I went down she wouldn't be around to give me breath.

I stayed briefly with Mr. and Mrs. Sutton. He had been a foreman at the Briggs Bodyworks until felled by arthritis. In the week I knew him I never saw him without a newspaper. Even when he got up to greet me he carried it in his left hand. They had taken other orphans. None could have been less forthcoming than I was. "Well," he said, after we came to an abrupt halt, "it's going to be a long summer for the Tigers. I'm afraid this isn't their year."

I was so stunned by the world outside Margaret Tessler's I couldn't speak.

Mrs. Sutton led me to an attic room. One of the windows was closed off by an exhaust fan. She didn't have a key for me. She said they'd have one made. Meanwhile, I'd have to be in by their eleven o'clock bedtime. It turned out that I had arrived in the middle of a quarrel that in the next few days reached its crisis. Her ferocious monotone penetrated ceilings and walls and I stayed away as much as I could, looking for work.

I found nothing as good as Clamage's offer.

I saw a range of positions on a sidewalk blackboard outside an employment office—short-order cook, handyman, welder, mechanic, Fuller Brush salesman—I didn't bother going in.

I wasted time riding buses, waiting for appointments in personnel offices. I barely managed three or four applications a day. Of the positions that seemed interesting, most were taken before I arrived. The two leads I found—busboy at Greenfield's Cafeteria and helper on a laundry truck—I didn't follow up.

Each evening about six I sat at the counter of Blakeney's Chili Parlor across from the Margaret Tessler grounds and watched the day end. I heard her distant whistle, summoning the boys to dinner. The playground emptied. The new janitor lowered the flag, then shut the great carved double gates. Shadows spread over the ironwork fence and the elaborate gates with the letters MT scripted in brass, then the hedges of forsythia and the great elms and the blood-red brick with the sandstone coping, the towers, the gables. At dusk lights appeared, first in the refectory, then spreading above and below until all of Margaret Tessler was ignited. At nine-thirty Miss Wyman began her rounds. In her wake light vanished, first on the top floor where the youngest slept, then on the third floor. By ten everything was blanked out except the red exit lights on each floor and her rooms on the ground floor and the threshold lanterns and the streetlights on Six Mile Road and the reversed Blakeney's Chili Parlor sign.

One night the counterman at Blakeney's leaned over and in a low pleasant voice, so as not to offend the other customers, said to me, "You've been using up that chair for three days now. I've got customers waiting." He nodded toward the bowling crowd that had arrived. "You come in every night, spend fifty cents for a bowl of soup, load up on oyster crackers, leave a nickel tip. Listen, Big Spender, why don't you take your business someplace else? I can afford the loss."

I was an orphan in the world. I had no place to light. I had to keep moving. I was breathless, as if I'd been running. Dreams devoured my sleep. I awoke in panic and started moving again. I looked for work in the neighborhood of Wayne University. The summer session had just finished. The campus was empty. Clerks manned the admissions office. I didn't have the appropriate credits for admission. I barely missed a job at a bookstore.

A week after leaving the orphanage I was down to twelve dollars.

Out of necessity—I was exhausted, it was a boiling day, my shirt was soaked, I limped from tight shoes—I found a room near

Wayne. There was a For Rent sign in the window of a three-story Victorian. The door was open. I looked into a dark cool vestibule and a carpeted stairway. The landlady was out front watering the lawn. Something Prussian in her manner was confirmed by the German accent. She softened "t's" and hardened "th's" and put dents in "w's."

She introduced herself, Mrs. Marta Tuchler. There was a room available for a clean, reliable tenant. She didn't want drinkers or noisemakers. She guessed I was a Wayne student. She had other students as tenants. It was a good place to study, quiet, cool, clean. The rooms were furnished. Each had kitchen facilities. Rent was eight dollars a week. There was a shared bath off the corridor.

I followed her to the second floor where there were three rooms and a bath. My room was at a corner near the bath. There was a cot by the wall with a crocheted spread. There was a round oak table in the center of the room. There were two straight chairs and a rattan armchair. The kitchen alcove was the size of a large closet. It contained a counter and sink with cabinets above. There was a countertop refrigerator and a two-jet gas burner. The braids on the rug were unfurling. The rattan was broken on the armchair. The table was unsteady.

I paid on the spot.

I left the Suttons that afternoon. He was locked into silence behind the spread sheets of the *Detroit Free Press*. She ran the vacuum around his feet. They were barely interested in my going.

"Leave an address and phone number," she said, "in case someone wants to get in touch."

I left Tuchler's number and spent the night in my own place.

I dreamed of my father. I entered my room and he was sitting at the round table, dressed in a robe, his face in his hands. I said, "Dad, you're alive." He turned to me and burst into tears. "Oh, my boy," he said. "I've missed you so." I picked him up and sat with him on my lap and I hugged him and said, "I miss you too, Daddy." I woke up. The old man downstairs was coughing. It was still night. I felt dreadfully orphaned. I yearned for the sounds of Margaret Tessler—the morning prayers and exercise, footsteps on waxed linoleum tiles, the echo of Mr. Atkins' tenor in the small amphitheater adjoining the shop. Our breath at night. I dwelt inside the noise and smell of the Home as if they were my skin. The sound of buckets in the corridor signaled the rituals of Sunday morning inspection, then chapel, and afterward the best meal of the week. The stillness of Harold Mitchell in the cot beside me was promise of trouble ahead. There were uncalculated inferences to be made about my future state from slight changes in the skin of noise that located me.

At Tuchler's every creak, every rattle, every clank needed attention because I wasn't at home.

The next day I didn't go out. I had four dollars left after paying the rent. I drifted into fantasy. I imagined a heart-shaped island. I stood on a quivering pier. I saw a line of cottages above the beach. There was dense forest. I began to create my dream of Arcadia. Benign days, a lovely breeze, lemon-scented air, fish-dappled water, blackberry bushes, wild strawberries, gull cries, my island.

I don't know how far into my dreams I would have declined if I hadn't been summoned by Mrs. Tuchler in her German English. "Mr. Smith! The telephone! Downstairs. It's for you." When

I came down she said, "Next time give them the number of the upstairs phone. My phone is not for the use of tenants." I walked through her lacy, pillowed bedroom to the phone. Miss Wyman was at the other end.

Had I found work yet?

I gloried in her voice. I would have done anything to have ready access to it. Did she want me for Clamage? I was willing to serve.

"Eugene, I think I've found something tailor-made for you. It's perfect."

And the next day I entered those gates again. I was back in her office, which I knew better than most, always from the perspective of a school chair, looking through the innards of an ancient Smith Corona across a huge walnut desk at an erect, matronly woman in a squealing swivel chair, the fish tank perking, a fluorescent light illuminating a miniature seascape with caves and swaying plants and fish and snails that were glued to the glass. Truman had replaced Roosevelt on the wall near the window. Above the desk, Margaret Tessler was ornately framed, a prettified young lady with protuberant eyes and a creamy bosom and full lips and chestnut hair. Taken in the flower of her youth, the Home endowed in her memory. Every other object in that room subdued.

"Well, Eugene. How do you like being a free man?" A large, innocent smile, as though she hadn't choreographed my destiny and brought me to this moment in precisely the attitude she wanted.

I was available for anything she had for me.

A job with Elton Kramer, proprietor of Elkram Real Estate.

She told me about Elton Kramer before he arrived. He was a hustler from the day he had come to the Home, eight years old, undersized, underweight, eyes so huge they seemed to be devouring the rest of him. He was called Knobby by the other kids. He had knobs on his cheeks, a knob on his chin, knobs on collar bones and shoulders. She used to be relieved to see him eat. He hustled to be first in line. He was first for seconds. He ate and ate but his bones never vanished from sight. She considered his survival her triumph. As she described it, he insinuated himself into a crowd, wiggling and elbowing, and arrived up front, his tray at the ready.

His success was a tribute to the Home. After serving as an agent for a large developer, he had started his own real estate business and at twenty-six he was on the verge of a great success. "Believe me, Eugene. The world will hear of Elton."

He was her boy. He returned to see her two or three times a year. I saw her pleasure when he entered, lighting up that worn room. He wore a checked suit, a hankie in his lapel pocket. He brought a bouquet of roses for Miss Wyman. He kissed her on the cheek.

"Business? Terrific!" As much as he could handle. Right here in the Margaret Tessler neighborhood. A hot area, in transition from Catholic to Jew. The Catholics were heading for Royal Oak and Birmingham, while the Jews moved to Six and Seven Mile Roads.

"Miss Wyman tells me you're smart, one of the brightest. Terrific. But can you sell? Without hustle you could be Albert Einstein and you'd go down like a lead balloon." He thought I was young to be selling. Maybe I could grow a mustache. A blazer and gray flannels would help. He liked the college look. We could have terrific fun, two Margaret Tessler boys taking on the city of Detroit. But he gave me warning. He wasn't going to carry me. It was a tough world. I would sink or swim on my own. I wouldn't get a free ride just because of the Margaret Tessler connection.

"Well, kid. Are you interested?"

Miss Wyman stared at me and I said, "Terrific. Yes. I will," despite the protest of my heart, which longed to be free of her breath in the land of my dreams.

THREE

Just Molly and Me

I've described her as matronly, and that's how she intended herself to be seen, although she couldn't have been forty years old when she introduced me to Elton. She cultivated the matronly appearance in dress and bearing, her auburn hair secured in a knot, her work uniform a humdrum sky-blue smock over a black skirt; yet there was often a hint of something not matronly.

We saw it in our morning exercise. She put on ankle-high, white gym shoes, otherwise her regular work outfit. We exercised in the playground, weather permitting. She called out the rhythm for jumping jacks, hup-hup, hup-hup. With a "HUP!" her arms went sky-high, her legs split, she landed on her toes, and with another "HUP!" her arms clapped her thighs and she sailed from her straddle position, springing lightly, her breath unflagging. She gathered strands of auburn hair back into the band that secured her knot without pausing.

She must have seemed absurd to anyone passing by—a tall, full-bodied woman in billowing smock and skirt and gym shoes leading our workouts. She didn't seem absurd to us. She seemed quick and graceful, the buoyancy in her jumps suggesting a body that was something other than matronly.

Saturday nights when she checked the dorms before leaving, we saw her in a plain brown tweed skirt and jacket, a white blouse buttoned almost to the throat, but her appearance softened by her released hair, thick and red-brown down to her shoulders. In summer, Detroit steaming, she wore short-sleeved print dresses for her nights out, no longer our familiar Miss Wyman. Lenny Lucca, seeing her in a summer dress, open at the throat, murmured, "She could fly with tits like that." He meant, I suppose, that there was lightness at her center as if she were lofted by her breasts but that's not all he meant and I told him to shut up.

He pretended to be puzzled as if I'd heard what he hadn't spoken. He knew what reaction he'd get to any disrespect to Miss Wyman and enjoyed needling me. But I saw what he saw. We all guessed at the true body that she kept under wraps. She was the center of our lives, under constant watch. When our janitor lay on the concrete, beneath the flagpole, felled by a heart attack, she knelt at his side, pulled out his tongue, rolled him on his stomach, mounted his back, tried pumping him back to life, unaware that her skirt had risen, her thighs exposed. I recovered from the shock of our janitor's dying but the thought of her thighs remained vivid and intense. No use warning myself, Stop! Respect the dying! Respect the woman who tried to save the dying! Don't think of her thighs! The fantasy had an unalterable course and only after it was done could I see her again as matronly, not to be thought of as anything else. She discouraged probing into her personal history. Once in her office when she seemed warm and available I said I'd heard a rumor that her dad was a farmer.

"He was more than that," said in a tone that made it clear I was broaching on forbidden territory.

She believed that Elton was a model of what hustle could accomplish. He would discipline my dreamy, Arcadian side and set me in motion.

Elkram Real Estate was located in a shack at the corner of a General Motors used-car lot. We faced a traffic-choked Livernois Avenue. The lot around us was strung with lights and pennants. Despite the exuberant surroundings, there was nothing inside our shack—not a piece of furniture, not a breath of air, not a sound—that signified ease or pleasure. His desk butted against my card table. There were a file cabinet, two folding metal chairs, a bookshelf containing city codebooks and listing directories. The only wall decoration was a framed, tinted photo of Harry Truman, straddled by tiny U.S. flags, in imitation of a similar picture of FDR that had once hung in Miss Wyman's office.

Our shack resonated to the idling diesels stopped near the intersection of Livernois and Six Mile Road. The heavy traffic turned the air to metal. Hot days fried the tarpaper skin of the roof. A swiveling fan on the green file cabinet made us anchor everything that could fly. Elton was stripped down to a diaphanous, short-sleeved white shirt with ribs of opaque white, his tie loosened, his collar opened wide. The seersucker jacket he used for summer business hung on the hat rack.

This was the rundown he gave me on Detroit real estate. World War II was a few years past and the Korean War underway. The economy was still revving up to satisfy consumer needs. Housing was in extremely short supply, the entire country a red-hot residential market. Detroit, with its vast wartime migrant population, had to be reinvented every day. There were no boundaries to what it could become. The two of us were in a great position to take advantage of the times. We didn't have to worry about being drafted for Korea. He had chest problems. I was rejected as unfit after I admitted to an army psychologist that I had shared in the delusion that killed my mom and dad. Lucky us, Elton said. He meant lucky, I supposed, because we were unencumbered and free.

"We're the ones can make things happen. We don't have to sit around and wait for the world to call. We go out there and call the world."

He picked up the phone to show me one way of doing business, his finger on a listing in the classified section of the *Detroit News*. "Hi, there. This is Elton Kramer of Elkram Real Estate. I understand you're not represented by an agent. Do you sincerely believe you can get the best value for your home representing yourself? I warn you, Sir, you won't save a red cent."

He didn't waste time with rebuffs, just a, "Thank you, Sir," then hung up and dialed the next home listing.

"Do you get the idea? Stir things up. Make things happen."

The message he sent out was that, in a turbulent world, no address fixed, you'd be lost without a guide, and, he, Elton, was the man to conduct you to your "blue heaven."

Sometimes after he closed a deal he hummed, off-key, what he mockingly called the Real Estate Anthem. "A turn to the right, a little white light, will lead you to my blue heaven."

"We sell the whole package," he told me, "the picket fence, the smiling face, the fireplace, the cozy room, the little nest in roses, where Molly and baby wait for Mr. Nine-to-Five."

At first he couldn't bear listening to me work the phone and tried to reform my phone voice. "You sound like you expect to be cut off. You sound like you hope you'll be cut off." He told me to control my voice as he controlled his. "Do you want the client to think he's talking to Eugenia Victoria Smith instead of Eugene Victor Smith? We need to hear sincerity and a guy with a soprano voice doesn't sound sincere."

"I'm not a soprano."

"Whatever. The point is you're a nice guy and you got doubts and it shows in your voice because you feel you're obliged to tell the truth. The truth isn't your business. You don't have to let the client in on your doubts. You're under no obligation to let every-thing hang out when you open your mouth. You have doubts, who doesn't? but the sound I want to hear is the sound of convic-tion. You're trying to get a client to make the biggest investment he's ever made and it's not enough for him to think you're a nice guy who always tells the truth. He won't put his life savings in your pocket just because you share his doubts. He hasn't come to Elkram Real Estate looking for a buddy. He comes here because he expects to find someone who knows the score, someone who can make him believe that, when he buys, the market is going sky high, and, when you tell him to sell, he better jump before the property melts under his feet. The message that sells property has to be delivered in a voice—" here he slowed down and spoke with deep emphasis—"that sounds like the absolutely authentic lowdown. Take Edward R. Murrow calling from wartime London, for example. You're too young so you probably didn't hear him broadcast in the middle of a London buzz bomb attack but you can catch him now on TV and get some idea of a great selling voice. The city could be blowing up and Edward R. Murrow makes us feel we don't have to run down to the cellar and hide. We can stay on the rooftop with him, our eyes wide open, watching the whole air show, the searchlights, the anti-aircraft, the buzz bombs hitting, and we're safe because we're with him. Listen to him on Sunday nights, the voice of conviction, the voice you want. When a client comes to you thinking of buying and isn't sure if it's the right deal, you're the one who'll tell him. He'll hear it in your voice. Keep it low and sincere and there's a chance you'll make the sale."

I tried, not wholeheartedly, to sound like Edward R. Murrow. My effort didn't convince anyone. There was no baritone in my box. Elton gave up on the voice project as he did on the mustache he suggested I grow. He thought it would give me a more mature appearance. After two weeks he looked at the growth and said, "Shave it off. It doesn't work."

He gave me an advance on salary and led me to Hughes & Hatcher, a downtown men's store, where he chose a seersucker suit that matched his own. He studied me in my new outfit and shrugged. "We'll take it anyway. You can wear it until it gets used to you." He also chose a fall outfit for me, a navy blue blazer and gray flannels, hoping I'd become adequate to it.

He invited me to hang out with him so I could learn how to be in the world. He took me after work to his rented duplex off Palmer Park. He rarely ate in, he never entertained; his rooms were meagerly furnished, but the few pieces looked top of the line—a cherrywood king-size bed, a leather sofa, a leather arm chair, a leather-topped desk, and a dark mahogany office chair. He owned a few dishes and skimped on cutlery. His main investment was his wardrobe, and that's what he wanted me to see, three large closets, crammed with suits and sport jackets and matching trousers and ties and winter coats and sweaters and perhaps a dozen pairs of shoes and several hats.

His investment in appearance reflected what he meant to be— identifiable everywhere as a man headed for the top. He drove a white Buick convertible. He had a signet ring on his right index finger, a gold number 45 on a black jade backing. He wore a diamond studded Masonic ring on his middle finger. One ring signified a college graduating class he had never belonged to, the other a fraternal organization he was about to join under the sponsorship of his friend and mentor, Andy Sermon, a Detroit developer.

He asked to see my place.

"It's not your kind of place," I told him. "I already know what your reaction will be."

"What will it be?"

"You'll tell me to move."

He showed up uninvited. I heard Mrs. Tuchler answer the door, his loud query, then her brusque answer, "He's on the third floor, the room on the left." He came running upstairs and I met him at the top.

He looked over the room quickly.

"Move. The sooner the better."

I told him the room suited me fine. "Why should it trouble you where I choose to live?"

"Why should it trouble me? What should trouble you and doesn't trouble you is what troubles me. You share a third floor john with two other guys. I hear some old geezer croaking downstairs. It's a loser's set-up, a lousy neighborhood. You can't have big dreams when you come home to this."

I liked the location close to the Wayne campus.

He wanted me to relocate to his neighborhood of hustling young professionals.

I couldn't afford Palmer Park.

"Why not?"

It was too expensive, out of my league.

"If you don't have the nerve to go into hock for your future, you got no future." He offered to lend me money to pay the rent. "It's not charity. I'll get it back with interest. I believe in you, kid."

I had my own ideas about my future and stayed in my funky room in the shadow of Wayne University.

Until Elton's business took off, a major source of his income was agenting for Sermon, Inc. The Sermon Corporation owned tracts of farmland and orchard skirting Detroit. What Elton called empty land—only used for apples and corn and hay and potatoes and dairy—was transformed by Sermon into living space for young families. The production method was efficient and simple. Bulldozers knocked over trees, filled dales, scraped down to raw earth and leveled fields. White clapboard homes for the less affluent and larger brick colonials for the upwardly aspiring were dropped on blank land—plop, plop, plop—one after the other, and anchored in coils of pavement.

Andy Sermon admired Elton's hustle and put him in charge of Ponchartrain Estates, a development in Northwest Detroit.

"It's a terrific opportunity," Elton said. "We're linked with Sermon. If we do a good job everything will open for us."

He thought I mourned the passing away of the Detroit countryside and blasted my ignorance. Was I stupid enough to regret the vanished forests and farms and apple orchards? Was I put off by the shrub-like evergreens? "Give those trees a chance. They're midgets now; in twenty years we'll have another forest."

We stood outside the Ponchartrain Estates office on summer weekends, in our blue striped seersucker suits, waiting for couples to enter our domain.

"Elton Kramer here." He offered his hand to a hesitant couple. He presented his Elkram card and introduced me. "My associate Eugene Victor Smith." We led them to a model home.

Most of the home seekers, brand new to private ownership, approached the models timidly. They were reluctant to stray from the plastic runners that trailed over carpet and tile. Elton encouraged them to take charge. He opened windows, ran faucets, prodded them to flush the Kohler toilets that could swallow anything and after a roar come to complete silence with no grumbling, leaky aftermath. He took them to the small cellars to see the new oil furnaces. There would always be clean fuel in the pipeline. They'd never have to trouble with coal deliveries. They wouldn't have to navigate dirty coal bins or suffer choking coal dust. He reminded them of icy Detroit winters and the advantage of wall-to-wall carpeting. No more frozen feet in winter. Each unit had floor-to-ceiling drapes and electric kitchens. Each unit had a small backyard with room for a sandbox, a playpen, a small garden to accompany the evergreen shrubs.

I'd never lived in a house and I was at first as much in awe of these Ponchartrain models as any of our clients. The first time I turned the lever to demonstrate a flush I felt as if I were intruding on someone else's property.

"You're no orphan anymore," Elton said. "Take charge."

We operated from an office just beyond a stone gate and welcoming arch that carried the subdivision name, PONCHARTRAIN ESTATES. A steady stream of clients was channeled between overhead pennants and rows of cardboard arrows first to our office, then to model homes.

Our clients were part of the Southern influx that had manned the Detroit war industry. After the war they found work on auto assembly lines, at auto parts suppliers, and in construction. According to Elton, Ponchartrain was a terrific deal for these people. Most of them came from a meager background of outdoor plumbing, pumped well water, and pot-belly coal stoves. Sermon, Inc. released these migrants from their cramped trailer parks to expansive living.

"They've come to 'blue heaven.' Like the anthem says, 'Molly and me and baby makes three.' 'Three' is almost as far as these hillbillies need to add. Oh, maybe they'll get to six or seven or eight or even a dozen but you and me, buddy, we're aiming for a million, not kids, but bucks." He mocked our clients as Okies and Arkies and hillbillies, even though, as I later found out, his own family origin was rural Arkansas.

Elton mocked what I loved. Summertime brought flocks of young nest-seekers, the wives swollen with coming family, and I could imagine one of these slim, sandy women who entered our model homes—a kid inside her expanding middle—cozying my nest.

On weekdays Elton drove me to work, stayed awhile, then left to do Elkram business. He called in frequently to check the action. He returned in the afternoon to complete what paperwork was necessary. On weekends, our busiest time, Elton remained all day.

He wasn't around when I made my first solo sale. A couple entered, my age, perhaps a few years older. Her belly flowered, the rest of her still in bud, slim and fair and graceful. The husband said, "We're looking to buy but to tell the truth I'm pretty sure this is out of our range. The wife said to let's stop anyway, so if it's okay with you, Sir, we'll have a look."

His name was Dave Bell, a lanky, handsome man, his sun-burnished face shaved close, the sleeves of his white shirt rolled, muscular arms and throat. I was reminded of a photo of my young father, just married and back from war. Dave was also a war veteran. He worked as a welder on the Dodge assembly line. He called me "Sir," as if I, who had barely entered life, outranked him. While we talked she wandered the plastic trail of the model interior, abstracted and dreamy. He told me they had saved for three years and now had a few hundred dollars for a down payment. They couldn't afford to make a mistake. They'd seen dozens of places and were still looking.

I imagined myself nesting with a slender, ripening blue-eyed Molly like the one now running the bathroom tap and offered them my dream of home. "Buying a house? Maybe it's scary when you first think about it but it turns out to be the easiest thing in the world. Consider what we have for you here at Ponchartrain."

An elementary school was under construction nearby. A church of their choice was in walking distance. I showed them the tiny wedge of sunny yard where they could put in a vegetable garden. The mud flat out front would soon be sodded. They would have a community of their own kind—young couples with kids, everyone just starting out, no worry about traffic or violence or strangers. Later, when the nest was full, they could use their equity to finance something in an even better neighborhood. The first step was the hardest, but they couldn't go wrong. Ponchartrain Estates was a sure investment.

I took time with them. I knew I was convincing, even though I was a tenor, not a baritone. Finally he called her over—she had listened to me while wandering—and asked if they should do it. She looked at me, wide, blue, inquiring eyes. I nodded and she nodded and it was a thrill to have her acknowledge me. When Elton returned he did the paperwork and closed the deal.

I told Elton how I had made the sale.

"Yes!" he said. "You got it. Sell the dream and you'll score nine times out of ten."

Of three kinds in an entrepreneurial set-up, the seller, the buyer, the looker, Elton considered the seller the top dog. The seller controlled the action. What could a buyer do but resist? The best of sellers were themselves buyers and so knew the language of desire.

The looker—the mere looker who never plunged—was stuck in front of the show window, only his eyes alive, just killing time.

"I wouldn't have wasted my time on a couple like that. I'd have spotted them as 'lookers' and brushed them off. You did a great job."

I sold to another couple a week later. The rangy, dark woman, also pregnant, did the negotiating. She had a vibrant, deep, Southern voice. Her husband Bobby had fought in the South Pacific as a Seabee and accompanied General MacArthur when he returned to the Philippines.

She asked about financing. I told them they'd have no trouble qualifying for a low-interest GI loan.

She opened and closed the drapes. She tested faucets and tried light switches. She was delighted with the all-electric kitchen. "Beats a pump and a well, don't it, Bobby?" He was a thick, balding slag hauler at the Ford River Rouge plant. He stared glumly out the French doors at the tiny yard with its raw earth and stubs of evergreens. The only decent object he could see in that space was a fledgling plum tree with marble sized purple fruit.

"Isn't that a beautiful tree, Bobby?"

He didn't answer for a few seconds then said bitterly, "I could buy a tree like that for a buck and a half. We're nowhere out here."

I put myself in his shoes. To buy a house for that tree? To be confined to this barren view for a lifetime?

I spoke to her, but pitched to him. I summoned up a different vista than the one he looked at and imposed it on the blank fields of Ponchartrain Estates. A creek was at the rear of the development, a dam was planned for the creek, and one day there would be a pond stocked with fish almost in their backyard. They were buying into a hot neighborhood. Prices were bound to go sky high. It was an absolutely sure thing. Housing was still tight six years after the war, the population soaring. There was a drive-in fifteen minutes away on Ten Mile Road. The Wyandotte Inn, a saloon that featured country music, was in walking distance. A mall was under construction on Eight Mile Road that would give them all they wanted of city life—movie theaters, restaurants, a Hudson department store, an A&P market, a Cunningham drugstore, a Woolworth five and ten, liquor stores, bars, coffee shops. Everything was on the map of their imminent future. There was a bowling alley going up on Northwestern Highway. How could he be better located? He didn't have to worry about being stuck at Ponchartrain Estates. There was nothing more marketable than a Sermon home. In a year they'd be able to sell at a profit. I could see they had a baby coming and needed a home. Why prolong the agony?

I won Bobby over by assuring him escape was possible.

When my sympathy was engaged and my own dream of Home ignited I was a surprising salesman. I was selling to myself. I sold fifteen Sermon homes before I was fully licensed. Elton did the paperwork and gave me a piece of the commission. I had the trust of clients who figured a nice kid like me wouldn't con them and I didn't con them. I had a pride of authorship in this Ponchartrain Estates village, fashioned in small part by my dreams. The yards were greened. Housewives pushed strollers. Toddlers roamed the lawns and sidewalks. Moms yelled at them to stay out of the street. Street traffic was slow and drivers attentive and no one was at risk in the traffic circles of Ponchartrain. The men gathered on Sundays after church, in their leisure clothes, slinging footballs, talking about cars and work and sports. I heard radios broadcast football games on Saturday. I heard cries and laughter. The barren, eviscerated feel of the place was quickly transformed into something fertile and alive.

I received a letter of commendation from Andy Sermon. He'd heard how young I was, and how successful. He told me to come see him to discuss my future with Sermon, Inc. I was too shy and never did.

Elton, too, had a pride of authorship. He had authored me. His tutoring had shown me the future he wanted me to aim for.

The fact is, my plans didn't include Elkram or Sermon, Inc., or for that matter Elton Kramer. I was enrolled part-time at Wayne University and saved to make it full time.

Monday and Wednesday nights I put aside real estate and went to the grimy brick main building, a high school in the early 1900s. It was still in use while a new campus was being constructed around it. I overheard students rating faculty at the nearby Webster Hall cafeteria. Professor Huston Fuller seemed interesting and I signed up for his Twentieth Century Civilization, a general education requirement.

Smeared blackboards encircled the classroom. The room quickly filled. There must have been more than forty of us, some standing. I heard the scraping of iron and plywood chairs, the squeal of wooden arms unfolding, briefcases unsnapping, notebooks and texts thumped down, the glum sound and smell of childhood classrooms. I considered leaving before the class began. I had nothing in common with these students. I should have been out in the world hustling homes.

Fuller entered before I could leave. He was a tall, slim, spectacled black man with a grizzled close-cropped beard and mustache. He walked with an easy, erect, youthful stride. His age was ambiguous. He was perhaps fifty. He unloaded his briefcase, arranged books and papers on the desk. He sat down, still not looking at the class. He started calling the roll from a sheet. "Louise Lehman?" He had a pleasant, calm voice. He looked up, scanned Miss Lehman to get her in mind. He did the same with each name he called.

"Eugene Victor Smith?" I included the 'Victor' to distinguish myself from the horde of Smiths.

He raised his eyes in search of a reason to remember me. Louise Lehman he wouldn't forget. She was a confident, poised young woman, easily remembered. At the next meeting he would call, "Miss Lehman," and find her at once. When he called, "Smith," he'd again have to scan the room, not knowing where to fix his gaze until I answered, "Here," and he'd try again to hold me in mind.

He stopped after calling my name. He smiled, studied the enrollment card, "I presume it's not by chance you're named Eugene Victor? Do you know who Eugene Victor Debs was?"

"I was named for Mr. Debs."

"Eugene Victor, see me after class."

He took his time before addressing us. He shuffled his notes, as if looking for a point of entry. He told us what he would expect of us—papers, exams, attendance, class discussion.

Again a long pause before getting down to business. His subject, he said, was the twentieth century, viewed through world literature.

"My friend, the writer Saul Bellow, once said to me, 'The twentieth century, despite its enormities, is a century of progress,' and I asked what could he possibly mean? A century with two world wars, most recently the Korean war, the holocaust, the slaughter of the Armenians? That's just for starters. That's not to mention race riots, lynching, poll taxes. A century of progress? What could my friend, a most perceptive and intelligent writer, have meant?"

This was the question we would consider in the coming semester. He, too, in spite of everything, believed this had been a century of progress. He had faith that there was a clear direction to history despite all the hesitancies and turnings and retrograde movement. We had risen from primal muck, emerged from the sea. We had graduated from hunters and gatherers to become peasants and farmers. We had moved from cave to village to city to nation state. Though the progress hardly followed a straight line, its long-range direction was up, up in quest of perfection. We would never achieve the ideal society, but it was a goal we could strive to approximate. What was an ideal society? No distinction of class or race or nation, no mine, no thine, no war, no oppression, enough food and shelter for everyone. That wasn't his exact language, but it was so close to my father's statement of belief, I knew I wanted to study with him.

He passed out a syllabus and a reading list—he would begin with a foundation in the past. He assigned for the next meeting the first books of Plato's *Republic.*

I came up to him after class.

He asked, "Do you know who Eugene Victor Debs was?"

"A socialist."

"A labor leader, a war resister, a heroic man."

"In jail during the First World War as a pacifist."

"Correct. You're the bearer of a good name. But I have a problem with you, Eugene." The class was an upper division course. His hands were spread out over the roll sheet where I was identified as a sophomore.

I told him I was limited to part-time study. I worked during the day. I'd been at Wayne long enough but hadn't accumulated enough credits for his class.

"What work do you do?"

"I sell real estate."

He gave me the studied glance he used when taking roll.

"Not the kind of work I'd imagine for Eugene Victor. What sort of real estate do you handle?"

"I sell houses in the Northwest area."

Still seated, he gathered up his books and notes and enrollment cards and put them in his briefcase.

He looked up quickly and smiled. "Can you get me a house in Northwest Detroit, Eugene?" Before I could answer he asked how he could refuse to admit the namesake of Eugene Debs. "I'm sure you can handle this class. See you next Wednesday." As I was leaving, he said, "If you find a nice house in a nice neighborhood, let me know."

Everything about Professor Fuller suggested control and order. He wore a gray turtleneck, the collar precisely rolled. His nails were manicured, his beard closely trimmed. There wasn't a wrinkle in his Harris Tweed jacket.

He lived not far from me. He rented a large flat three blocks from the university. He had a white wife, a dangerous coupling in the Detroit of 1953.

A few minutes in his classroom and black-white became an irrelevant distinction. On campus, when I later walked with him, I felt proud to be in the company of a noted Wayne professor. Within a radius of three blocks from the campus center, still University territory, his color had little relevance. Beyond the compass of Wayne his color became dangerous.

It was a relief not to have to tell him there was no chance he could buy into Ponchartrain Estates.

And why go there? Here, in the shadow of Wayne, he had an opening to the world. I could have stayed happily within the confines of this neighborhood. I'd never settle with Elton Kramer in Palmer Park or plan on graduating to a posh suburb.

Huston Fuller led us from Plato's *Republic* and Mumford's self-contained village to Florence and Rome and Paris and New York. Despite the slums, despite the unnatural massing of people, he saw progress toward a benign freedom, even in Detroit.

Elton complained that the time I spent at the university affected my work.

"What can you learn there that you can't learn better on the job?" If I were taking a course in marketing or sales or accounting maybe I'd learn something useful, but he couldn't understand my interest in ancient history. He couldn't be persuaded by my enthusiasm for the *Iliad* and ancient Troy. "Troy? Troy, Michigan? Naw. You don't mean Troy, Michigan. There's no action there. Where's your Troy located?"

"It's not on your map. It's a town of the mind."

"Then nowhere." He expected me to be full time at Elkram Real Estate. If I put my heart into it that would be my future. Sermon's letter of commendation guaranteed my career. "Andy Sermon is a power. His trail leads to the top."

He took me to Vesuvius Ristorante, off Six Mile Road near Gratiot. We shared a carafe of Chianti and when we had mellowed he told me he was considering making me a junior partner at Elkram. Not now, but someday when I was more experienced.

Why? He didn't need me. I was a novice. What did he see in me?

He answered in terms that moved and troubled me. We were Margaret Tessler boys, linked together by our memories of the Home. Weren't we as close as kin, almost brothers? We'd grown on the same food, slept in the same air, breathed the same ammonia compound that drenched corridor tiles and the same piney cakes that disinfected the urinals and the same cabbagey kitchen odor. We had slept through the same night cries and sighs and snores. We orphans went everywhere together, whether to chapel or the occasional Saturday afternoons at the Riviera Theater. He knew me as he knew few others. Whom could he better trust? It was a natural union. Miss Wyman understood that and put us together.

He interrupted his appeal when the food arrived. He ate fast and methodically, clearing his plate. When he saw I wasn't going to finish he moved to my plate. "Do you mind?"

"It's yours." I watched as he took my half-eaten chicken down to the bones.

"My rule is, 'leave nothing on the plate.'"

Vesuvius became a Friday-night custom. He was insistent and needy and it's true that we had Margaret Tessler in common. He talked freely about himself. His folks came from a farm town outside Little Rock, Arkansas. The Depression and the drought killed farming, and they moved to Detroit on the promise of a job at a Dodge assembly plant. They couldn't adapt to city life, and his mom cracked under the pressure. Elton rapped his head. "Her lights went out." She was sent to a state asylum. "When she came back she wasn't back." It was too much for his dad. "He put in a forty-eight hour week when he was lucky. What was his future? There was me, eight years old, and two other kids under three. He must have felt done for. One night he was there and in the morning he was gone. He left fifty bucks and a note. 'Dear Martha, I'm taking off.' Period. That's it. He took off. No explaining. Bye bye." Elton marveled at the simplicity of his father's action, disposing of a fate hopelessly entangled with a madwoman and three needy kids, his unraveling as bold as Alexander's cutting the knot. His mother went back to the asylum where she dwindled and a few years later died. The little kids were taken into foster homes. He was sent to Margaret Tessler.

"'Here's fifty bucks. Goodbye.' No hassle. Cute and simple, that's the ticket."

"The ticket?"

"To freedom, kid. That's the last I heard of the man."

I'm not sure how he wanted me to respond. What I felt was,

"Not cute and simple. Monstrous. Unforgivable." Maybe he wanted the "cute and simple" confirmed so that he, too, might be justified in some terrible unraveling.

He prodded me to tell about my own loss. The story I had to tell seemed tinged with craziness and yet what I'd witnessed felt utterly real. I held back, uncertain how he would take the story, but he wouldn't let me withhold and one Friday night, loosened by wine, I told about the trip we had planned from Syracuse to the Lake Michigan Island.

"So what happened?"

"You don't want to hear."

"Sure I want to hear."

There was little poetry in him while I was stuffed with dreams. I hoped he could handle the differences between us and described how I was jammed into the back of the old Ford. We drove all night and reached Dearborn by dawn. We were outside the Ford River Rouge plant when something loomed up beside the road, a delusion, the result of fatigue and poor light. Dad lost control. We flipped over.

"What did you see?"

I knew it would be hard for him to understand and that I had better shut up but he insisted. I told him that what I saw probably wouldn't stand up to the light of day. It didn't happen in the light of day and what loomed out of the dark was terrifying. Something like a dinosaur or a dragon. Dad twisted the wheel and we crashed. I flew out and was saved.

"You saw a what?"

"It looked like a dinosaur. It breathed like a dragon. My mom saw it, too. She said, 'What is that?' the last thing she said."

He picked up the menu and studied it. He snapped his fingers for the waiter. "Want anything else?" I said, no. He ordered coffee and dessert for himself. He poured the rest of the wine and waited for silence to expunge the dinosaur story.

"You should realize whom you're inviting to be your partner. Real estate is not in my blood." Whatever I saw had orphaned me and so was as good as real. It didn't matter if it was a delusion.

He slammed the table. "Just shut up. There are no goddamn dinosaurs in Dearborn!"

"Of course not."

"The only place there's a dinosaur is in your head!"

Yes, I said, he was right. My head was dinosaur country. No room for ordinary real estate there.

"She stuck me with a goddamn nut. Just shut up for awhile."

The dessert arrived. He concentrated on a bowl of bread pudding topped by a scoop of vanilla ice cream. After a few spoonfuls he shifted to the solid ground of orphan memories. He recalled desserts made of leftovers. Bread pudding like this, but without the ice cream. Corn flakes baked in honey. Tapioca pudding with strawberry jam. Jelloed fruit. He, too, had memories of morning exercises in the schoolyard. Freezing mornings, puffs of breath. She shouted, "Isn't it a beautiful day to be alive, boys?"

"Alive? I froze my skinny ass off."

Al Clamage, the radio repair entrepreneur, was one of the older boys when he arrived at the orphanage. "Al wasn't the brightest star in the sky but he was a star in shop." They were among a group of orphans who one Saturday afternoon went to the Riviera Theater, accompanied by Mr. Atkins, the shop teacher. Elton had a vivid recollection of the movie they saw, *A Star is Born* with Janet Gaynor and Frederic March. In the climactic scene the suicidal Norman Maine plunges into the ocean and swims toward the huge setting sun. The ocean is endless, the sun unattainable, Norman Maine's death by drowning a sad, weepy climax to a sunny afternoon. The scene weighed down on them—"the orphan blues," Elton called the mood—until Al Clamage said, in a flat, unaffected voice, "The guy's after the beach ball and he's not going to make it."

"That's not a beach ball, you moron! That's the sun!"

The power of the scene was undermined, grief defeated, as Al Clamage intended. The boys howled with laughter, ruining the moment for everyone in the theater who treasured sorrow. Mr. Atkins led them out before the movie reached its maudlin end. It was late afternoon, the sun still up. They gathered at the bus stop, still laughing. Mr. Atkins exploded. "The Riviera donates tickets to Margaret Tessler. You clowns got no gratitude?"

"Al Clamage was the kind of guy—still is—that wants everyone to be happy. If Miss Wyman asks him to give a kid a job it may be a tight squeeze but he'll fit him onto the payroll. The same goes for me. When she asked me to take you on, I said, 'For you, Kate, anything.' And it still goes, even if it turns out she stuck me with a loony. So don't worry. I'm not my old man. I won't run out on you. I'll bring you along, nut case or not."

"Where are you bringing me?"

"To the top. We're on our way. No getting off now." He was after a nest, all right, but no Ponchartrain Estates blue heaven. He'd have the right home, the right woman, the right location. He now had the wherewithal to make his move. His investments in real estate were paying off. He meant to rise in status from broker to developer. I would be there with him. That was his plan. "Forget Troy. Forget Florence. Forget dinosaur bullshit. I'm bringing you along."

He would accept me, whatever I was; he was a true friend, and I thought it wouldn't be the most terrible fate to be Elton Kramer's junior partner.

I asked him one night if he was ever lonely.

"Why should I be?"

"You live alone. You eat all your meals in cafes or restaurants. You don't have a girlfriend."

He was annoyed that I would think he could be lonely. He didn't have time to be lonely. As for girlfriends, did I mean sex? He had all the sex he cared for. Was that what I wanted to know?

"Not exactly."

"I go downtown to the Book Cadillac, see what's doing at the bar. If someone looks good, I'm not shy. I buy her a drink, talk her up and if I get lucky I take a room at the hotel for twenty bucks. If I don't score I go to my fallback position. Her name is Frances Rex. She has a place off Dexter Avenue. For ten bucks Frances cures loneliness. It's her full-time job. Are you lonely, kid?"

Often, I said.

"I'll take you to see Frances."

"I don't think so."

"She'll get the dragons out of your head. It'll be my contribution to your mental health."

He kept on pushing, and if I hadn't been interested I could have made my refusal convincing. One Friday night he drove me in his Buick convertible to Dexter Avenue and the apartment of Frances Rex. We entered a four-story tan brick apartment building. We took the elevator to the third floor. We walked down a carpeted corridor past a dozen apartments and at the very end, next to the illuminated exit sign, Elton pressed the buzzer of F. Rex. The door opened a few inches, the chain in place.

"It's Elton, Frances. I come with a friend."

The chain was released, the door opened. Frances, in housecoat and slippers, could have been any housewife in that building.

"My boy here"—Elton indicated me with his thumb—"is a cherry. Take care of him, Frances."

I felt reduced by the introduction, my inexperience revealed, my failure guaranteed.

Elton stayed in the front parlor while she led me to a bedroom. She was immediately and indifferently naked. She hung her housecoat on a hook in the bedroom door, and turned to face me with no need to represent herself as anything other than what she was. She had the ripeness of a woman Miss Wyman's age, her gourd-shaped breasts ample, not so huge as the breasts I remembered Mrs. Alfieri swooping into her brassiere. She was a faded blonde, the skin of her face loosened, slightly swollen beneath the chin, her mouth wide, her lips thin, her blue eyes indifferent. She wore no makeup.

It was my first sight of an entirely naked woman. I didn't look closely. If I'd have met her afterward at the A&P I might not have recognized her.

Perhaps she wouldn't have recognized me either, though she had an intimate view, soaping me with as much attention as a good housewife might give to her silver. She led me to the bed and sat me down and asked in a voice as neutral as a grocer's what I'd like. I didn't know how to answer. She shrugged and bent to me. I watched her smooth, rounded back. The thrill she induced didn't spread beyond the flesh she raised. She lay down and pulled me on to her and it was quickly done, of no more significance to her than a minor household task. I squeezed her bottom to discover where I was. She said, Careful now, and I let go, not sure I'd been inside her. Elton paid at the door.

"How did it go?"

"Terrific."

"A lesson from Professor Frances Rex beats anything they teach at Wayne, right?"

I thanked him for the loneliness cure. I didn't admit my shame and disappointment.

It wasn't enough that we were both Margaret Tessler boys. We had different kinds of loneliness and needed different cures.

By fall I'd saved enough to concentrate on Wayne. My application for full-time status was accepted. I had to make a decision whether to enroll for the winter semester. I was encouraged by Huston Fuller, who promised to guide me to the best of Wayne.

If I were to quit Elton, it would have been only fair to give him early notice. I delayed, still not sure.

We were almost finished at Ponchartrain Estates. There were only a few units left unsold. We were due to pull out after Thanksgiving, when the real estate season entered its doldrums.

The place was alive, pumpkins drying on doorsteps, turkey pictures in the windows, football games pumped into the air from passing cars. Plumes of smoke rose from chimneys. I felt like a founding father of a new colony.

One breezy Saturday afternoon Elton took off, leaving me in charge. He said he had business and would pick me up later and drive me home. I sat in the office. Puffy clouds were moving fast, heavy clouds on the horizon. A rainstorm had passed; another was brewing. I smelled wood smoke from Ponchartrain chimneys. All around me I heard the sound of Saturday-night gatherings. I suppose I could have dropped in on old clients and would have been welcome but I didn't know how to get beyond my position as a Ponchartrain official and reveal myself as the inexperienced kid I was. Elton called to say he would be very late.

"Go next door, grab yourself a bed and relax. I got lucky. I could be all night."

I closed the office and went next door to the model home I had been showing for a good part of a year. It was furnished for display. In the bedroom there was a made-up bed. The double bed, though lacking sheets and blankets, was covered with a chenille spread. I turned up the heat, turned on the bedside lamp, sprawled on the bed with a novel I'd heard the group from Webster Hall praise, listened to distant thunder and entered the wintery mood of Gide's *Symphony Pastorale*.

A blind girl lived in the snowy countryside with her foster father, the local pastor. The book took a turn toward incest. I was immersed in the snowy world of the blind girl and her imminent tragedy. I drifted into a dreamy state, centered on Gide's blind girl.

How did she learn she was beautiful? Perhaps through the sudden formal, deepening voices of men. She could hear their avidity. She would be confused and vulnerable. She had little sense of what was underfoot or in her close neighborhood. There was something about being blind that resembled being farsighted. The farsighted, too, could be clumsy dealing with ordinary affairs. They might have the power to see beyond horizons and guide us to transcendence but needed a helping hand to survive the commonplace. I imagined what it would be like to be the guide of the beautiful blind girl. I imagined being the one whose touch brought her into focus and led her to safety, and imagined the deliverance she would offer in return.

I was in the dreamy other world of *Symphony Pastorale* when I heard the party next door breaking up. It was the house I had sold to Bobby Orleans, the once-reluctant Ford slag hauler I had talked into buying.

The party moved outside and I heard Bobby leading a boisterous group toward the parking lot near the office. Bobby spotted the bedroom light and guessed the model was occupied. He yelled, "Gene, you there?" I didn't answer. It wasn't yet nine o'clock, too late for business, too early to shut the night down. Bobby must have wondered if some intruder had taken over the model and he beat on the door. "Gene?" I opened to a group of seven led by Bobby and his almost-delivered wife. Behind them was my first sale, the Bell couple. Dave Bell was the man who resembled my young father. Alongside him was his wife, one of my dream Mollys, a baby wrapped in her arms.

What I promised Bobby had come true. Ponchartrain Estates was just what he wanted. His new buddies were all around the neighborhood. His wife was about to deliver. It was easy getting to the bowling alley and the Wyandotte Inn. Bobby was content. He waved to me whenever he passed the office on his way home from work. He yelled, "What's doin', Gene?" then a ritual exchange: Come on by, he said. When business lets up, I said. Play a little, kid. All work and no play, you know. Say hello to the Mrs. for me, I said. He said he sure would.

Bobby had with him a pal from Ford, Jack Schultz, and his pregnant wife, Georgia. Schultz was a big, redheaded man, with a fiery mustache.

Bobby had just been talking about me to the Schultzes. "I'm trying to sell them on Ponchartrain Estates, Gene. Doing your work for you. I told Jack all he needs is a kick in the ass and your smooth talk and he'll be ready to move in. Georgia is already with me on this. Isn't that right, Georgia?" The tall, pregnant woman shrugged and laughed.

Bobby admitted he hadn't trusted me at first meeting. He had considered me just another slick salesman and he braced against being conned, but I'd told him the truth when I sold him on Ponchartrain Estates. Great pals lived on either side of them, wonderful neighbors like the Bells.

Schultz said he'd like to come back when he was more in a house-buying frame of mind. "I'm right now a little bit relaxed and it's not houses I want to look at."

Lagging behind, a bitten apple in hand, was a seventeen- or eighteen-year-old, a loaded tote bag over her shoulder. Maureen was Dave Bell's niece from Toledo, staying the weekend with her aunt and uncle. She wore an oversized man's sweater. She resembled a Modigliani painting I had seen on exhibit at the Art Institute, tall, slim, with a slight overbite, plump lips parted, her dreamy eyes either fixed on a far horizon or simply indifferent to what was under her nose. She was as unexpected as a dream materialized. She had been conjured up by my vision of Gide's blind girl. She answered with a mumbled, "How do," to my "Good to meet you."

I told Schultz not to rush off. It was after hours but I'd be glad to show them through the house. "This is one of the units still available, a great location, near parking, near the new pond coming next year. I have a standard spiel—" here I smiled—"that will give you a better idea of how Ponchartrain Estates can fit your plans."

I ushered them down the corridor toward the kitchen. Maureen came last and brushed me with her hip. I spoke the language of real estate to the Schultzes and a different language to her. I opened the cellar door, the Schultzes passed down, and Maureen and I brushed again and for a moment lingered. She had finished her apple and held the core. I said, Let me take that. She touched me with sticky fingers.

I went through the regular litany of oil furnace and carpeting and drapes and the possibilities for the backyard and the burgeoning neighborhood, and the increasing value and the low interest rates, the ardor in my voice heard as a quality of salesmanship by the unwitting. I meant her to hear something else.

Jack Schultz liked the house and the location. Dearborn and the Ford plant were just a half-hour commute down Scheafer Highway. Most important, these were their kind of people.

I was on fire with touches that happened in full view and appeared as the ordinary contact of people in close quarters. We were on a plane of feeling I thought invisible to the others.

When it was time to leave I told the Bells and the Orleans how pleased I was that everything had worked out for them. They must have thought I was a nice guy, concerned for their welfare. My concern was for the niece. Mrs. Bell asked, Are you spending the night? I said I was waiting for Elton but it looked like he wasn't coming and I'd probably sleep over which was fine with me since I had a good book, a good bed, not a bad place to be with a storm on the way.

I walked them outside. There were already splatters of rain. The Bells and Maureen turned to the left toward home. Bobby and his wife turned right with the Schultzes toward parking. We shouted goodbyes left and right. She murmured, Seeya, and I said cheerfully, The sooner the better, nothing more than what a salesman might say to clients, but encoding a desire I hoped she'd guess.

I returned to the bedroom and saw her tote bag on the floor. I lay down with *Symphony Pastorale* but couldn't read. How could she get away from the Bells without their knowing?

The storm began with a thunderclap and immediately flailed the house; I figured she now wouldn't come for her tote. It was almost midnight when I heard the knock and opened. She was wearing her uncle's yellow slicker.

"I came for my bag."

"I should have brought it over."

"That would have been dumb." She dumped the wet slicker on the plastic floor covering and, absolutely confident that she had read all the cues correctly, walked right over, looked me in the eyes, opened her mouth, and we were on each other.

"I knew what you were thinking," she murmured.

"Yes," I said.

"Let's get in bed."

"Do they know you're out?"

"They're asleep."

It was my dream realized, though her body wasn't the body I had dreamed. She was nothing ethereal. The momentum was there and we did what she had done before and in the moment of climax I was in my dreams again and blurted, "Live with me!" It was stupid because almost immediately I wanted her out of there. It was too rude to ask her to dress and go home. I had little to say and let her talk.

She was with her uncle because things weren't working out at home. Her folks kept tight control. She'd screwed up at school. She admitted she was hard to handle, a trial to anybody, but got along fine with the Bells. She had an easy, unreflective voice. It was a complete misjudgment to have placed her in a Modigliani painting or a Gide novel. I said she'd better get home in case the Bells woke up and found her missing.

"Naw. They don't wake up once they're under."

I coaxed her into dressing and we both had our clothes on when Bell pounded on the door. "You in there, Maureen?" he yelled over the storm. "Come on out of there."

I told her to put on her shoes.

Bell wore sweats and carried an open umbrella. He refused to enter.

"Damn you, Maureen. Come on out of there." He didn't look at me and didn't say anything until she was in her slicker. "She's not even sixteen years old. I'm disappointed in you, Sir."

I wanted to get out of Ponchartrain, out of selling, away from self-delusion.

Elton showed up at three in the morning.

"Sorry, kid. I had a live one and she wouldn't let go. Had anything to eat?"

It was then I told him I was quitting.

"What the hell you talking about?"

I couldn't stand trafficking in houses.

"You gone crazy?"

I could no more believe in selling a house than in selling bodies. We lived in our skins; a home was an extension of our skin. Selling homes was as brutal as selling bodies.

Again he realized he'd been saddled with a loony.

We drove to my place, the rain so dense he must have driven on memory. He got to my place and grabbed my arm when I was about to get out. No, Sir. He wasn't going to let go of me. He'd made promises to Miss Wyman and he was going to keep me in real estate even if he had to listen to the crap I'd picked up at Wayne.

"Selling homes? Nothing to it. The same principle as selling shoes." Were my shoes part of my body? I was inside my shoes, wasn't I? He clutched my arm. "Besides," he said, "I need you, kid."

I told him I was through with Ponchartrain, never wanted to return.

"No problem. We're done there," he said. "We got new business coming up."

FOUR

Elton Rising

Elton called me at home one miserable winter afternoon. He told me to meet him in the office. I asked why the meeting. It was terrible weather. Were buses even running?

Be there, he said, and hung up.

I entered a blizzard, waited half an hour for a bus. It was bumper-to-bumper traffic, almost no visibility, the thumping wiper blades barely clearing the snow. The used-car lot around the office was drowned in snow. I entered ready with apologies for being late, but he wasn't there. I huddled near the electric heater, my coat on. He showed up an hour late, frost-marked and exuberant. He went directly to the phone without removing his camel hair overcoat or his gloves or his tan leather cap. In mock rage he said while dialing, "What a miserable fucking place. What are we doing here, kid? Are we nuts? You'd expect to find a couple of bums in a dump like this, not big shots like us. Why don't we take off?"

"Where do we go?"

"Up, up, up," always his intended direction. "It's time to rise, Eugene."

He reached Paolo, the maitre d' at Vesuvius. "Did you get the champagne for Saturday night? There'll be three of us. Around seven o'clock." He hung up and, while dialing again, told me we were celebrating at Vesuvius tomorrow night.

"What's the occasion?"

"We're saying goodbye to the old, hello to the new."

"What's the new?"

"I'll tell you tomorrow night. I'm inviting Kate Wyman."

"She's agreed to come?"

"I'm calling her now."

"You're inviting her on one day's notice? Not a chance."

"She'll come when she hears my proposal."

"Her Saturdays are taken. Saturday is her night out."

She was on the line and he motioned me to draw near and listen. "Kate, it's Elton." He announced himself as if he were still at the center of her thoughts and she wasn't preoccupied with a new crop of orphans.

He invited her to join us for dinner at Vesuvius.

"For tomorrow night?" She laughed. "I'm sorry, Elton, you have to give me more notice than that. I'd love to catch up with you boys but I already have plans. Call me again soon, won't you?"

He told her we were celebrating a new venture that we wanted her to join.

A business venture?

"Definitely business. Business you already have a stake in."

What business? What stake?

It was too complicated to explain on the phone.

She had time between three and four tomorrow afternoon in her office.

He tucked the phone between throat and shoulder, removed his gloves, unbuttoned his coat, pushed back his cap. "An office visit isn't what I had in mind, Kate. I need to talk to you about a matter that concerns Margaret Tessler, something you're probably not aware of."

"What is it?"

He paused, reluctant to bring up a subject that might be disturbing. It would take time to make it clear. "I'll tell you this much. Kate, are you under the impression that Margaret Tessler is safe?"

"Safe? From what, Elton? From fear? From theft? From vandalism?"

"Worse." he said, "From developers."

"Developers? Developers of...?"

"Your board is either now under pressure to sell or will be soon."

"What are you saying, Elton? I've felt no pressure. We have nothing to sell."

"There's the Margaret Tessler Home for Boys to sell."

"The Home for sale? Margaret Tessler is not for sale. Why on earth would anyone want to buy an old, dilapidated building with more than a hundred orphans? It's absurd. Where did you get such an idea?"

"It's five acres of Detroit in a hot residential neighborhood, worth a fortune to a developer." He reminded her of the authority of the Board. Henry Tessler, an auto magnate of great wealth, had enshrined the memory of his daughter in the Home. He meant our Home to reflect the world he wanted, not the world as it was. He had the money and influence to bypass city and state agencies. The Home was almost free of regulation. Old Man Tessler spared nothing in designing a self-contained world with its own schools, its own curriculum, and a staff he had chosen. All of this was common knowledge, the lore of the Home, passed on to us by the staff. We also knew Tessler had dropped the first director when we orphans had turned out to be a disappointment, not the noble savages he had meant to produce. He hired Kate, barely out of school, almost a kid herself. She was lovely, strong, innocent, dedicated. He entrusted her with the memory of his daughter. "Am I on target, Kate? Hold on. Let me finish." Henry didn't plan on dying. He left a Board, not constrained by regulation, to deal with the world as it was. "You think this a Board of Utopians, Kate, all out for the kids whatever the market tells them? Maybe the trustees can ignore what the market says and keep the property for the exclusive use of a hundred orphans, but I wouldn't bet on it. They're going to see some tasty offers and, believe me, they'll bite."

Insane, she said. A malicious rumor. She couldn't believe it. "Do they say they want to buy my boys, too?"

A sale would bring a big payoff. A new facility could be found for the boys, somewhere out of town, at a fraction of the Margaret Tessler sale price. "Kate, this is no rumor. A developer I know is about to make an offer."

"A friend of yours?"

"Someone I do business with."

"This is home, Elton. This is where you and Eugene grew up. It's not a place you buy and sell."

"Someone in my line of business doesn't look at it that way. He looks at Margaret Tessler and he doesn't see my life or Gene's life or your life. He doesn't see 'home.' He sees what the market tells him to see, a five-acre parcel of prime Detroit real estate in a city busting its seams, a developer's dream, more valuable torn down and cleared away than restored."

"Is that what you see, Elton?"

"Kate, your interest is my interest. I don't forget where I grew up. I don't see Margaret Tessler as just a property. I'm on your side. Trust me. I'm working on a plan for you and the Home. That's what I want to talk to you about. A big change is coming and I'll help you get through it. The three of us working together—how can we not come out winners?"

She agreed to rearrange her Saturday night and meet us at the restaurant.

"We'll pick you up at six-thirty."

"I prefer to drive, Elton. Where is the restaurant?"

"It's on the East Side, hard to find. It'll be simpler if we come for you."

"I can't get away before eight."

"We'll pick you up at eight."

"The gate will already be locked."

"We'll wait for you outside the gate."

"It might be after eight."

"Whenever you get out, we'll be waiting."

"Well," he said after hanging up, "she's coming."

He rang Vesuvius and gave Paolo the change in time.

"What do you want to say, kid? I see that ugly look on your puss. What's on your mind?"

I told him that he'd staged his usual melodrama. He'd hustled her as if she were just another prospect. The matter was always urgent. We were always on the brink of great change. He made immediate action seem necessary. She was an innocent with no clue to how he operated. She was embedded in routine. She secured us in discipline. The celebrations she allowed in our lives conformed to tradition—Easter, the Fourth of July, Thanksgiving, Christmas. She didn't celebrate at Vesuvius. She didn't look for novelty. She didn't want change. She was completely vulnerable. He confused her and frightened her. "I'll bet every cent I've got that you're part of any tasty offer for Margaret Tessler."

"Was I talking melodrama? Stupid me. I thought I was talking Detroit real estate. Herr Professor calls it melodrama. He's the wise guy here, isn't he? Kid, you don't know crap. All this time you've been in the business and you haven't learned shit. A property like that in a city with pants so tight there's no room to breathe—five acres, prime residential area, underused—a hundred orphans living in a brick heap—how's it going to escape the vultures? You sit still in this market and you'll be taken for dead and eaten. That's plain and simple fact, not melodrama. Sure, Andy Sermon is interested. Lots of people are interested. I'm interested, too, I don't deny it."

I told him she was the only real mother he ever had and he hustled her as if she were someone he had spotted at the Book Cadillac bar.

"Get this through your dumb, thick skull. I don't hustle her. I'd never hustle her."

"You call her Kate as if she's one of your pickups."

"What should I call her?"

"It's Miss Wyman to you, not Kate."

His lips curled, his frost marks disappeared. "You're damn right she trusts me. She knows it's me who'll look out for her. It's me who'll never abandon her. She means more to me than you could ever know." He set his cap straight and laughed. "I know you think the world of me, kid. Don't keep it to yourself. Let everyone hear about your pal, Elton Kramer, who showed you the real estate game and now wants to make you rich. You still think like an orphan, full of suspicion, scared you're being conned. Get over it. Practice thinking like the big shot you're going to be." He buttoned his coat, pulled on his gloves. "We used to call her Miss Wyman. Now it's Kate. So why did I want you here? Oh, yeah. We're moving. Pack up your stuff. Use the cartons under the table. We're finished with this dump. It's goodbye Livernois Avenue. We're setting up in a fancy office on Eight Mile Road, so load up. Just the books and records and your personal stuff. Load it in my car trunk. I'll buy you lunch, then drive you back to your rat hole."

Detroit was muffled in snow. Snow had piled up for days. The salted avenues ran with icy slush.

Elton sailed his big boat down risky streets. He swung confidently through skids. When we stalled in traffic, I warned him not to turn down the side street. The side streets were almost impassable, cars buried at curbside, deep center ruts pressed into ice. He said, "My boat goes anywhere," and rode the sidewalks around roadblocks. Somehow he navigated without hitting a pedestrian. He'd had a special horn installed in the Buick. It whooped like an emergency vehicle warning traffic out of the way.

We parked across from Blakeney's Chili Parlor at the entrance to Margaret Tessler. The snow-covered playground was rimmed with snow ridges gathered from the cleared walks and driveway. Globe lights on arched stanchions lit the glittering snowfields and the long, curving approach. The dorm lights were on. The carriage lights on each side of the door were on. Her office was lighted. Someone else would darken the Home tonight, probably Mrs. Hempleman. I could imagine Miss Wyman standing at the threshold of each dorm, checking out her boys before leaving. She'd be in her brown tweed suit. Her Saturday night, usually taken by someone we didn't know, now belonged to us.

The door opened shortly after eight. She stood in the doorway, searching her purse. She wore a heavy dark wool coat, scarf tucked in, dark leather gloves, something like a beret over her auburn hair. She wore ankle-high galoshes. She stepped carefully down three steps, then trod gingerly along the icy driveway walk. She opened the gate, locked it, put the key back in her purse.

We both got out. Elton told me to sit in back.

"I intend to."

She restrained his embrace, her hands on his arms. She turned her cheek to receive his kiss. She hugged me and I relished the simple, powdery scent. I opened the back door.

"There's room for us all in front, Eugene."

I told her it would be more comfortable if I sat in back.

"That's right," Elton said.

She insisted I sit beside her. She maneuvered me between herself and Elton on the bench seat of the convertible. "It will be cozier this way."

Elton said, "Crowd in," and took off before we were settled.

He thanked her for coming.

"I had no choice. You convinced me it was urgent."

"It's very urgent, but that's not going to stop us from having a fun time. I'll tell you about it at Vesuvius."

She asked me how I was.

"I'm fine."

"He's still with me," Elton said, "still trying to get away from a marriage not made in heaven. But, yeah, he's fine. Sometimes too fine."

I was in my third year at Wayne, attending on a part-time basis. I planned to go on to graduate school. I'd saved enough to put my plan into action.

"What are you studying?"

"Philosophy. Literature."

"Is that practical?"

"My question exactly," Elton said.

"Being practical doesn't come easily for me, Miss Wyman."

"That's what always troubled me, Eugene."

I felt her warmth, breathed her scent. It was cozy in Elton's great boat sailing to Vesuvius. I rejoiced that I had always troubled her.

Elton had everything mapped out, what each of us would order, what we would drink, how the evening would build to his revelation.

We sat beneath clusters of artificial grapes hanging from ceiling latticework, the walls circled by pastel Italian views, beginning with Venice and its canals and gondolas and gondoliers, around to the opposite wall, ending in Southern Italy at Mount Vesuvius. On the corridor wall leading to the toilets there were photo blow-ups of family and staff lined up in front of a restaurant in Naples also called Vesuvius.

Paolo stood beside Elton, waiting for the wine order.

"Did you get my champagne?"

"The Dom Perignon."

"Vesuvius doesn't usually carry it, but for tonight I got the best."

"Please," Miss Wyman said, "no expensive champagne. I'm not a wine drinker. I have a touch on special occasions, but only a touch."

"I'm about to make a proposal that's going to make you rich. That's very special. This occasion deserves more than a touch of ordinary wine. It deserves a lot of the best. Bring the Dom," he told Paolo.

"I'm afraid it would be wasted on me. I can't tell the difference between an expensive champagne and a cheap champagne."

"I want to waste it on you. I can afford it. Tell her I can afford it, Gene."

"He says he can afford it, Miss Wyman, so maybe he can."

Paolo asked if we wanted another look at the wine list. Vesuvius carried an Italian sparkling wine that he could recommend, a fraction of the price of the Dom Perignon.

"Paolo, don't do me any favors. Bring on what I ordered."

"Fine, Mr. Kramer. The '49 Dom Perignon."

"Bring the other one, too, your Vesuvius cheapie. We'll try

both. We'll taste and compare and learn."

She said it wasn't necessary. He didn't have to impress her.

"Kate, let's not get hung up on the champagne. It's just a start."

"A start of what?"

"The start of thinking big."

She sat between us, close to me, our arms, resting on the linen tablecloth, almost touching. She wore an outfit much like the brown tweed she usually wore on her nights away from Margaret Tessler, a brown checked jacket and skirt, a white blouse, the top button open, her strong throat exposed. Her hair was down. I breathed the scent that once enveloped me when I was in need of comfort. It might be a turbulent world but she knew where she stood and where we ought to stand and revealed it in calm, clear diction.

Paolo rotated the champagne in its ice bucket, wrapped it in a towel, opened it with a slight pop. The presentation didn't have the effect Elton wanted. The idea of consumption so conspicuous didn't please Miss Wyman. When Elton urged her to drink, she sipped and put the glass down without comment.

"Drink and enjoy," the miffed Elton demanded. "I paid enough."

She laughed and so did I.

"Elton, you could buy the elixir of the gods and I still might not like it. Forgive me. I have very simple tastes."

"At least I got a laugh out of you. Kate, we're going to finish this bottle and try the other one and learn the difference."

His excess won her over and she sipped more of the champagne.

"Someday," he said, "you'll be able to drink this stuff and not worry about price." He raised his glass. "To the woman we respect and love, Kate Wyman, who I hope to see bathing in champagne."

He had us laughing. That's the mood he wanted. He told her he was going to talk about Margaret Tessler but first another subject. Our waiter was ready for our orders. Elton suggested the seafood. Vesuvius brought in frozen lobster tails from South Africa, fresh fish from the East. The filet mignon was superb.

"I don't care for seafood. I'll have the Caesar salad."

He was outraged and she finally agreed to a more ceremonial squab.

I had the steak. He had the lobster. He poured more of the champagne and prepared the ground for his proposal.

He belonged to a group of real estate investors, Ponchartrain Associates, organized by his friend Andy Sermon. Ponchartrain Associates specialized in the purchase of undeveloped properties in and around Detroit. Elton's participation had already brought him to the threshold of wealth. He owned three hundred acres out Plymouth Road on the way to Ann Arbor. He had acreage out Grand River and beyond Thirteen Mile Road. "I've got property all over the landscape."

"Where is this leading to, Elton?"

"A million bucks is what it's leading to."

"What has this to do with the sale of the Home?"

"Everything. Listen to me. Follow me." He was serious. He was after a million. Not nine hundred and ninety-nine thousand and ninety-nine dollars and ninety-nine cents. That final penny was important.

She asked if he imagined he'd be a new man with a million dollars.

"Absolutely. Brand new." He described how out of that brew of dollars a new being would be precipitated, an Elton with no stain of having been orphaned. He had in mind settling in an eminent location—Bloomfield Hills or Birmingham, or even Grosse Pointe—whose address would confirm his standing in the world. He had the formula for becoming rich. It was in his power to make her rich and me, too, his untrusting partner. He couldn't tell exactly how close he was. His money was tied up in deals for land. He plunged ahead, took great risks. That's why he was getting there.

Our meals arrived and Elton offered to share but we declined. He tasted my steak. He finished the champagne and summoned Paolo to bring the sparkling wine.

"Kate," he said, "you look gorgeous in that outfit."

"It's very old. People probably think I'm your granny."

"They'd have to be nuts. Who compares in this room? You see anyone, Gene?"

I didn't look up from my steak.

He returned to the subject of money. He knew how to make money grow. He could make it double, triple, quadruple. The more money you sowed, the bigger the harvest. You only had to open your eyes to see what was happening to Detroit. Everything was in ferment. Everything was changing. Everything was available if you had the nerve and intelligence to act on what you saw. He had the necessary nerve and hustle. Our time had come. Detroit was cracking open. Every part was in motion. It was our luck—our terrific luck—not to have any attachments to neighborhoods. Old neighborhoods were doomed. He saw us orphans as the children of turbulence. Great arterial roadways would bring new blood to a city that had been strangling, four lanes in each direction, from the heart of the city west to Chicago, other arteries opening to the state capital in Lansing. We would be sprung from the city. What we dreamed of and could only enjoy briefly on summer holidays—open meadows, high grass, the lake country—would be ours the year around. Ann Arbor streets, lined with flowering plum and weeping cherry, once reserved for residents of palatial sororities and fraternities, would become available to every Detroiter. At sixty-five miles an hour, non-stop, we'd arrive at a house in the country in the time it once took us to abut against city limits. All the wasteland outside Detroit—nothing but farm and orchard and forest—would be developed into new towns.

It was there to be had. We had to think beyond neighborhoods. We had to think regionally, nationally, even globally. He was lucky to have Andy Sermon as a teacher. Sermon knew the country as few Detroiters knew their own street. He was informed about the path freeways would take. He saw patterns of growth. His imagination was unbounded, his intuition always on target.

"Kate," he said, "it is my intention to make you a rich woman. It's the least I owe you."

"You don't owe me anything, Elton."

She had hardly touched her squab and Elton did what I knew he would. "Okay, if I pick at this?" She shoved her plate to him. He poured the Italian sparkling wine for all of us, disregarding her protest. He ate, drank, and talked.

"I owe you," he said, "more than you can imagine," and raised a forkful of squab breast to his mouth and still chewing told us the secret of becoming rich. The secret was leverage. The proper application of small capital could pry loose substantial parts of Detroit. The city flaked off and you had gold in the form of land. All it needed was knowledge about the path of growth—Sermon had that—and five percent down. Ponchartrain Associates chose land that could be turned over quickly at a healthy profit. The land was held for six months to earn capital gains credit, then sold and the profits reinvested, the next time a larger parcel bought and six months later a larger profit. He had started the process five years ago with a mere ten thousand dollars. His holdings now had to be worth in the neighborhood of five hundred thousand dollars. He was putting much of it into a huge Livonia parcel Ponchartrain Associates had bid on. The entire deal was worth several million dollars. The hard part was that for six months you had to hustle to make payments on your note. For six months there would be a struggle to meet payments. But where was the risk? He could always borrow against his holdings or even, in an emergency, sell early and forego the benefit of capital gains.

He wiped his mouth, done with her squab.

"There's hardly any risk, Kate. This is land. It won't spoil. It isn't wheat or pork bellies. It's not stocks. This is land we own. I spoke to Andy Sermon and a quarter share in Livonia is reserved for you and Gene to divvy up."

We needed five thousand in cash for a down payment, five percent of the valuation. Monthly payments would be about five hundred dollars, steep for us, he knew, but he promised that in six months the value of the land would increase by as much as a half—it was along a pending freeway route, information only available to insiders. Our small investment would at least quadruple. In about six months Miss Wyman and I would have twenty thousand dollars to divide between us.

She said it was impossible. She was not a rich woman. She would have to use almost her entire savings.

The twenty-five hundred I'd have to put down was all I'd saved for my degree and graduate studies.

"Change your way of thinking," he told us. "You're going to be rich." He was so sure of success he would cover any of her losses. "I'll pay out of my own pocket. But losing isn't going to happen."

She would have to speak to a friend who advised her on financial matters.

"Who's your friend?"

"Someone who knows my affairs."

"I don't want our plans to get around. No outsiders. But to please you I'll talk to him. If he's got any business sense he'll tell you to jump on board." He assured her that once she took the plunge her fears would vanish. It was necessary for her to get into the swim. It was the only way she could avoid sinking with Margaret Tessler. A year from now Ponchartrain Associates would join with Sermon, Inc. in a downtown development. All the partners would be invited to participate. The twenty-five hundred she was now putting on the line would then have multiplied.

"You'll be rich. It's not Dom Perignon talking, it's your own orphan boy, Elton Kramer, and he's telling you we're going to be rich. And then—" he paused, "—we're going to build the Katherine Wyman Home for Boys."

She couldn't believe what he was saying. It was madness.

He told her the demise of Margaret Tessler wouldn't be the

end of her world. "Your board is going to let Margaret Tessler go. You'll beat your head against a wall if you try to stop it. It's a valuable property. It brings no income. It's the boys we're concerned about, isn't it? When Margaret Tessler goes we'll find a new place for the boys, somewhere upstate where the land is cheap and the costs are low and we can do something brand new, something glorious, the Katherine Wyman Home."

"How can you not understand, Elton? Margaret Tessler is my life. I'll be shattered."

"It was your life. But no more. We're moving on, the three of us. We'll be with you every step of the way. Gene and me are here to help. Listen, we can arrange it so that Margaret Tessler stays open until the Katherine Wyman Home for Boys is established. You'll have your own board."

"You frighten me, Elton. I can't dream of a new Home."

"Start dreaming, Kate. The idea will grow on you. Dream the Katherine Wyman Home. Say it and it'll become real. The Katherine Wyman Home."

"You've had too much champagne and I've had too little."

"We need another bottle." He summoned Paolo despite her protest and ordered another bottle of "the good stuff." "This is no fantasy. I leave fantasy to Gene. My dreams come true. Trust me, Kate." He invited us to drive into the country the next day to look at his holdings and look at the Livonia parcel and understand how he could make dreams become fact.

"Tomorrow is Sunday. We have chapel and inspection, then the staff is off. Not Sunday."

We had to decide before Monday morning. That's when the

ownership of the Livonia parcel would be decided. Sunday was her only chance to consider the investment.

She wanted to get away from him and back to the Home and solid ground; she agreed to survey his land Sunday afternoon.

"Now," he said, "how about dessert?"

We both refused and he was willing to let us have our way on dessert.

I told Elton I didn't want to be rich. My twenty-five hundred in savings was enough to see me through graduate studies at Wayne. I'd happily settle for that.

"So why are you going along? Just to make me happy? Do you think you're Saint Eugene Good Guy? Come on, kid. Admit it. You're scared but you want the action."

Not true, I said. Not true. He dropped me off and was on his way.

The next day when we came for her she told him she had changed her mind. She couldn't come along. She couldn't remember taking a Sunday off. She felt Margaret Tessler sliding away from her. Many of the staff were gone on Sunday. She respected his intention; she knew he meant well, but in the light of day, all this talk of investing her savings in land and the demolition of Margaret Tessler and a new home was unthinkable. She needed time to absorb such terrible information. She hadn't been able to get in touch with her financial adviser. She apologized for her vacillation, she was ashamed to shilly-shally, but she needed time and couldn't go with us.

He told her she didn't have time. Monday morning was her

deadline. Our quarter share blocked the closing of the deal. Any further delay would jeopardize the deal and we'd be dumped. She'd be no better off if she waited. Her problems would still be there. The Margaret Tessler offer was on the table. If she didn't act everything might be lost; there'd be no Katherine Wyman Home.

He pulled her along, inch by inch. She left Mrs. Hempleman in charge of Sunday's activities and we took off in early afternoon. This time I sat in back.

It was a brilliant day, snowy fields blazing. Elton wore sunglasses. I felt distant and disconnected. It was in part the weather, cold, dry, breezy, luminous, exhilarating. Every detail of every tree and every shadow of every tree were precisely outlined, nothing hazy or blurred. As we sped by, the countryside unrolled for us, each feature brilliant and exact, the landscape surreal despite its familiarity.

Dazed and dreamy, I looked at Miss Wyman from in back and imagined that if she turned around, I'd see someone else. I said to her, as if talking to someone on stage, "I'm not sure what to call you. It's always been Miss Wyman. I feel I need permission to call you Kate."

"My boys who have graduated usually call me Kate or Katherine, sometimes Miss Wyman. No need for formalities."

"My friends call me Gene. Sometimes Eugene. Never Mr. Smith."

We took off for Ann Arbor along Plymouth Road. The windward sides of barns were heaped with snow. Powder flew from steep pitched roofs. The protected façades were clear and stark red.

We sailed into Elton's surreal world stunned and disconnected.

He was entirely there, vibrant, driving fast, whipping around to explain the sights to us, whipping back to return the Buick to our side of the road. The strong wind drove snow powder over the centerline and it wasn't always clear what side we were on. When we shimmied over apparently clear patches of road covered with invisible ice, he didn't slow down. She asked him to please slow down, to please keep his eyes on the road, but he didn't slow down. He had too much to reveal and too little time. He had promised to get her back before dinner and he wanted to show us the world he owned.

"No need to rush, Elton. It's all right if I'm late. Edith's in charge." She tried ordinary conversation to calm him down. "After your million, Elton, then what?"

After a million? He would join forces with Andy Sermon. He would become a major partner in a planned downtown development. He would upgrade himself from realtor and investor to builder and developer.

But what was there for him after development?

He meant to have an elegant wife, a woman with fine bones and light hair, not a taint of poverty in her voice or shape. With a million anything could be his. He would be brand new. This wasn't idle dreaming.

We drove through the white countryside in his white convertible to acreage outside Farmington. A harvest of stakes with red ribbons sprang from the snowy fields. He said, Mine! He waved down a lane that traveled straight out to the horizon where a red barn stood on a hill. Mine! He pointed at right angles down the Farmington Road toward a distant chimney, a plume of smoke jerked into the freezing, brilliant sky. He claimed hundreds of acres outside Novi. Returning to the city, he showed us the Livonia property reserved for us, a small piece of the vast Ponchartrain Associates parcel. All it needed was our signatures on a note and we, too, could say, "Mine."

"That was mine," he said as we closed in on the city. "And that. And over there." We looked at a row of new homes going up in Oak Park. "It was my land." Now it was a Sermon, Inc. development.

He laid claim to my earth, my sky, my horizon. They were staked out by this knobby, hungry, big-eyed orphan in an expensive camel hair overcoat and sharp tan leather cap. His appetite was enormous. Not two hundred thousand. Not three, four, five, et cetera, but a million. Not a penny less. A million dollars of Detroit. And no doubt afterward a second million, a third, arriving at higher stages of being as he reached new cardinal sums until—what? A billion? The numbers were infinite, but not the years of his life. If he extended his claims far enough, he'd come to the end of his days. Then what? I asked. A monument to a dead billionaire?

He accused me of faking a sour view, disguising my fear of rising beyond the boundaries imposed on me. Detroit, said this new conquistador, belonged to anyone with the nerve to plant ribboned stakes and claim the ground. As he talked I lost sight of the knobby hustler, my fellow orphan, and saw a man on the rise to a higher state, a man with a vision of development, building from nothing, from less than nothing—from slum and decay. He wanted to eviscerate the blighted interior of Detroit. Down with ancient relics so begrimed with a seedy history there was no cleaning them. "Yes, Margaret Tessler, too." Rip it out. Nothing there to redeem. A rotten gut. He and Sermon were of one mind. Bulldoze the foundations. Get down to something raw and untouched. Build from there.

We ended the circuit of his claims in our new office on Eight Mile Road. Eisenhower was on the wall with the crossed American flags. Elton had a grand office, mine far more modest on the other side of the lounge.

He sat us at his desk, placed the note and copies in front of us.

She balked at the last minute. "I can't sign until I talk to my friend. I'm not ready, Elton."

"You got no time. This deal closes tomorrow A.M. Kate, I promise that you're covered. I guarantee you'll get your investment back. There's no risk for you."

"It's all new. It's all strange."

"Enter the new world. Take the plunge. It's the only way any of us are going to make it."

The pen was there and the notes.

"What if I change my mind?"

"You got till tonight. If tonight you change your mind give me a call. Tomorrow is too late."

I asked what about me.

"Quit crapping around. Decide who you're going to be."

He called in the woman from the next-door office, invited there for the occasion though it was Sunday. She was a notary and had brought along a friend to witness the signing. He passed the note and copies to me and I signed. She grabbed the pen, wrote her signature, signed the copies, pushed the notes away. "I've done it," she said in a tone she might have used after swallowing a fatal dose.

The notary stamped and recorded the notes.

He asked us to write checks for the down payment.

She didn't have enough in her account to cover the full down payment. She could give him two hundred dollars now, the rest in a week.

"Give what you can. I'll carry you till next week."

He knew my checkbook was in my desk.

"I can give you a hundred now, the rest tomorrow."

He brought out a bottle of champagne from the corner refrigerator.

"Absolutely not. I have to get back to Margaret Tessler. I have work to do and boys to take care of. Please, take me home."

She didn't speak to me after we both signed the note, my awkward signature to the right of her beautiful, strong, unwavering Katherine Wyman. Did she feel I had failed to protect her? She had given me permission to say Kate but I didn't say it. I wanted her to stay Miss Wyman. It was already a strain to connect her to the woman who had led me through Margaret Tessler.

She called me late that night. She had been trying to get in touch with Elton but he wasn't home. Did I know where he was?

I had no idea.

"I can't go through with it, Eugene. I talked to my friend. He's furious. He believes Elton wants to deliver us into the hands of developers. Eugene, have I made a terrible mistake? Can I trust him?"

"He told me that you mean everything to him. He says he'll never abandon you."

"You're young and able to take risks. I can't afford to lose my savings. I rely on that money."

"Elton says he'll cover you."

"What if he's unable to? My friend tells me I'm gambling with my future."

I told her Elton knew his trade. He worked with Andy Sermon, one of the top men in Detroit real estate. "He'll never abandon you. I believe that."

"Eugene, I can't go through with this. I know I may be losing a wonderful opportunity but I need time."

I told her I would try to find Elton. How late could he call her?

"I'll call you."

I phoned every half-hour but he didn't answer. She called me at midnight and I told her Elton hadn't answered.

"I thought he was going to be available." She sounded forlorn and her mood affected me.

"I'll try him again."

"It's too late. We have no choice."

"Kate, he's always come through for me and he will for you. It will be all right."

"You think so, Eugene?"

I was confident.

I didn't find him in the office in the morning. He arrived at noon long after our notes had been delivered and our checks deposited.

"She tried to get in touch with you. She thought you were going to be available. I kept on calling till midnight. She could have used some reassurance."

"Kid," he said, "you are now a Ponchartrain Associates partner. I need the rest of your down payment by tomorrow. I've set you up at our Oak Park subdivision. You are going to work your ass off. In six months you'll be my pal again."

There were two hundred homes at Sermon, Inc.'s Oak Park development. The site was still raw, more homes under construction. I saw foundations dug, concrete poured, joists and girders placed. Framers raised the walls. A swarm of plumbers and electricians strung wire and installed pipe. Plywood skin was dressed with tarpaper, then clapboard exteriors. Carpets were stretched out on newly poured walks and streets and cut to size. Refrigerators and stoves arrived in cartons. Finally the painters and drapers and gardeners came in to tidy up details. In the office, the agents joked about interchangeable houses and spouses and kids. And interchangeable subdivisions and cities and planets, Martians not knowing whether they had arrived on Earth or had blundered back to the red streets of home.

My commissions covered the monthly payments on the notes.

I managed two night classes that semester.

I didn't speak to Kate Wyman for several months. She was in almost daily touch with Elton, who briefed us on the state of the Livonia parcel. He had all her money and all mine. In late June we met at Vesuvius, the six months up. He looked grim. I was prepared for bad news.

"What is it, Elton?"

"First the champagne." He insisted on the same process and only when she got up and said she would leave did he laugh and produce the checks. "I hoped it would be more, partners." We each had checks for ten thousand dollars. This time she took the full glass of champagne.

"Chicken feed," Elton said. Now was our big chance. Ponchartrain Associates had bid for a Farmington property, a huge undertaking. We had the right to purchase a half share together. It would take all our money. We had a few days to make the commitment. The partners would assemble in a couple of weeks at the Sermon offices and we would meet Andy Sermon.

I asked what the monthly payments would be.

"Thirteen hundred for the two of you."

"Impossible!"

"You'll do it," he said. "You'll sweat for six months but you'll find a way."

Kate stood up, shocked, no doubt, that she had survived one ordeal only to be plunged into another.

"You can take the money and run," he said. "I know the strain you're under. But it would be a huge mistake. A few more months and you'll have it made."

She said to me, "I have absolute confidence in Elton," a tone less of confidence than despair. She surrendered to Elton. She told him to keep her check and to my surprise and resentment I surrendered mine as well.

FIVE

Financial Advice

She called him her financial adviser, so I expected a mature, avuncular consultant in the mold of Bernard Baruch, adviser of presidents. We prepared the arguments that would reassure him. Her investment had already quadrupled and she could exit at any stage. We would guarantee that when Ponchartrain Associates began the riverfront development, Kate Wyman would become a rich woman.

Our intention for a calm, reasoned approach went out the window once we met the man. He was no Bernard Baruch, no avuncular consultant. He was far more than a financial adviser. He was the one who used her Saturday nights, and at the first sight of big, meaty Gordon Pickering it seemed obvious that those nights weren't devoted to finances.

His attitude was, "She's my territory," implying an intimacy it hurt to think about. I didn't want to think of her with Gordon Pickering.

Elton needled me afterward, not admitting his own chagrin. "What did you think they were doing? Reading poetry? She's a woman, not your mother. What right do you have to be jealous?"

It wasn't jealousy. She balanced my world; her connection to Gordon Pickering threw everything out of balance.

I first entered the Margaret Tessler office when I was ten years old. I returned regularly till I was almost eighteen. The office hardly changed in that time. The portrait of Eisenhower succeeded that of Harry Truman, who had followed FDR between the little crossed flags on the wall. The heavy Smith Corona typewriter rose from a well in the massive walnut desk. Behind the desk she would swivel to face visitors whom she invited to sit in any one of three school chairs. The ferns in a wicker stand beneath the window may have been the same plants I saw a decade before. The bubbling fish tank behind the desk was still there. Angelfish, goldfish, miniature catfish, and exotic fishes I couldn't name hovered at various levels, the scene so familiar I could imagine the fish hadn't changed position in ten years. Snails vacuumed the tank. On the bottom a Japanese bridge and caves and clumps of moss offered the illusion of safe harbor to the guppy spawn released into the tank to survive or be eaten. She replaced the resident fish to correct accidents and imbalances, but there was otherwise little novelty.

The art of the tank, she once told me, aimed for balance. She set conditions for life underwater and intruded as little as possible. Her motto, she said, was "Balance in everything."

On the way to the meeting, about to enter her office, we heard a man bellow, "For godsakes! What world are you living in!" and when Elton shoved the door open she was standing in front of her desk, braced backward on her hands, leaning away from a very big man, and the Home—my home—became unbalanced.

He was well over six feet tall, a massive chest scrunched into an open tweed jacket, slightly rounded shoulders, his helmet of dense brown hair cut close, U.S. Marine style. He wore an incongruous red bow tie. I didn't see anything fine or subtle about him. His nose was big, his chin and mouth were big. He barely listened to introductions before starting in on us, first in a ponderous, lawyerly voice, then in barely smothered rage.

He was here to challenge the note which committed her to a $650 a month payment for one quarter share of a Ponchartrain Associates purchase of—he looked at the note and read the parcel coordinates—a subdivision of Southfield, then tossed the note on the floor as though it were already worthless. She immediately picked it up, a cowed underling, not my Miss Wyman.

He accused us of forcing her to sign. If she'd waited for his advice she wouldn't have signed. "I don't know what you guys are trying to pull off, but she can't afford this note and she isn't going to pay this note. We want it voided."

Elton told him the check was cashed, the note was on record, and it couldn't be voided, but what was his problem? We were going to make Kate a rich woman. Did he object?

He said in a booming voice, "The idea isn't to make her *rich*. The idea is to keep her *safe*."

She said that she didn't ask to be rich. Being rich wasn't what she was after. Her only concern was the Home.

The big guy said in disgust, "Then why the hell did you put yourself in hock and risk everything!"

I shouted that she wasn't in hock, she wasn't at risk. WE were watching out for her. WE kept her safe.

He ignored me and spoke to Elton, "I'll give you the benefit of the doubt, Kramer. Maybe you got good intentions—how the hell would I know?—but when I see you gamble away her retirement it looks to me like you don't give a damn about her safety."

Elton said Ponchartrain Associates made rock-solid investments. There was no risk for her.

"No risk? You put her retirement into undeveloped property with real estate already sky-high and you say 'no risk'?"

I couldn't hold back. Yes! No risk! Real estate was sky-high and going higher!

"Aim for the moon, Sonny. That's maybe a target you can hit."

"We're aiming past the moon! We're shooting for Blue Heaven!"

He brushed me off with a wave of his big mitt and focused on Elton. "When you take your fall, Kramer—and you will—I don't want her going down with you."

She urged us all to please sit down and be calm, but no one sat down.

He said he knew how the real estate game was played by all the young hotshots. On one side were the hustlers and connivers; on the other side the innocent and self-deluded. The market wouldn't dive until the last gull was raked in. The connivers and hustlers would end up on top while the small fry went down the drain. He wasn't going to allow that to happen to Kate Wyman.

Elton said he didn't know about "hustlers and connivers" but he'd learned the real estate business in the school of hard knocks. He'd raised Elkram Real Estate from ground level, shooting for the top, and in less than eight years, he was almost there. If anyone knew the market, he and his partner, Andy Sermon, did, and they could guarantee that the Southfield investment was a sure winner. "So where do you come by your know-how, Gordon? What hard-knock school did you learn in? What do you know that I don't know?"

"Gordon is a teacher," Kate said, "a wonderful teacher."

Gordon told her he could give his own résumé, he didn't need her help. "My training is in economics, if that's what you want to know."

"An economist? Great. Wonderful. Where is it you work, Gordon? At a bank? A brokerage? A university? Do you consult?"

He stressed each denial. "I'm NOT with a bank, NOT with a brokerage, NOT with a university, I DON'T consult. I'll throw you meat for your grinder, Kramer. I'm a high school teacher. A mere high-school teacher. I teach civics and economics. Go ahead. Try to make something of that."

Elton grinned. "I guess Detroit real estate isn't your specialty."

She intervened to elaborate Gordon's résumé. Gordon wasn't just any teacher. He was a great teacher, twice selected Teacher of the Year at Central High School, faculty sponsor of the Central High debating team, a volunteer wrestling coach.

He saw us grinning and knew her claims for him sounded absurd. He told her to stay out of it. Didn't she see that every claim she made only diminished him in our eyes? "I'm not trying to impress these guys. I don't give a damn what they think. All I'm trying to accomplish here is to get us released from that note."

I said, "'Us' released? You were never connected. How can you be released?"

He waved me off again, a sharp, infuriating, hacking gesture. I told him to quit waving at me. He didn't have to use sign language. I wasn't deaf.

"Eugene," she said, "Please."

Elton assumed the voice of cool reason and urged me to calm down. "Yelling doesn't get us anywhere, Gene. Can't you see what's worrying Gordon? He doesn't know us and as far as he's concerned we're just two conniving orphans trying to fleece Kate Wyman. I'm not offended by his hard line. I'm glad Kate has a tough friend to guard her interests. And, anyway, Gene, quarreling with the debating coach is not a bright idea." He turned to Gordon. "The note is a done deal. Kate is a co-owner of property in Southfield. That's a fact and we can't void facts. But like I told Kate, she has my absolute guarantee—and I keep my promises—that I won't put her at risk. So this is what I'm prepared to do. In a couple of weeks there's a partners' meeting and we'll get the lowdown from Andy Sermon himself about where we're headed. All your doubts will be cleared up. Everyone will be satisfied. If for any reason Kate still wants out after the meeting, I'll buy her note. She'll get back every cent she invested and keep the profit. It's a no-lose deal for both of us. She'll end up with four times what she had when her retirement was sitting in a bank. Me, I'll be holding an extra quarter share of a gold mine. My only regret is that Kate, who is family to me, won't be along for the ride."

I told him he wasn't only a realtor. He was a politician.

He grinned. "Watch and learn, kid."

Gordon asked if Elton was saying she could get out of the note.

"If that's what she wants, absolutely."

"That's what she wants."

"You don't have to speak for her," I said. "She can tell us what she wants."

She said slowly, emphatically, "Gordon, I signed and I honor what I sign. I trust my boys."

"The guy says you can get out of the note."

"I don't want to do that."

"You don't owe them your life's savings just because they were once your BOYS. When your BOYS sold you that note they put your security on the line." He turned back to Elton. "I don't want her going to this meeting alone. I want to be there with her."

Elton told him it was partners only. "But don't you worry, Gordon. She'll have her BOYS with her."

"That's not good enough."

"Gordon, he's offering what you asked for. Can't we leave the subject until after the meeting with Mr. Sermon?"

Elton said Kate was right. What, after all, was the quarrel? Weren't we all after the same thing? To make Kate a little money? More than a little? "Can't we agree on that, Gordon?"

He shrugged.

"Come on, Gordon. What do you say we shake on it?"

Elton offered his hand and Gordon stared at the rings on the right hand. He asked, as if not believing, "You're a Mason?"

"Any day now."

"The other ring tells me you graduated in '45 from the U of M.

Is that what you claim?"

Elton dropped his hand. "You know what I admire about you, Gordon? When I look at you I don't see a pantywaist economist or teacher. I see a warrior who can't be conned, someone tough, exactly the kind of friend Kate needs. And, coach of the wrestling team! I bet you wrestled yourself."

He grudgingly admitted he'd wrestled at the university level.

"I bet you were good."

He was a bronze medalist, representing East Michigan University in the state competitions.

"You look ready to go for the gold right now."

Staying fit remained a priority for him.

"I can see you've been working at it."

Kate said Gordon was faithful to his body, even when the regimen wasn't easy to keep up.

Faithful to his body? Was he married to his body?

She frowned. "I mean, Eugene, that Gordon is very disciplined in his exercises." She asked Gordon to tell us about his fitness routine.

He described a routine he, no doubt, thought would impress and intimidate. He ran the high school indoor track five times a week, swam a mile in the pool each lunch hour. He lifted weights. He could still bench-press three hundred and seventy-five pounds.

Elton whistled. "What a powerhouse. That's more than one of me in each hand. You must be one hell of an economist."

I broke out laughing and she glared at me. She told Gordon to wait, and led us outside, away from the orphans who were on the playground at recess time. She bawled us out. We had judged

Gordon without knowing him. He was a devoted friend—an absolutely loyal friend—maybe too easily angered, too easily provoked, but a dear, dear friend. We had seen him at his worst. "You were cruel to a man who is usually generous and giving."

I asked what he gave. Hammerlocks?

She said the mockery was not to my credit. I was hostile to Gordon without giving him a chance. She expected better of me. Perhaps if I knew the strain he was under, I would be more understanding. His wife had been wheelchair-bound for years and Gordon served her unstintingly, never a complaint. He medicated her, massaged her, fed her, bathed her, utterly loyal. You could always depend on Gordon. What saved him from despair was his service at Central High School.

"And your service to him," I said.

Yes, her friendship meant a great deal to Gordon and she wanted him treated with respect.

Was it Gordon who used her Saturday nights?

"What are you implying?"

"I'm asking, not implying."

Elton interrupted. "The guy's had rotten luck and I appreciate that he sticks by his wife, but that doesn't excuse his worrying you about your investment. Kate, the guy doesn't know diddly about real estate. All I ask is that you listen to Andy Sermon. I promise that after he briefs us you'll be very happy with the Southfield deal."

"I want Gordon to be at the meeting."

"Not a chance. Like I said, it's partners only."

"Ask Mr. Sermon if he'll make an exception. It's important to me, Elton." She turned to me. "What I do with my nights is absolutely not your business. I don't care for your innuendos." She returned to her office before I could tell her she was at the center of my life and that seeing her with Gordon had thrown me out of orbit.

I shouldn't have asked what she did with her nights. She didn't have to justify herself to me. Why should I even have any relevance to her? She handled orphans in batches and I was in an old batch, long released, with no right to her attention. That wasn't easy to accept. And then that wave of dismissal—Gordon had rubbed the air with his big mitt and erased me—was I obliged to accept that, too?

Elton told me it was stupid to let him get under my skin. "So what if he can hoist a few hundred pounds? Big deal. I'll get him a job in construction hoisting I-beams and make him happy."

I called the Home to apologize and was told she wasn't available, and it was the same later. I needed to explain myself and couldn't let go of it, and that evening I squeezed through the gates just as the groundskeeper was locking up.

He ordered, "Halt!" a military command from a very old, unlikely soldier. "We're closed! You can't come in!"

I said I was a former resident, Miss Wyman's friend, and before the befuddled old man could figure it out, I pushed past and entered the Home.

It was after dinner and orphans of all sizes streamed from the dining hall toward the dorms. I'd been gone from that scene for four years but I felt instantly part of it again—the familiar dinner smell, the same sound of chatter, the same rumble of shoes on the corridor tiles and up the stairways. I could have fallen into that stream and flowed with it and I would have been washed clean of anything I'd experienced outside.

She was under one of the fluorescent panels that lit the corridor. She was in her work smock, hair knotted, prim and severe, talking to Edith Hempleman, who obligingly retreated down the corridor when I joined them.

"It's not visiting hours. What are you doing here?"

I needed to be forgiven. I'd been caught by surprise, not prepared for Gordon, but for someone else, a financial adviser. I'd behaved stupidly. I shouldn't have said anything about her Saturday nights. I was thrown off balance when Gordon implied I'd do something to hurt her. I would never do anything to hurt her. I said what I'd never even said to myself. I loved her.

Miss Sample and Mrs. Hempleman and the groundskeeper gathered down the hall. They were joined by Mr. Atkins, still wearing his shop apron, his sleeves rolled, his arms bare and folded, prepared to be the village constable.

She was in no mood to forgive. "I want you to leave now."

Cast out again? No longer part of it?

"If you have any respect for me, Eugene, you'll apologize to Gordon."

"Apologize for what?"

"For ridiculing him."

He was the one to apologize. He had treated me with contempt.

Enough, she said. Leave.

"I'll try to apologize."

"I hope that you do. But leave now."

He lived on Elmwood, off Linwood, near the Central High School campus, a mostly Jewish neighborhood. A few blocks away on Twelfth Street you could see the beginning of a Negro presence—a store here and there, a few Negro rentals in apartment buildings, some kids on bicycles, scouting foreign terrain. I knew—everyone knew—that the neighborhood was under the threat of change—as if its history wasn't a history of change—and, as far as the neighbors were concerned, it wouldn't be a change for the better. We heard about associations formed all over the city to stem the tide. The image was of a black tide with real estate agents organizing neighborhoods to hold back the surge. The message from the associations was, in effect, "Everybody stays put. Nobody sells to colored. Be loyal to your own."

I waited out of sight on a quiet Sunday afternoon, a frigid day for late spring, the weather hovering between winter and summer, a bite in the air to remind us that, however beautiful Detroit might now seem, there were hard days behind and ahead.

He came into view pushing a tiny bundled woman in a wheelchair, a long scarf wrapped around her shoulders and throat almost to her mouth, a knit hat down to her ears. He wore an athletic jacket over a T-shirt, walking slowly, oblivious to me, almost disconnected from the woman he pushed. There was no spirit in his pushing, no apparent intimacy with the woman. He could have been a hired attendant.

I walked in step across the street behind tall elms arrayed on both sides of Elmwood, the street dappled by leaf shadows.

It was a block of mainly two- and four-family brick homes, built in a 1920s style once favored by immigrants moving from poverty into middle-class comfort. Thirty years later we offered a different style to Ponchartrain Estates homebuyers, also trying to move upward. These '20s offerings, squat, ponderous brick buildings with modest, scruffy front yards and deeper backyards, were more substantial than ours.

Gordon's house didn't fit the neighborhood. It was a very large Queen Anne anomaly on a half-acre lot, dating perhaps from the mid-1800s, with a wraparound porch and insets of dark, warped shingles on the façade, three stories under a steep shingled roof. There was a peaked cylindrical tower on one side and a screened-in gazebo on the other.

I watched him push the wheelchair, a slow, spiritless walk, a grimace twisting the big, rocky face into a clown mask of pain he couldn't have meant anyone to see, not even the woman he wheeled. He pushed her up the driveway to a wooden ramp fitted over the stairs. I made out the lettering on his brown and yellow jacket, EMU EAGLES, beneath the arch of a spread-winged eagle.

I imagined calling out, "Pickering! Gordon! I've come to apologize," but I didn't have the heart for apology and didn't know how he'd accept an apology. I stepped in and out of hiding. A neighbor, passing by, asked if I was looking for someone. I said, no, I was waiting for a friend and thanked the man who kept watching me as he turned into his home. Gordon, backing up the ramp, set to wheel his wife through the door, saw me. There was nothing for it but to come into the open. I smiled, waved, crossed over, said to him cheerfully, pompously, insincerely, "At Miss Wyman's request, I've come to apologize."

He stood hands on hips, as unforthcoming as stone.

I cautiously approached, didn't know what to say next, blurted out blithely, unable to pretend remorse, "I apologize for not being respectful. I shouldn't have laughed." I said this laughing. I meant it to come across as self-disparagement, not mockery. He must have heard it as mocking laughter, and that was the last straw.

He abandoned his wife, jumped down the stairs, hooked me under my armpits, swooped me up, his arms fully extended.

"Three hundred and seventy-five pounds!" he snarled, teeth bared. "You're nothing!"

I hung from his grip, wanting to make it a joke, and kept on laughing.

"Want to laugh? I'll give you something to laugh about!" He slung me over a rock-hard shoulder, as easily as a butcher handling a carcass. I slapped his back, still laughing, "I get the idea. Put me down." Anyone looking must have thought it was a joke. He carried me up the driveway alongside the house.

"I yield. Put me down."

He unlatched the backyard gate, passed through and kicked the gate shut. The high fence of pointed wooden slats closed out the neighbors. All they could have heard was my out-of-control laughing. "Enough, I surrender, put me down." He kept going across a deep yard framed by oak and maple, across a brick patio, down a flagstone path, across a lawn, through a vegetable garden, between tomato vines in wire cages. We came to a shed and a compost heap against the rear fence and there he dumped me. I landed on my back in moldy leaves and ripe fertilizer. He jeered, teeth bared, "New earth for my garden. That's how I use her BOYS." The contempt was virulent. I watched him swagger back to his wife.

I lay there a moment, got up trembling, brushed myself off, followed him out front. He was on the porch, behind the wheelchair.

He looked at me, leaned over to her, spoke loudly. "Nothing to worry about, Sarah. Just a goddamn real estate agent."

I shouted loud and clear—I didn't know it was coming—"'EARTH THAT NOURISHED THEE'—YOU ASSHOLE!—'SHALL CLAIM THY GROWTH TO BE RESOLVED TO EARTH AGAIN!'" He shrugged and pushed through.

I'd behaved like an idiot. My laughing had made it worse. I couldn't let go of the scene. I tried bottling it up, hoping it would smother and die, but instead it unrolled again. When I finally told Elton, I kept the story light, as if it had been a joke, accompanied again with self-disparaging laughter. I told about the street, the house, the backyard, about being dumped into ripening compost, a shock, but I wasn't hurt. Gordon handled me carefully. The compost was soft and moldy, the smell not too awful. It was absurd, silly. I'd been caught by surprise. To tell the truth, I even felt sorry for the man. I put myself in his shoes and felt his loneliness. I was moved by the anguish in his clown face. I could understand Kate's sympathy for him. My jealousy, or whatever I'd felt, was gone. He'd swooped me up, held me high, said I weighed nothing compared to the three hundred and seventy-five pounds he could lift. Did he mean that compared to the burdens he carried, I was trivial, no three-hundred-seventy-five-pound grief, but a weightless nothing? Was I the clown, letting everyone take potshots at me, accepting the damage as if it were no more than the punch line of a joke? I'd shouted words I'd stored away ever since I threw them at Harold Mitchell years ago, and they again lightened me. I was okay now, not bad at all.

"What do you mean he lifted you?"

"He hooked me under my arms and hoisted me. He's a powerhouse. He could have launched me into space."

"And you let him?"

"I had no choice."

"And you think it's a joke?"

"I was airborne. I had no leverage. I could have kicked my legs like a kid in a tantrum, but I had no choice, so I rode with it."

"Why were you even there?"

"She wanted me to apologize."

"You were going to apologize?"

"He didn't give me a chance."

"And you still think it's a joke?"

"I'm a fool, Elton. You've told me that often enough."

"You're a fool," he said, "but not just a fool. You're worse than a fool. You're stupid. You're a 'good boy' looking for a gold star from Teacher. Don't you get it that a gold star from this teacher isn't worth shit outside the Home? She's got no more sense of how the world operates than you do. Do you know what would happen if someone dumped ME into a pile of compost?"

"I'm sure you'd make him pay."

"I'd KILL!"

"I don't want to kill. I'm not even pissed off anymore."

"Of course you're not pissed off. Good boys don't get pissed off. Good boys think it's the guy who dumps them in shit who needs hugs and back pats and—who knows what else she gives him? I'm not like you. I'm no 'good boy.' I want the bastard to feel what it's like to get dumped. And I want her to learn to save her hugs for someone who deserves them."

I asked who that might be.

"Not some heavyweight loser. And not you, kid. Oh, absolutely not you."

The wound was deep. Gordon had not only made me weightless, he'd taken over my thoughts.

I checked on his house. It was built by an Elliot Pickering after the Civil War, when the neighborhood was still rural. It was once a ten-acre estate with apple and cherry orchards. Only the house and oversized lot remained, a Don Quixote of a house, hip to hip with its inferiors, grandly out of place, once considered for landmark status but judged too run-down. Without a significant architectural signature it wasn't worth preserving.

Everyone on Elmwood, except Gordon Pickering, was a newcomer. He should have long ago moved with his peers to a rich suburb and become part of an established Detroit aristocracy, a social rank to which he was entitled. He was somehow stalled on commonplace Elmwood. He would never win the gold. He was a self-styled economist stuck at Central High. He was able to haul me through his garden and dump me in compost, but he couldn't get beyond Elmwood Street. Elton had called him a loser, and he was a loser, and it was a relief to come to that judgment. I wanted to see him as a clown, maybe a sad and crazy clown, but merely a clown.

Elton let me know three days before the meeting that Andy Sermon had made an exception for Gordon Pickering. "I got him an invite."

"Why?"

"She asked, didn't she? And we give her everything she asks for, don't we? Now you'll have a chance to laugh it up again with your buddy, the weight lifter."

I didn't want him there. I'd met him twice and that was more than enough. I wanted him out of mind and out of sight. I threatened to skip the meeting. "Why should I be there anyway? You'll tell me what I need to know."

"I told Sermon you'd be there. It's your big chance. I've set it up for you and you're coming."

I called Professor Fuller, no hint I was asking for asylum. I told him I needed to change my line of work and was applying to the Ivory Tower. Could he think of me as a colleague? Was there a vacancy? I was willing to start anywhere on the ladder.

"What exactly is it you're asking for, Eugene?" It was a relief to hear his deep, mellow voice and know that he belonged to a place where it was unimaginable someone might be tossed into compost.

"I'm inquiring about a college job, Professor. Do you know if there's a place for me?"

"You ask *me* for a place? A real estate agent asking *me* to find *him* a place? That's a complete reversal of roles, Eugene. I'm the one who's free floating in limbo. My wife keeps nagging me to find her a respectable address and I tell her it's impossible, forget it, it's not in the cards. This is Detroit."

I said I'd try to help. I didn't know what was available but I'd see what I could find.

"Eugene, you look for a place for me and I'll look for a place for you and let's see what we come up with."

We met in the evening a couple of days later. I was outside waiting for Elton to pick me up for dinner and the professor walked by arm-in-arm with his wife. They lived in the neighborhood and often came this way. It was only chance we hadn't connected this way before. He said he had news about his end of the bargain. "First let me introduce you to Marybeth."

In those days a mixed-race couple in the wrong neighborhood was in serious trouble and most neighborhoods were wrong, so I had expected a cautious woman who knew enough to appear unobtrusive. Marybeth Fuller was not a cautious woman. She was twenty years younger than Fuller, vivid and flamboyant. She stood under the intense mercury streetlight in a sleek black leather jacket, a mane of black curls forming a broad halo. In high heels she stood a couple of inches above me. She seemed almost luridly white with sharply contrasting dark eye shadow and lipstick. Long silver earrings with ruby inserts glittered when she moved.

"Some babe, no, Eugene?"

"Lovely" was the safe word.

He introduced me as Eugene Victor Smith, named after a famous World War I radical. He told her I was his student, always around, using up all his course offerings, and he had nothing more to teach me. The only thing left to do was move me over to his side of the lectern. "Eugene, I've found you a place. Not much of a place. It's on the bottom rung. You won't get rich, but you're on the ladder, where you said you wanted to be." He'd arranged a readership for me with Professor Hunneke of the German department. "You'll be reading for his introductory German. Think you can handle that?"

I'd studied with old Hunneke. I could handle his introductory German. The bottom rung was where I belonged and money was no problem. I'd hold on to my day job until I'd climbed a few more steps.

"And I might be able to find you a section of my Contemporary Civilization."

"My god! I'll be rich!"

"Not on slave wages, my friend."

Marybeth spoke with an actor's voice, projecting for the benefit of hundreds even though the two of us were her entire audience. "Isn't it wonderful, Eugene, how Huston goes to bat for his students?"

I couldn't begin to tell her how pleased I was. "Professor Fuller has changed my life."

"Then, Eugene, maybe you can return the favor. Huston tells me your day job is in real estate. You sell houses, correct?"

I said real estate was only a temporary profession. I waited for my true calling.

"Then maybe you're the man we're looking for. Do you think so, Huston?"

"He probably is, but let's not get pushy, sweetheart."

"Eugene," she said, affecting a patrician haughtiness, "we are candidates for your largesse. We need a home." Then changing to a brassier tone, "We need to get out of where we're living. Where we're living is crap. It was supposed to be for three months but we've been stuck there for almost three years. It's not as if we're asking for the moon. Almost anything will do, just so it has two baths and plenty of closets. Three bedrooms, at least. Four would be even better. Office space for each of us. And a big yard."

"Located where?"

"Not here. A place in a good part of town. Price is no consideration."

"Whoa," Fuller said. "*En garde*, Eugene. Watch out for her." He warned me that his wife was an accomplished actress, experienced in twisting hearts, wringing out tears, soon to be seen at the World Theater in *Antigone*, the title role, and I shouldn't buy into her drama too readily. He feared we were about to hear a blatant appeal to pity. Their home was not, as she said, "crap." He said it was a stunning apartment with a great view of Woodward Avenue traffic. "If she'd only stand back and think about it she'd realize what we've got is a bargain. Do we pay for the music of grinding streetcars? Not a penny. And every time we open a window the place is perfumed with exhaust fumes, but does the scent cost us anything? It's absolutely gratis. She claims the landlord refuses to repair the windows but I tell her it's only because the noble gentleman practices the virtue of thrift. And that's also his good reason for not fixing the plumbing. It's true that someday a gas leak will kill us—it's bound to happen—but why not look at the bright side? We're located a mere three blocks from my office. We can make all the noise we want—so can the neighbors—and no one complains. I could name a hundred other blessings, but I'm afraid nothing satisfies the drama queen."

She dropped her brittle manner. "I'm not kidding, Eugene. Our situation is no joke. I may be a little frantic—we intend to have a kid—it's time we got aggressive. Huston is too easy. I've warned him if he doesn't get tough real quick he's going to lose a wife to the nut house. He doesn't like me to come on this way—he wants to keep it light, that's his style—but you're his student and you know how special he is, and you're also a real estate agent, right? So I am very aggressively asking for your help. Get us out of Uncle Tom's Cabin and find us a place where we can spread out. A big yard, a vast yard. Trees. Flowers. Grass. A place where we can entertain the queen—it doesn't matter which queen—a drama queen or any queen who happens to drop in."

"A big yard, grass and flowers?"

"And don't worry about price. The sky's the limit."

"I'll see what's available, but to be honest, Mrs. Fuller, it won't be easy."

"Of course it won't be easy. I'm not asking you to do something easy. I'm giving you a chance to help save your favorite professor's marriage."

It was then Elton drove up and blasted us with a crescendo of whoops from his horn—Whoop, whoop, WHOOP. I introduced the Fullers to the owner of Elkram Real Estate.

She asked Elton if he realized he was attracting attention when he whooped like that.

"I want attention." He pointed to the embossed red lettering fixed to the side of the white convertible. ELKRAM REAL ESTATE. "I blow my horn for Elkram." He turned to Fuller. "Professor, I hear from Gene you're the Wise Man on Campus, so let me ask you a question. How does a wise man like you let this not-too-smart kid get into your program? Haven't you found out how simple he is?"

Fuller said I was far and away his best student and predicted a bright academic future for me.

Elton shook his head. "Can't let you have him, Professor. I got other plans for the kid. He's got a bright future, but not with you. I have too much invested to let him get away. He's all mine and you can't begin to match the returns I can offer."

"I'm sure we can't. What we offer will barely keep him in poverty."

I said I might prefer poverty.

Marybeth interrupted. "If you're whooping up business, Mr. Kramer, you have customers right here." She described their predicament. They needed to get away from Wayne and they'd had no luck. They were looking for a house in a good neighborhood, a place with a great yard, at least two baths, three bedrooms, office space, a modern kitchen, and near good shopping.

He took out a notepad, wrote down their address and phone number. "What price range are you looking at?"

Price was no object. She had an inheritance. "We'll spend whatever we need for the right place."

"That should get you somewhere. I'll call if anything turns up."

"Don't take forever, Mr. Kramer. I'll expect a call soon."

Elton liked the Professor. "He's a sharp dresser. Notice the shoes? Gucci. He's got a problem, though, and it's not his feet; it's the pushy wife, right?"

I asked if he could do anything for them.

"Know what would happen if they showed up at a place like Ponchartrain Estates? There'd either be a lynching or a mass exodus."

I told him that Professor Fuller had opened the world to me and I wanted the world opened to him.

"Bring them into our neck of the woods and you'll start a riot. This city's a tinderbox. You know that."

I owed it to the professor to try.

"Forget it. End of subject."

Not for me. I had made promises.

"Stall them for a few years until they give up."

I had no intention of doing that.

The Sermon offices were on the 43rd floor of the Penobscot Building, nothing in Detroit above us, the spire more than 550 feet from the ground. Tall, arched windows lined the north-facing conference room. I saw Canada across the Detroit River. To the far left there was a glimpse of Grosse Ile. Lake Erie was off to the right. I saw a line of barges heading toward Buffalo. Closer in the Ambassador Bridge spanned the river into Canada. It was a view of two nations conjoined at the Detroit River.

Even this grand perspective couldn't match Andy Sermon's vision, laid out for us in miniature scale on a narrow platform that ran along one wall the entire length of the conference room. The platform carried models of Sermon, Inc. Detroit projects, past, present, and future, constructed in wood and plastic. It was a fantasy Detroit, unspoiled by the gritty intrusion of things as they were. The details of Ponchartrain Estates and vicinity were all there, the street signs, the road markings, shrubs, puffs of trees, green lawns, ponds, fountains, churches, schools, busy malls with tiny, plastic people. I saw models of the Livonia project and Southfield.

Beneath the tall windows, there was an elaborate model in gleaming white of the planned riverfront development, a grouping of high-rise and mid-size office buildings and hotels and condominiums and a convention center. The development was to be situated close to the site of the original Fort Detroit, now a seedy riverfront.

The only person I knew among the dozen or more in the room was Gordon Pickering in his tweed jacket and red bow tie.

He must have realized, as I did, when he entered the enormous room and saw its imperial vista, that he was out of his league. He could have taken on the whole room in a wrestling ring, stripped to his shorts and T-shirt and gym shoes, with ear protection, his genitals secured in a plastic cup. He would have seemed formidable. Or he could have maintained his academic demeanor behind a desk at Central High. But here he was an alien, entirely alone, and even a familiar enemy could be mistaken for a friend.

He walked over, no menace in his approach; in fact, deferential and subdued, trying to make his rock face smile. "This is awkward, not easy for me. I find it difficult—maybe impossible—to explain myself. What I did was inexcusable."

It was said honestly, hard to resist, but it caught me by surprise, and I answered flippantly, "No excuse necessary. As you can see, I'm still ambulant. No harm done."

"It's been a hard time for me. I don't behave like that. It was insane and, if it will do any good, I apologize."

It was a complete reversal. I couldn't understand it, couldn't believe it, didn't know how to handle it, didn't want him around. I told him—anything to get away—that I'd enjoyed the ride and perhaps we could talk some other time in a more appropriate place.

"Whenever you'd like."

I didn't want him near me.

He asked if I knew where Kate was.

"She's in Sermon's office being introduced."

"How long has she been in there?"

"I wouldn't know. I just got here myself."

Sermon's executive secretary entered the room, a gaunt, gray-haired woman with horn-rims perched on a substantial nose. She introduced herself, Muriel Evans, and announced that Mr. Sermon would be with us in a few minutes. She invited us to pour coffee from a silver urn on a side table. She showed us where we would be sitting. There were seventeen of us, twelve partners, two Sermon, Inc. executives, Muriel Evans, Gordon Pickering, and Andy Sermon himself. My seat was at the foot of the conference table, a good distance from Sermon. Gordon was on my right, a Dutch importer, Willem Frucht, on my left.

Frucht, boyishly good looking, spoke without a tinge of accent. He asked Muriel Evans if she could give us a rundown on the displays.

She led us down the line of models, offering details. When she came to Ponchartrain Estates, she turned to me. "You made quite a name for yourself here, Mr. Smith. How old were you when you made your first sale? Nineteen? Mr. Sermon was impressed."

It was a pleasure to be acknowledged. From where I had been placed at the table, far from Sermon, I'd felt consigned to insignificance.

Frucht asked about elaborate sketches, matted on the wall, resembling Escher prints.

"Those?" She laughed. "They're what our Chairman calls his Futures Projects. These are his plans for Ocean City and Moon City. Mr. Sermon has quite an imagination, as you can see."

Sermon entered, arm-in-arm with Kate Wyman, Elton following.

Elton became clearer when I saw his derivation from Sermon. Sermon also came from Arkansas but it wasn't origin or appearance that connected them. Sermon was tall, white haired, florid, his paunch crossed by a broad leather belt. He wore a Western shirt under an open tailored tan suede jacket. Military twills and embossed cowboy boots completed the rancher picture. His belt was secured by an oversized silver buckle in the form of the letters AS. ("And that doesn't spell 'ASS,'" he said, in a stentorian drawl he could bring down to a whisper or raise to a jokey squeal.) He had a light touch that Elton lacked. What they had in common was their enthusiasm for development, their optimism for the future, their flat-out energy, and low boiling points. There were clear echoes of Sermon in Elton's real estate patter. In fact, Elton channeled Sermon's thought in almost every word he spoke about development.

Sermon shook hands with each of us. To me he said, "About

time we met. How come I haven't seen you around?"

I said stupidly, "I'm a little shy," intimidated by his booming authority. That was all he needed to hear to drop me from his scheme of things. He looked away, his interest gone. "Not easy succeeding as a shy salesman."

Elton, following in his path, grimaced and shook his head.

Gordon was the next in line. "You're Kate's friend?"

"Yes."

"Not a partner, though."

"I am not a partner."

"Make yourself at home, Gordon."

He moved on to Willem Frucht. "You're the German, right?"

"Almost right. I'm from the Netherlands."

"A Dutchman."

"A citizen of the United States, Sir." Frucht was interested in the availability of warehouse space in the proposed development. His import business was expanding and he needed a riverfront location.

"We'll talk about the riverfront later. That's where all this is headed." Sermon moved on to the head of the table, waiting for Kate to join him.

She stopped with Gordon, a hand on his wrist, glowing from whatever was said in Sermon's private office. "If this ends early enough I'll have time for dinner, but I need to be back before bed check. We'll talk after the meeting."

He stared at her and said nothing.

"All right, Gordon?"

He shrugged and looked away.

Once Sermon had us seated—Kate Wyman to his left, his

secretary to his right, Elton Kramer next—he offered an account of Sermon, Inc., a story of himself. He had developed projects from Mexico to Canada. He was as boastful of his achievement as a Homeric hero establishing his credentials at the campfire the night before battle, a wholehearted advocate of momentum, the author of Elton's faith, unreservedly on the side of enthusiasm. He'd risen and fallen, but, by his account, always ended on top.

Detroit, he said, had been strangling and had undergone necessary surgery. The highways were the key. "We had a corset on her so tight she couldn't breathe. Now she's unhooked and can spread out. It is my intention to take this run-down old bag of a town and make a lady out of her." He leaned toward Kate Wyman. "Pardon me, Kate, but you're one of the boys now."

She was used to being among boys.

Gordon, next to me, was stiff as a board.

Sermon saw an unlimited future for our city. Detroit was number five in population, behind New York and Chicago and LA and Philly, but catching up fast. We had the biggest economic engine in the world. We were the Motor City. We were Henry Ford's town. We were the hub of GM and Chrysler. We had pioneered freeways leading from the city center out to the world. Our future lay beyond present boundaries.

A screen lowered at the front of the room with projected highways superimposed on Macomb and Washtenaw and Wayne counties, city and counties speckled with Sermon developments.

He mentioned the current Southfield subdivision only in passing. It would generate some of the cash for the riverfront project.

Construction would begin in the spring of next year. The project would take four years to complete. Occupancy of some units could begin as early as two years after the start of construction. That would help with cash flow and take the pressure off our debt. He hoped to sell some residential high-rises and lease the commercial space. Once the rents came in we would have no financial worries. The sale of the high-rises would recoup our capital investment and pay off the banks. He anticipated at least a twenty percent annual return from the commercial leases.

The future of Ponchartrain Associates after the downtown development was still unwritten. He defied anyone to come up with limits to development.

Frucht asked, "The moon?" and nodded toward the wall sketches.

"Why not the moon?" Sermon imagined domed cities and covered passages and manufactured air. It was feasible technology for the next century. The oceans? There could be domed villages under the oceans. Even space could be tenanted. Even Mars was possible. We would someday leave the solar system and prospect the galaxy. "Not in our time, but it's my belief that as long as we have the will and the vision we'll never run out of real estate. The direction of the future is up, up, and aside from a glitch here and a glitch there, always up."

It was then that Gordon asked, clearing his throat, to allow his deep, gruff debating voice to issue, "Before we go under the ocean or up to the moon, Sir, there's the current Southfield investment. What happens if the economy turns, value declines, you don't get your cash and are stuck making payments?"

It took nerve to speak up. Sermon could have asked him to

leave. He answered in language almost identical to what I'd heard from Elton. This was land. People had to be housed. The population was booming, the economy expanding. We weren't beginning to fill the need. It was true that some property didn't move. But Southfield? Repeating Elton's assessment, Southfield was more sure than gold. "We are going to get out in six months. The worst scenario is that we'll come out with a smaller profit than we planned and that would take an economic disaster and delay our riverfront project no more than a month or two." He repeated again as if it were a mantra that the direction of the future was up, up, up. There could be temporary reverses. Those of little faith would drop out. That would leave even greater opportunity for investors with strong nerve and clear vision. "If you're blind and can't see where we're going you shouldn't be here. You don't belong on our team. Ponchartrain Associates is not for you."

Gordon persisted. What if there was more than a glitch in the economy? What if there was a serious decline? Consider the Great Depression, that had lasted twelve years and had left Detroit a seedy, desperate place.

Sermon shook his head. "'Depression' is not a word I care to hear. It's not a word that applies to Detroit. Downturns, yes. Sermon, Inc. has survived and profited from many downturns. A downturn is an opportunity, not a disaster. I take advantage of downturns."

"Some analysts say that we're overvalued and due for a big correction."

That was enough for Sermon. "What analysts say is not worth a pig's fart. With nothing on the line it's just talk for the sake of talking and as far as I'm concerned they're talking crap. I don't need to hear from analysts."

So much for Gordon Pickering and other doomsayers who spoiled the mood he wanted. He gave snap answers to a few other questions. When asked for a specific time frame for the riverfront development, he turned the meeting over to the Sermon, Inc. executives, who offered a detailed agenda for demolition and construction. They discussed the bank financing, the schedule of payments, and an estimate of how long it would take for the money to roll in and for our personal obligations to be discharged.

The proposed date for the start of demolition was sometime next year in early spring, depending on weather.

Sermon sat through the rest of the meeting, his part done. He lit a cigar after getting Kate's permission. He smiled when Kate Wyman leaned over to whisper to him, perhaps an apology for Gordon's behavior.

She approached Gordon as soon as the meeting ended. "You promised you would just listen. You embarrassed Elton, who got you invited."

"I don't give a damn whom I embarrass. Were you embarrassed?"

"Yes, Gordon, I was."

"Well, that's frank enough. It's your investment I'm trying to protect."

"I intend going ahead with the investment."

"He convinced you, did he?"

"He was reassuring."

"You were reassured by that sci-fi garbage about cities on the moon and cities under the ocean?"

She nodded toward the line of models. "Look at what he's achieved, Gordon."

"I bet you're asking yourself, 'And what has Gordon Pickering achieved? Where does he get the gall to stand up to the great man?' I'll tell you what Gordon has achieved. Precious little, if you want to know. Precious little. I don't blame you for going with Sermon."

"There's no comparison," she said, meaning that she didn't measure one against the other. "You've done a great deal. I honor you for what you've achieved."

Honored him? For what? His chairing social studies at Central High? For his meager view of La Salle Avenue from an office shared with ten others? Who was she kidding?

"We'll talk at dinner." She started toward Sermon. "Let me say goodbye."

He wasn't going to dinner. He had to get home. He had an invalid to take care of.

"Stop it!" It was a tone she might have used with a whining orphan. "I'm truly grateful that you came with me this afternoon. I know you mean to help and you have helped. You have meant so much to me. Let's not have a scene."

"'Have meant so much to you?' The past tense?"

"For godsakes, Gordon."

"A mistake," he said, and turned to leave. "A mistake from the beginning. My mistake," and left.

"Eugene, would you please go with him?"

Did she still consider me family? I was at her beck and call, and chased after him. I caught him at the elevators. We rode down to the lobby together. There were other conferees with us and we said nothing till we were outside.

"I lost her," he said.

He lost her? He didn't own her. He had no right to her. Why should he be different from any orphan separating from her? What I said was, "Maybe you lost her but she hasn't lost you."

"What could you possibly know?"

"I lived with her for eight years and never saw her lose anybody."

"Don't put me in your shoes. I'm not one of your crowd." He walked fast and I ran to catch up. I walked him to his lumbering, ancient Packard, once top of the line, proof of class and station, now a mess. When he started the motor, it made the sound of an invalid.

I leaned into the car, said we should get together someday and erase the memory of our first encounter. I didn't mean it seriously; I meant it as an easy way of saying goodbye forever.

"Get in. I'll drive you home."

"I still have work to do. Some other time."

"I'm on the edge," he said.

"The edge of what?"

"The edge of blowing up."

"Who, yourself?"

"Me, you, her, the Great Man, the whole goddamned world. Get in and I'll tell you about me and Kate Wyman."

"I guess it's my obligation to protect the world from being blown up," and I got into the car.

On the drive he told me what I wanted to hear but wished I hadn't heard. He described their relationship with almost poetic inflation, no explicit details, but filling them in didn't take great imagination.

He'd met her years before at a charity function in the Central High School auditorium. He'd been asked, as resident orator, to chair the event. She talked about the plight of orphans, their isolation, the effort of the orphanage to restore lost children to the community, the need for increased financial support. She was balanced, intelligent, lucid. She seemed handsome, but no beauty. Her beauty was in time revealed.

He was then in turmoil, nothing calm about him. He clamped down on rage, but it seeped through in his treatment of other faculty and his no-nonsense instruction, and especially his obsessive exercise routine. Weight lifting was better than blowing up.

He had married his high school sweetheart. Though neither of them knew it at first—the symptoms weren't obvious—Sarah was already afflicted with rampaging MS. When it became apparent, he accepted that she was his obligation. He would never cut loose from her. They were destined to sink together even if her decline used up his life.

Kate Wyman saved him. At first he only saw what everyone else saw, an aloof woman whose composure seemed impenetrable. He wouldn't have tried breaking through. He introduced her to Sarah so that she would understand his inability to express what he felt. She was terrifically moved and her sympathy took a surprising turn. She came to him without reservation, no blue smock, no hair tied in a bun, no strained flirting, no need for seduction. It was her doing, could I believe that? She came to him unguarded and available, hair down, "Wide open," he said, to see how I would react.

She was seduced by her own compassion. Otherwise he couldn't understand why he was chosen.

Once a week he was released from rage and despair. She entirely let go and then—this made him crazy—she gathered it all back, abruptly formal, as if the letting go had no meaning. They lived in contradiction and he feared—justifiably it now seemed— that what was so easily given could easily be taken away. He knew guarantees were impossible, but he needed reassurance and he couldn't be satisfied when she answered his, "Why?" with, "I love being with you." That was a lie. It would have been more truthful if she'd have said, "You're a bad habit I'm trying to break. You scare me." He was scary because he was scared and that was unbearable. Where was the justice of it? She didn't acknowledge his real stature—he was a Pickering—a failed Pickering, yes, but an original Detroiter, born high, fallen low, while she was merely a farmer's daughter from Traverse City, Michigan, her history a blank. Did I know she had no history, no connection? She was nobody. She was connected to nobodies. "Farmers, fishermen, on a Lake Michigan island. Nobodies, nowhere." Easy for her to rise when she had begun so low. It was intolerable that she condescended to him. He wouldn't tolerate it. He loved her, she was everything to him, but he was quitting her service. She could latch on to a con artist like Andy Sermon or whoever else came along, but he was finished.

He began his account with reverence and ended with grandiosity and slander, painting a portrait of a totally unfamiliar Miss Wyman.

All this on the way to my place and then, after he'd parked, spilling what he'd never before confessed.

Why confess to me, the kid he'd dumped? We weren't made closer by his confession.

He warned me not to think he was after pity or sympathy. He used me as an audience, no more. He said in a deep, threatening voice, "I don't want any of this getting back to her, understand? This is between you and me." I'd heard nothing I cared to repeat and got out of the car.

He yelled after me, "We're finished. No more follow-ups."

His rage had too much force and I expected follow-ups. We weren't finished.

Elton was annoyed that I'd wasted a great opportunity. "Why did you have to tell Sermon you were 'shy'? When are you going to learn that some stuff you keep to yourself?"

The three of them had dinedat the London Chop House after the meeting. She had a great time with Andy Sermon. They clicked, as Elton knew they would. Who else had Sermon's energy, power, and charm? And she, of course, was our incomparable Kate, a perfect match. She barely made it back to Margaret Tessler to supervise the bed check. According to Elton, there was no mention of Gordon at dinner.

A few months later when I saw her again, I asked if she knew how he was doing and she said they were out of touch. She was by then swirling in Sermon's vortex, almost swallowed, just as Elton, now fully parented, intended.

Elton helped with my monthly payments. I couldn't have managed otherwise.

"We're on the verge, kid. What's a little more debt?"

Again it turned out as he said. In six months we sold the South-field parcel at the price we needed. For a moment I held in my hand a check for twenty thousand dollars, Kate Wyman the same. I could have lived for seven years off that money, more if I had invested even modestly. Elton was in kissing distance of his million. This time we didn't hesitate endorsing our checks to Ponchartrain Associates.

Elton had a clear map of his future. He stuck to all its turnings, waiting until blue heaven came into sight and he could step aboard.

Demolition started a day late, March 28 instead of March 27. There was a downpour on the 27th and the 28th was perfect, the air clear and crisp, the sun high, a beautiful spring morning, the Canadian shore as clearly outlined as if it were a cut-out placed by a set designer. We assembled at the waterfront site, all the partners, friends and family, and onlookers who had seen the newspaper notice. We joined Sermon and his crew of contractors and engineers and architects and city officials and union heads, all of us in Sermon, Inc. hard hats. We were not far from Indian Village where Chief Pontiac once encamped.

The mayor, together with Andy Sermon, snipped the ribbon. Photographers caught the picture. The machines were poised. A massive orange bulldozer initiated the assault on a slum that contained remnants of an original Detroit, pre-Ford, pre-Edison Illuminating Company, a gaslit Midwestern port city, center of the stove business. The freshly painted bulldozer drove straight into the ribs of a bedraggled Victorian. The building groaned, buckled, came down to its knees, a tower on one side, a porch in front. The house twisted in distress. There was no cleaning that house. The rot and grime were in its flesh and foundation. A brigade of cleaning ladies and carpenters and painters couldn't have done the job. Painters scraping at old skin would have carved through to vital organs. It was the province of rats and roaches and had to come down. And yet, twisting like that, exposing neglected features—fluted wooden pillars, ornate moldings, gargoyle heads carved above the pillars, the fairy-tale peaked tower, the swell of bay windows—it seemed the sad death of something once valued and too long neglected.

The bulldozer backed off, then charged up the inclined walls; the building folded on its side, the porch tore free, the tower hit the ground. The machine went over the top, its blade pointed almost skyward for an instant, the treads grinding, then descended to the other side. Afterward, back and forth, reducing the house to splinters and rubble.

The rest of Sermon's fleet joined the assault. Cranes and steam shovels and jackhammers and bulldozers and dump trucks were spread out over the site. Generators and compressors established a pulsing rhythm that shivered the ground beneath us. Sermon had a regiment working for him on the fenced-in site. The neighboring streets were reconfigured, downtown city traffic dominated by our project.

Elton shouted to me over the stunning noise of demolition, "Do you finally get what it's all about?"

Yes, I got what it was all about. I was about to be rich and freed from bondage.

I stood with Elton and Kate Wyman and the other partners. I asked what she'd heard from Gordon.

He never answered her messages. There was an inkling of concern, brow wrinkled, lips pursed, but on this day not enough to affect her excitement at this great demolition. "Isn't it amazing? Just a few of us and we've changed Detroit."

Sermon led Elton to a cluster of city officials and introduced him to the mayor. Elton was thirty-three and already among the city's power brokers. He accepted a cigar from Sermon, drawing it in as if he had been born to smoke Havanas. His eyes blessed everything they touched. He was refashioned by his own hand, worth a million and more. I loved Elton then. I admired his focus and boldness, even his ruthlessness. I told him all that.

"Kid," he said, drawing on his cigar, "everyone loves a winner."

I returned to watch the progress of demolition. I saw a burlesque theater go down, a grimy brick church, an abandoned stove factory, warehouses, a line of vacant storefronts. Hills of debris were hauled away, other hills piled up. The ground was leveled in places, deep pits excavated elsewhere. Massive stacks of rebar and lumber and plywood and sand and gravel and steel beams and sewer pipes and water pipes were hauled into place around the periphery.

Radical surgery was the cure for that forlorn neighborhood with its outworn history. Development was our future—up, up, up the direction of our century despite all enormities—if we had the nerve. These developers had the nerve. And, in the exuberance of the moment, so did I.

SIX

It's All Real Estate

For a short time I came to the development almost every workday, fascinated by my ringside view of a great show. I had the illusion that those steel skeletons, rising from dead ground, belonged to me.

A plywood fence wrapped the project. Window slits were cut for passersby. I was inside the fence, near architects and supervisors and engineers who examined blueprints spread on a makeshift table. We perched at the edge of a great pit and observed foundations rising.

I first arrived in the company of Andy Sermon, so no one questioned my being there. Sermon barely acknowledged me, just a nod, but the nod was my ticket to admission. A safety officer gave me a hard hat and I blended in.

I asked a supervisor how we were doing.

Smooth as silk, not even the usual foul-ups. We were on schedule.

Work started in a din of jackhammers and compressors and generators, then other noise joined in, trucks and bulldozers and giant cranes. Cement trucks, long tubes extended, poured concrete around rebar studs. Rebar lattices, set against the sides of the deep, squared pit, were hosed with concrete.

The noise, the dust, the heat, the hustling workers, shirtless and sun weathered, were proof our development had an inexorable thrust.

Sermon showed up one Saturday with Kate Wyman. They were on their way to lunch at a time when she should have been on duty at the Home.

He was dressed as usual in Western shirt and military twills and red-tooled cowboy boots and sky-blue hard hat. There was no modesty in his dress or bearing: sleeves rolled, a lordly slouch, chest in, paunch out, tall and immodestly at ease. He didn't have to be modest. This was his ground. He commanded everything, including Kate Wyman. He kept her close while consulting with officials, his hand on her hip. An architect called his attention to a blueprint modification. "I have no problem with that," and his will was done. When a crane swung a massive beam toward the pit, he pointed and said mockingly, "Behold!" as if he were a god and wanted her to see what he had set in motion, his crane, his trucks, his crew establishing his foundations. She turned to look, twisting against him, and his arm came around, close to her breasts. She unlinked herself but he clamped down again, a public intimacy that should have embarrassed her. He advertised that he knew her true age from the shape and feel of her true body. He said in an Arkansas bass rumble which I didn't accept as his true voice, "As soon as we get out from under this"—he nodded toward the construction—"we're gonna take care of Kate and her kids. We have a great location near Walled Lake." He didn't speak to me directly, facing one of his engineers, but he meant me to hear. The engineer nodded as if pleased by the news.

She was a changed Kate Wyman. She wore a summer dress, and when she stood in the sun I could almost make out her body outline through the thin fabric. I told her—I had to shout against the noise—that she looked ten years younger. She took it as criticism, but it was more than that. She disappeared inside that dress.

She shouted back, "I'm forty-five years old, Eugene, and I have no illusion I'm getting younger."

"Maybe it's the dress."

"Perhaps it's a mistake wearing this."

I told her she was going to be rich and needed a manner to which she was not born. "You need a dress like that."

Sermon, speaking to me without looking, said he'd asked her to wear the dress. "It's perfect."

At lunchtime the noise diminished and, accompanied by his entourage, he went down a ramp into the pit to inspect the foundation. Kate and I were alone and could talk.

She said she heard mockery in my comment. "I wish you wouldn't make a fuss about what I'm wearing."

I didn't mean to mock. I was teasing. I was used to seeing her in her work outfit and the dress surprised me. She was beautiful in that dress.

She told me it was a gift from Andy Sermon and the dress

changed nothing significant. For good or ill, she remained the same Katherine Wyman.

None of us were the same, I said. We were all changing, released by our share of Ponchartrain Associates to go in different directions. Elton was located at the Sermon offices, almost out of reach. I was preparing for my new life at the university. She was entering a world from which I was excluded. I'd heard a rumor that the Home was about to be sold. That would be an enormous change, our past erased, and, yes, that made me worry that she, too, would soon be out of reach.

"It's no rumor, Eugene. The board told me three weeks ago the Home is sold." The buyer was Andy Sermon. No, she hadn't protested. Of course, they had solicited her opinion and she assured me it was a good deal all around; there was no reason to be upset.

I denied I was upset. "Upward and onward, let the bulldozers roll."

She told me a new home was already planned, a vastly improved and expanded version of the Margaret Tessler Home. Each senior boy would have his own dorm cubicle. The workshop would be equipped with metal lathes and table saws and drills for advanced instruction. The kitchen would have top-of-the-line restaurant equipment and a professional crew. It was Andy Sermon who had guided the planning and inspired her to believe in the Katherine Wyman Home for Boys. The name was an embarrassment and would be changed—back to Margaret Tessler if possible—but, whatever the name, the important thing was her heart would always be with her boys, with the boys she'd had and all the boys to come, no one neglected. Her commitment wouldn't change. She believed Andy Sermon was a rare combination of visionary and man of action. Anything he imagined he could bring into being.

From what I'd seen, anything he imagined he could erase from being.

Sermon, returning from the inspection, caught her arm and towed her away without giving me so much as a nod. After they left, one of his entourage—the safety officer who had issued the hard hat—told me I was no longer welcome on site. I had no business being there. It was a liability issue and in the future, if I wanted to see what was going on, I could join other viewers outside, and watch through a fence-slit window.

I resented Sermon—no, stronger than that—I hated the man—not only because he had dismissed me as a hopeless contradiction, a shy salesman, who had no business being on site, but because he wrapped his arm around Kate in the same way he wrapped a fence around this chunk of the Detroit waterfront.

I considered Elton an older brother: impatient, condescending, yet always supportive. He'd set me up at a Southfield subdivision where I was doing work I didn't have the heart to do but was obliged to do. My university pittance covered food and rent, little more, and I couldn't have kept up payments on my note without his help. I owed it to him to put in five days a week at the subdivision. But when I started teaching it became too much. I had to scramble from university to subdivision, often late.

I went to the agent in charge to get relief.

His name was Sy Landis, a jovial, outgoing salesman who had

mastered the art of luring clients and closing deals. He loved the work. His ambition was to climb the Sermon, Inc. ladder. He had cultivated a mellow baritone to help him along. It was the kind of voice Elton had once urged me to develop, a voice I didn't trust. I had no sense of who was hiding behind the affability.

Sy was no more comfortable with me than I was with him. He must have heard my voice as pompous—he would have said "snotty"—and he was probably right. I was influenced by Huston Fuller, whose voice, natural to him, sounded false when it came from me. In time it would meld with what was mine and mine would become authentic, but I wasn't yet close, so Landis and I spoke different languages in different voices, unnatural to each other. I'm sure he'd have liked to shout in a crude, authentic Landis voice, "Smith! You aren't getting the job done! Get your ass out of here!" but I was Elton's hire and Elton was his superior and he limited his show of dislike to shrugs and grimaces and not very subtle sarcasm.

I met him outside the subdivision office. He stood in the sun, surveying the action, a large, blond, handsome man, portly and tanned, in a beige linen suit and pale yellow tie.

He looked at his watch, "Late again, Smith?"

I admitted I had a problem getting to the subdivision on time. I knew it wasn't fair to him or the other agents. I hoped we could adjust my schedule so that it would work for us all.

He waved at me to follow him into the office. He sat behind the desk, legs up, while I remained standing. "Okay, shoot."

I told him I appreciated his patience and knew it wasn't easy rearranging schedules but I was having trouble keeping up with my two jobs. He didn't say anything, so I kept talking, going into unnecessary detail about my work at the university. I not only had my own graduate work, but I taught a section of Contemporary Civilization three times a week based on a Professor Fuller lecture I had to audit. I also graded student papers for introductory German language classes that I sat in on two nights a week. Everything was new to me. I spent hours in class preparation, then, after teaching, I had an hour trip to the subdivision, followed by four hours showing homes and an hour back to campus. I needed to cut down on my hours and change my schedule.

"How come it takes you two hours round trip?"

"I have to make three bus connections."

"How come you don't own a car?"

"I don't drive."

That did it. That pushed him over the edge. He dropped the smooth baritone and in a furious, constricted voice released his dammed up bile. What country did I think I was in? Uganda? Congo? This was Detroit, the Motor City, not the Third World. "Don't tell me about your goddamn teaching schedule. I don't give a shit about bus rides. Get a horse and buggy. Get a frigging car." He unleashed grievances too long suppressed. No tie? Rumpled jacket? Did I think this was Third World real estate and our clients were Kalihari Bushmen? He'd overheard my egghead bullshit that could only drive clients away. He'd heard me tell a home seeker, worried about buying into a market that might have reached its ceiling, "Enter the future without fear. Our destiny is upward." Enter the future? Destiny? Was I selling homes or offering Sunday sermons?

I admitted my two careers were entangled and sometimes the language of Contemporary Civilization spilled over into my selling routine, but clients weren't offended. In fact, they seemed to like the idea that the agent selling homes taught at the university. The point was, I was stressed and, if I were to stay on at the subdivision, I needed to shift from working during the week to limited weekends. I knew it meant a big cut in salary and commissions and I was prepared to accept that.

"You'll accept a cut in salary and commission? That's goddamn generous of you, Smith. Know what you'll get? Zilch. Nada. Who the hell do you think you are, trying to set hours for your convenience?"

He was right, I was wrong, his outrage was justified; negotiation wouldn't get us anywhere. I'd hoped to hang on till Thanksgiving, but I could see that wasn't going to happen. "Sy, for my sake, and yours, too, I have to quit."

"What do you mean you have to quit?"

"I can't do this job anymore. I can't keep it up."

"You say for my sake you're quitting?" He lurched from his chair, his hands poised to strangle, constrained by his desire to use them to climb the Sermon, Inc. ladder, and bellowed, "Smith! You are FIRED!"

I told him he didn't have the authority to fire me.

He told me to get the hell out of there.

I said, gladly.

In fact, it was a risky move. I needed Elton's support. I hoped he would help with payments on my note. I counted on it.

The next day Sy called me at the university, sounding grim

and subdued. Mr. Kramer had approved my request for a changed schedule and he would somehow manage to fit me in.

I told him I regretted the problems I'd caused him, but, no, I'd lost any enthusiasm I ever had for the business and it was a relief to be out of it.

"A relief? Damn you," he said, then again with more force, "Goddamn you! Just don't claim I didn't make the offer."

I left Elton a message telling him that Sy Landis had fired me and with good reason. It was irrelevant that I found him pompous and shallow; he was, after all, an effective manager. I'd lost whatever desire I had for the business. I couldn't do the work anymore. I was quitting real estate, but I wasn't quitting him. He remained my mentor, my Margaret Tessler brother, my closest friend, and I'd never forget what I owed him.

Mrs. Tuchler handed me his return message, which she had recorded in her labored, misspelled script. "What you owe me is four tousand buks. See me about arranging payments." She was miffed that I smiled at her note. "I am not your secretary, Mr. Schmidt. I am not hired for dictation."

I told her once again, "'Smith,' Mrs. Tuchler, not 'Schmidt'."

We met in the lounge of a Sermon office suite where he was now located. He didn't invite me into his private office. The plush lobby was blocked by glass walls from the company's inner workings. We sat opposite each other in leather and chrome armchairs. He asked if I'd brought the four thousand dollars.

"You know I don't have that kind of money, Elton. I'm only an impoverished teaching assistant who works for love. Until the

Ponchartrain bonanza comes in, I have to survive on savings, a university pittance, and your charity."

I meant it to be light and funny but he was absolutely cold, nothing brotherly in his response. "If you think I'm going to subsidize your fun and games, you're out of your skull. You made your choice, now live with it. I'll give you two weeks to come up with the money."

"I won't have it in two weeks. What happens then?"

"Then you can kiss your 'Ponchartrain bonanza' goodbye."

I couldn't keep up the light tone and blew up. I knew what was going on. He wanted me gone. He needed a grievance to justify getting rid of me and I'd given him one. His family was complete and I was an unwanted relic of another time. He manipulated everything, detaching Kate from Margaret Tessler, matching her up with Sermon. I called him a sycophantic marriage broker, a pimp.

"Fuck off," he said, and left for his inner office. I watched through the glass wall as he walked down a corridor of cubicles toward the senior offices. He made an abrupt turn and was out of sight.

Two weeks passed and nothing happened. I regretted blowing up. I'd accused him of what was probably only in my mind. I hoped we would find some compromise and reconcile, perhaps a part-time job at another subdivision with more convenient hours. I called his office, but he was unavailable. I tried reaching Kate Wyman and she wasn't in. I asked Miss Hempleman when she would be in. "I'm sorry, Eugene. I can't say."

"Can't," she had said, as if she were under duress.

It was more than two months before I heard from Elton again. He called to invite me to the beginning of his first solo project. He didn't mention the four thousand dollars I owed him. He sounded calm and reasonable. I told him I felt terrible about our last exchange and was delighted his development was underway and that he'd finally arrived at the place he'd spent almost ten years trying to reach. When I asked what the project was he told me to see for myself. He would come for me in the morning.

"I teach till eleven."

"I'll get you at eleven."

He picked me up in front of Old Main in a new Cadillac version of his white convertible, this one with a bugle horn, sounding what he told me was "mess call." He shrugged indifferently when I said he was my best friend; I missed him; I hoped we could work something out. What I meant sincerely came off as ass-kissing sentiment. He parked on Dexter Avenue, near Six Mile Road, no project in sight, and turned to me. "You never paid attention to what I kept telling you."

"What did you keep telling me?"

"Something very simple, but you never paid attention. I told you, 'Nothing stays put, everything moves; it's all real estate.'"

"I still don't get it."

He started the car, drove a few blocks, parked in front of Blakeney's Chili Parlor across from our Margaret Tessler home.

"Do you get it now?"

The Home was the center of that landscape and for a moment—a very brief moment—I didn't understand that it wasn't there. There was only a rubble field. I had a clear view all the way to the forsythia and the line of elm and maple and oak at the rear of the property where I'd once gone underground to establish my Arcadia. The ground was peppered with shards of red brick and concrete. The gate was gone; the paved approach remained, but now an approach to nowhere.

I visualized her office with the fish tank and the typewriter and the flags and the portrait of young, lovely, deceased Margaret Tessler, and imagined the lights popping on at dusk in the dormitories, the noisy clatter in the refectory and corridor, but those scenes were as immaterial as an amputee's phantom limbs.

A hundred and fifty apartment units were to rise where that red brick Home once stood, each unit with the amenities of modern kitchens and modern heating.

"Where are the boys?"

"They're taken care of."

"Where is she?"

"She's taken care of, too."

I left the car and headed toward a bus stop.

He shouted, "It's all real estate, stupid!" He whipped the white convertible around, exposing sides emblazoned in red, ELKRAM REAL ESTATE, and screeched off.

He cut the ground from under me, not hindered by sentiment.

She must have known and never said a word and that was the most hurtful.

I met Frucht, the Dutch importer, at his Highland Park warehouse and offered to sell him my stake in Ponchartrain Associates. All I asked in return was my original investment and repayment of my debt to Elton.

Frucht's office overlooked a crammed factory space, once an assembly for universal joints, now used as storage for his import business. Crates of merchandise were stacked almost to the beams. I saw workers unload marble slabs from shipping crates and transfer them to a lift.

Frucht came from the Netherlands, but there was no hint of his being Dutch. He spoke an unaccented, idiomatic English. He was a few years older than I was, boyish in appearance, blond, almost pretty, but I don't think anyone who ever did business with him took him at face value. Despite the apparent boyishness he almost immediately impressed as tough and shrewd.

He was at first suspicious of my offer. Why did I want to get rid of my share when the development was about to pay off? He knew I was connected to Elton Kramer. Did I know something he didn't?

There was no mystery. I was a mere teaching assistant and couldn't afford the payments.

"So why don't you go to your friend?"

I figured that Frucht was a man who would jump at a good deal, no hassle, no complications of friendship.

He agreed it was a good deal, but, unfortunately, he was already deeply invested and reluctant to get in any deeper. The best he could offer was to assume my debt. He refused to cover my investment.

I told him he'd make a fortune on my note and had to be more forthcoming. After some back and forth he offered an additional three thousand.

I told him it wasn't enough. I'd look for something better.

"Good luck, Smith. I hope you find what you're looking for."

Elton was parked at a no-stop zone near the entrance to Old Main, the convertible top down. He bugled his horn to catch me as I left the building, startling exiting students and faculty. I kept walking and he left his car and ran after me.

He'd heard about my dealing with Frucht. "That Dutchman will steal you out of your shoes."

I was disposing of my real estate and didn't need his advice.

"'Yours'? Do you know how you got 'yours'? I gave you a piece of my share out of pity for an orphan kid who didn't know his ass from a hole in the ground. I didn't give it to you so you could make that Dutch pirate rich."

"It's real estate, Elton—nothing but real estate. I'll sell to anyone who'll meet my price."

"I let you have it, so, okay, I'll let you off the hook and take it back."

I pointed to his car. A cop was writing a ticket. He yelled, "That's my car!" and took off. He shouted, "We'll keep it like it is. Just stay away from that Dutch prick."

Frucht raised his offer to five thousand dollars. I told him I had decided not to sell.

"Five thousand isn't necessarily the final offer, Smith. Maybe I can put something together that will satisfy us both."

I told him I had decided to hold on to my share of Ponchartrain Associates and gamble that fortune would come my way.

"Can you handle the risk?"

Aristotle had written that happiness required wealth, health, and leisure. Two out of three wouldn't do.

"If that's what it takes," he said, "be happy."

Elton's attorney sent me a registered letter with an enclosed legal document I was to have notarized and then return. Elton would assume my payment of $930 a month with the proviso that my entire debt could be called after thirty days notice.

I tossed the letter on my desk and left it there until a few days later I signed.

I dreamed I walked down a deserted Dexter Avenue, no evidence of life, no auto or foot traffic, everything shut down. I walked through the Margaret Tessler gate, no orphans there, no one at reception, no one in her office. I was bone-tired, went up to my bed in the senior boy's dormitory, stripped, got under the covers, glanced at the shelf above my bed. It was stacked with paperback thrillers, cartoon illustrations of naked women on the jackets. In my time, such reading would never have been allowed in the Krause Library.

I heard the clatter of an approaching group on the linoleum tiles. Before I could jump out of bed, a crowd entered, men in funereal suits led by the director, an aloof young woman in garish makeup. She turned to a hulking attendant. "What's HE doing here? Get him out!" I stumbled naked from bed, said I was once a resident in the era of the famous Katherine Wyman and had imagined—no doubt mistakenly—that I was at home.

She said contemptuously, "We know who you are. You weren't

anyone to her. You're no motherless child. Grab your forty winks and get out."

Huston Fuller used the phrase "free floating" to characterize himself. I floated in his wake, not yet free.

Three mornings a week I led a section of his upper-division Contemporary Civilization course. All sections—more than a hundred students—gathered in an Old Main lecture hall to hear him speak on a "Century of Progress." His initial assignment, as usual, was Plato's *Republic,* and, following his lead, I tried to make the reading significant to my twenty-five students.

I asked them to imagine what it would it be like if Detroit had halted all growth and stayed the size of an isolated village. No need for police or soldiers or national guard or customs officials or Great Lakes heavy traffic or overland trade or manufacture; no need for massive construction—no GM Building, no Ford River Rouge plant, no Fisher Building or Penobscot Building or Book Cadillac Hotel, no bridge or tunnel to Canada—no upturns, no downturns, no unemployment, all exchange simple barter. We'd be almost fully self-contained, issues settled by an agreement of families, no need for a complicated history, as the cycle of days would be uneventfully repeated—no radio, no automobiles, no airplanes, no movies, no Milton Berle, no *Detroit News* or *Times* or *Free Press* newspapers, almost no development, nothing but a village technology with as few connections to the world as we could get away with. A simple myth of origins—the Bible might do—would be sufficient. We'd get rid of the injunction to go forth and multiply.

Wouldn't we prefer that simplicity to the turbulence of modern Detroit?

A boring simplicity, the students unanimously agreed. Deadly, claustrophobic. That village model represented little they wanted. It wouldn't even include them. They were mainly blue-collar kids, children of immigrants or Southern migrants, with no desire for an archaic village. The future would inevitably be an improvement. They wanted a modern Detroit, even with the problems of governance that came with it. They wanted Hudson's Department Store, and the new mall on Northwestern, and freeways to the countryside and streamlined power autos and weekend movies and Elvis shaking his hips and all the distractions a dull village couldn't support. They accepted the police and army as necessary to maintaining the boundary between "mine and thine."

"If that's what you want," I said, "then consider Plato's design for avoiding the perils of development," and I led them further into *The Republic*.

I would have voted to stop with a village—with even less—an isolated self-sufficient ark, floating safe in a drowned world, picking and choosing whom we'd let on board while we waited for an empty shore to appear. I wouldn't have lowered a ladder for Elton Kramer. I didn't want a developer on my ark, though development was inevitable, village and ark only fantasy. We went forth and multiplied and death was the outcome if we didn't expand beyond a village. "Up" was our direction. Buccaneer developers appeared as our liberators. On the other hand, up, up, up was just another way to death.

Plato would have constrained the peril of development with lies—good lies, not the miserable lies I told myself.

SEVEN

Dancing Lesson

On Tuesday and Thursday nights I audited Professor Hunneke's introductory German 101. I sat in back taking notes and after class picked up student papers left on his desk.

The professor, a benign old man, everyone's favorite, was allowed to linger past retirement. At the beginning of class he stood tall at the lectern, almost martial. He at first seemed fit, though thickened in the middle. His carefully tended silver hair was bent off-center, left and right, along a healthy, pink seam. After announcing the next lesson assignment, he eased into his chair with a deep sigh, revealing his disabling arthritic pain and stiffness.

He spoke a German-British English, the fused accents producing a slightly formal speech, pleasant to hear, salted with corny jokes. The first night he briefed me on my duties. "I am an *Alter* and our good superiors have given me a crutch—you, my son—to keep me on my feet." He jokingly summarized his grading policy.

"What I ask of you, Eugene, is very simple. You will grade with a heavy hand."

"Why a heavy hand?"

"Why a heavy hand? I'll tell you why, my son. I am the good guy. You are—unfortunately—designated the bad guy. They should be angry with you, not with me. I forbid sadism but severe strokes with a red pencil will encourage discipline. You understand, of course, that I am teasing a little bit?"

He kept me there, complaining about the fading interest in foreign languages and the pettiness of school politics, until the janitor entered the classroom with mop and bucket. He invited me to join him at a late night cafeteria on Woodward Avenue.

We slid our trays on chrome rails that ran the width of the cafeteria, past appetizers, salads, soup in tureens, and entrées steaming in metal craters, past desserts and drinks. We sat and talked and ate.

He loved the old country. He loved the old language. He loved the *gemütlichkeit* of Göttingen. He couldn't abide the thugs who had taken over. He'd fled Germany in the late thirties, and in leaving he had left too much. His wife died soon after they arrived in Detroit. A son lived in Venezuela. His major work, a Göethe study, was finally complete, but there was little publishing interest and he feared his day was over.

"So be it," said the old man, trying to come to terms with his irrelevance. "We dream to become important, but at the end we find we are not so important." He apologized if he spread gloom. He didn't mean to. He accepted the world as it was, though that wasn't easy. "At your age, Eugene, you can not believe—and you should not believe—what in time you, too, will learn to believe, that what we struggle all our lives to tell the world, the world has little interest in hearing. So be it. We delude ourselves when we make drama of our despair. The drama is maybe necessary—it is maybe pretty—but it is a lie. There is no joy in discovering our unimportance." He apologized for afflicting me with the miasma of old age. He translated a mournful phrase of Goethe's, "I only breathe and already I am betrayed."

I was less impressed with his despair than with his noisy, zestful drinking and eating. He downed a beer. He finished a plate of brisket and vegetables, belched, lit a cigarette, and by the time we left the cafeteria he was flushed a worrisome red, but seemed content and affable.

"We must do this often, Eugene."

His teaching assistant was Louise Lehman, a language PhD who handled the other Hunneke classes. Louise checked my grading of student assignments before they were passed on to him. She was wiry and intense, with straight, bobbed black hair; her voice, when she corrected me, a commissar monotone. She wore no makeup, dressed in dark slacks and long-sleeved white blouses buttoned to the throat. She was determinedly severe and when later she eased up and smiled it was a surprise to see how attractive she seemed.

Louise was more than the old man's assistant. She was a guardian of his well-being, on campus and off. She scorned my "pitiful command of the *Sprach*." She implied I had my language job only because of Professor Fuller's intercession and not because of any language talent. I dismissed it as a jealous guarding of turf and refused to let her spoil my pleasure at being on staff.

I told her not to worry; my German was improving.

"You have a long way to go."

Old Hunneke wanted me to make peace with Louise. "You should try to be a little nice to her, Eugene. Not so cold. Buy her a coffee. Buy her a beer. It pains me that such good young people do not get along. If you will take the trouble to better know Louise you will become friends, I promise you."

"My problem with her, Professor Hunneke, is that she knows everything and listens to nothing."

"You are wrong," he said. "She is a wonderful listener."

Louise was important to him and I was new to his life and if the axe had to fall, it would be on my neck, not hers.

I invited her to meet me across from campus at the Webster Hotel lounge to clear the air.

I found her wedged into a couch near the hotel elevators.

"Afraid we'll be seen together, Louise? Ready to make a get-away?"

"I have nothing to be afraid of."

I told her I admired her greater knowledge of German but I was offended by her tone of superiority. I was new at the game and didn't want to be exposed to her putdowns, so would she please moderate the nagging critiques?

She was just as blunt. "The German language isn't your strong point."

"Getting along isn't yours."

She smiled. "I should try harder, shouldn't I?" and laughed.

I said I could almost like her when she laughed. She should do more of it; laughter brightened her.

She agreed to brighten up if I agreed to improve my German.

I said, "That's a bargain," and we sealed the agreement with a handshake.

Her attitude changed when I managed to reassure her I wasn't an enemy. Behind the pose of superiority, I found a generous, though insecure woman. There was no chemistry to complicate our relationship and we warmed into friendship. Hunneke was right; she was a good listener. I could trust Louise. It was easy opening up to her. She heard my orphan history, and how my life with Kate Wyman and Elton Kramer had abruptly ended. I admitted to moments of intense loneliness, but nothing I couldn't manage. I'd found my place at Wayne. My future was taking shape under the wing of Professor Fuller. I felt awakened, and sometimes—was it a risk saying it?—content.

"What's the risk?"

"My feelings don't have staying power." I had thought Kate Wyman was everything to me. I'd spent almost every day for seven years with Elton Kramer. We abruptly separated and I was fine, no problem, on with my life.

She was amazed I was involved in the riverfront project. "I can't even imagine you building a dollhouse for a five-year-old. You are not of this world, Eugene."

Why did she say that?

"For instance, you don't own a car."

"I can't drive."

She could do something about a car. She had a new Mercury

and her old Plymouth coupe was taking up space in her garage. She offered me the rattletrap plus driving lessons.

She lived in a duplex facing very upscale Palmer Park, not far from Elton. Her parents, long divorced, had new families, the father in Atlanta, the mother in Florida. Maternal grandparents had raised Louise. When they died, first Grandma and months later Grandpa, they left her a trust income and a new Mercury sedan.

"See," she said, "I'm something of an orphan, too."

She was a patient instructor, not disturbed by my clumsiness behind the wheel, and I quickly learned what I'd too long put off, finally liberated from transportation bondage.

Our friendship seemed easy and straightforward, until, one night at the Fullers', it became complicated and difficult.

It was a welcoming party for Fuller's students and colleagues and Marybeth's actor friends, a miscellaneous crowd of black and white, knit together by food and drink, but mainly by dance.

The seven-room apartment was on the upper floor of a shabby two-story clapboard building, the yellow siding peeled and mangy. The apartment had all the problems Fuller had described and more. When the music paused, you could hear the river-rapids noise of Woodward Avenue traffic. The windows were braced open with strips of lath, the living room floor uneven. At the outer edge of the floor, I felt slightly tilted. The toilet was cramped, the tiles stained, water pressure weak. The walls were bumpy with layers of paint. The kitchen was small, although I don't imagine Marybeth did much cooking. Nothing much was invested in that apartment and nothing much would have been lost if it were abandoned; yet, with all its defects, I wouldn't have exchanged that place for what Marybeth said she wanted. It had none of the features of a Sermon production—it was ramshackle, funky, full of life.

Huston and I stood at the living-room threshold, watching the dancers, Marybeth, at the center. There were perhaps twenty people dancing. Because of the heat everyone was stripped down. Standing fans at opposite sides of the living room swept the dancers. An enormous painting of an unmistakable Marybeth, emerging naked from fiery swirls of pink and red, dominated the room. Huston described the painting as a true representation by an artist friend who had summoned her spirit as well as her body.

A saxophone and piano drove the dance. After a few numbers, the saxophonist, a balding, light-brown man with a pencil mustache, wearing a sweat-stained Hawaiian shirt, parked his horn—the piano carrying on—grabbed Marybeth from her partner and began dancing.

"Look at her." Huston, bending close so I'd hear, nodded at Marybeth tightly linked with the saxophone player. "She says she wants to settle, but can you see what happens when she touches ground? She's up and flying. That woman," he said, shaking his head admiringly, "has no *sitzfleisch*."

She wore an embroidered Mexican blouse scooped low, sweat glistening on her shoulders, breasts, and back.

We'd been drinking; I tried to match Huston glass for glass. He seemed unaffected, while my talk tapes were loud and racing. I told him I could imagine what I'd feel that close to Marybeth. I could imagine what I'd feel if I were Huston watching my wife that intimately connected to another man.

"What do you think I'd feel, Eugene?"

"Jealousy?"

Not an ounce. He had defects but jealousy wasn't one of them. He had no more experience of jealousy than the tone deaf had of music. Jealousy was in the baggage of the young and he had no baggage problem since he carried no baggage. He didn't own a home; he didn't own a wife. He was married and that was something different from HAVING A WIFE. Could I imagine anyone HAVING Marybeth? He didn't own a wife, he didn't own a place. He was free floating—at least that was his intention for himself.

The saxophone player returned to work and Marybeth needed another partner. She fixed on me and beckoned.

"Your turn," Huston said. "Go to it."

No chance. I didn't want to dance and couldn't dance. The only instruction I'd had was in gym where I'd practiced ballroom dancing with boys as partners. She came over, took my hands, and drew me into the center of the crowd. No excuses, she said. She didn't ask for skill, only enthusiasm. "Just let go and follow me." We bumped into other dancers until we'd cleared a space. It was a problem getting close. Elevated by heels and the springy bush of curls, she was almost six feet tall. The heat triggered her perfume, a scent that I first braced against, then relaxed into. My hand was on her bare back and we came apart with a slight pop, and then returned to be glued together.

"I can't dance and I'm dancing."

"Keep going. You're doing great."

"Wine helps. You help."

She spun away, disregarding the crowded floor, rewound, and we again ended in tight.

She murmured, lips at my ear, what I expected would be seductive invitation, but was all business. "How come I never heard from you? It's been how long? Six months? More? You must have been looking, so tell me what you found. Nothing? Did you forget about me, Eugene?"

"How could I?"

The pianist quickened the beat and I lost the music and quit in mid-dance. She summoned a slender black woman, a secretary in the English Department, who took over.

The drink and food were on a table in the dining room, perhaps a dozen people standing and drinking. I'd already had too much but poured another glass to keep up with Huston.

"You looked good out there. That orphanage must have had some hip boys teaching dance."

Who wouldn't look good with Marybeth showing the way? I apologized for not doing anything about finding them a home. The fact is I was no longer in real estate. Had they tried other agents?

"You are by no means the first, Eugene, but I hope you're the last." He confessed he had no great interest in finding a home.

I thought he wanted to put down roots.

"Eugene, I am not a 'roots' man. I'm on the side of rootlessness."

Then why was he looking for a home?

"She's looking. I'm going along. The fact is Detroit is the last place I'd choose to settle." He didn't have to be told about the history of redlining, restrictive covenants, and the animus of neighborhood associations. He'd lived with that knowledge all his life and he didn't intend to be snared by avoidable trouble.

Then how could he claim in Contemporary Civilization that our century was a century of progress?

He had confidence in the future, not in this particular moment. Detroit had a past and maybe a future but definitely no present. "It would be stupid for us to buy a house here." It wasn't the fear of rejection that made him recoil from settling down. At his age to have kids? Here in Detroit? Her desire to settle wouldn't last. "Look at her dance. She's one hundred percent on the move. She'll soon enough drop the illusion of home and we'll take off. Do you know our direction, Eugene?"

It was almost exactly the question Elton once asked. "Up?"

"Up and away."

The music stopped, the musicians took a break, and she joined us. I told her I admired the painting in the parlor.

"Me, as harlot?"

Not a harlot. A spirit on fire.

"How sweet," she said, discounting the flattery. "So what happened to the house search? I haven't heard from you or your partner, not a word."

Huston enjoyed my confusion. "When she sets course, she plunges ahead, no digressing. She wears out old men and right now, my friend, I'm running out of gas. Marybeth, I leave you our philosopher-realtor. Keep him dancing."

After he left I told her I was no longer connected to Elkram Real Estate and couldn't do her much good.

"Come on, Eugene. You've got connections. What's the problem?"

White neighborhood associations discouraged home sales to people of color.

"You told me that before and I still don't accept it." It would be a month before the scheduled production of *The Bacchae* finished its run and then she intended to take a recess from acting and begin motherhood. "I'm thirty-four years old." It was time to get serious, too late to keep fooling around. "I want a kid." She filled another glass for herself. "So let's make an effort to find a decent home for my kid."

I tried to change the subject and asked what role she had in *The Bacchae.*

"Do you know the play?"

"A little."

"So what role do you think I'd have?"

I guessed Agave, the bacchante mother of King Pentheus, among the pack of savage women who tear her son limb from limb and impale his head on a spike of fennel.

"That would be a hell of a part for an aspiring mother, right?" No, not Agave, but Dionysus himself, polymorphous, man and god, always attended by a flock of women. Like one of the ferocious girls, wasn't he? She would be a great Dionysus as she'd been a great Antigone. She was good with the Greeks. She expected to see me at the opening, but right now, the piano starting up, the saxophone joining in, she needed more dancing. Was I up to it?

I wasn't up to it. I didn't want to risk my newly established reputation as a dancer.

"I'm counting on you, Eugene," and I understood that she meant the great house I was to find for her.

The faculty crowd was in the back parlor, where I met Professor Hunneke with Louise. The old man sat in an armchair, near a fan, Louise hovering alongside. She wore vivid makeup and a pink halter dress. She looked like a girl caught playing dress-up, shy and vulnerable.

The unseasonable weather, she said, justifying the dress.

I said, not to fear, she looked great, and, she did.

She said the heat and noise were getting to the old man and he had to go home. Did I want to come along?

Hunneke was ruddy with drink and reluctant to leave. What waited for him at home? Fedder air conditioners? True, he was hot—Detroit had deadly summers—and this year summer had pushed into fall, but better the heat at the Fullers' than the air-conditioned barrenness at home. If he still had legs he would be dancing with Louise. "Eugene, it would give me great pleasure if you would be my legs and dance with her."

She didn't care to dance. She wasn't much of a dancer, especially not to jazzy music.

"Dance," he ordered. "Let me take pleasure in your pleasure."

"It wouldn't please me."

"Dance with her, Eugene."

I risked nothing with her and led her into the front parlor, now even noisier. "We don't have to," Louise said. "Let's not." I pulled her into the dance. I needed rhythm imposed on me and Louise was too restrained, but wedged in tight, we caught the rhythm of the crowd, and lost restraint. She either lost herself or gained herself, joyful and quick, salvaging my unexpected moves from clumsy disaster. Two more dances with Louise and I was ready to take her and the professor home.

We moved through the crowd, edging past the other dancers.

I waved to Marybeth, who was involved with a musician and didn't take notice.

I asked Louise to hold on while I searched for Huston. I couldn't find him in the dining room or the kitchen. All the rooms were crammed. I opened a bedroom door and saw him in dim light, asleep on his stomach in a huge bed, arms in beginning pushup position, stripped to maroon jockey shorts, socks up to his calves, his coffee-colored back exposed. No goodbyes, no declaring the party over. He guiltlessly abandoned us. *I guard nothing. Take what you want.* Everything was available, even his wife.

We left with Hunneke and eased him into the front passenger seat. He mumbled, "I should not drink. I say, 'No,' to drink, but drink says, 'yes,' and I drink." I sat behind the old man, who nodded off as soon as we were underway. We arrived at his house and struggled getting him upstairs. He apologized for subjecting young people to the sight of an ancient ruin. "Learn the *Sprach* from me, children, not how to drink," he said, laughing, as if he enjoyed the contradiction between the professorial dignity he assumed when he gripped the lectern and the clownish old geezer he exposed when he let go. Louise shushed him, helped him out of his shirt, and knelt to pull off his shoes. He said she shouldn't have to do this shameful business. She was like a daughter to him but what was the use? Why trouble and why go on? She led him into the bathroom and shut the door. I heard the water running, her scolding, his laughter. She came out while he used the toilet.

"You help him undress?"

"He's had too much to drink and needs help."

He emerged wearing only boxer shorts and a ribbed undershirt, shuffling in bare feet, ankles red and swollen, not shy about revealing himself. He thanked us for our service, and told us to go home, he was going to sleep. "Goodnight, my children."

Everyone was stripped, no restraint, everything was possible, that was the lesson of the night.

"Do you often put him to bed?"

He was a great man, a gentle, lovely man who needed her help.

A man full of self-pity and she called him great?

She'd read his Goethe manuscript, a masterpiece that would one day be recognized and his stature acknowledged.

Putting the professor to bed was not part of the job description for a teaching assistant.

She was glad to be of service.

"Then how about serving me, Louise?"

"I'll drive you home."

"That's not the service I want."

There was a bedroom downstairs she sometimes used.

It was easy making love to Louise. Wine and heat, the parlor portrait of Marybeth, dancing with Marybeth; Louise's pink dress, the transforming makeup, and her service to the old man—her devotion and generosity and compassion, and our loss of restraint—all that provided the chemistry. What wasn't easy was dealing with the early morning aftermath, her face wiped clean, the dress rumpled, no sparks left from the night. Neither of us said anything until we were in her car.

She spoke before I could warn her that what happened was without consequence. She said what happened was the result of heat, and wine, et cetera, and she warned me not to make too much of it.

"My feeling exactly."

"I know that." We reached my place. She pulled over to the curb to let me out. I tried embracing her and she said, "No, thank you," and shoved me away. I thanked her for a lovely night. She shouted, "Don't condescend to me!" and took off.

When the old man invited us to accompany him to the opening of *The Bacchae*, I accepted reluctantly, preferring to go alone, but he was insistent and I couldn't refuse.

Marybeth on stage was far more than I expected, nothing like the breezy, bold, unreflective woman who wanted at least two bathrooms and a big, big garden. She was dazzling as the god-man, her black mane of curls tinted tawny gold, her face streaked red and black. She prowled the stage in a full-length robe of the same colors, vibrant and full of threat.

Afterward, an ebullient Huston Fuller, in black tux and bow tie and ruffled shirt, ambled through the crowd, accepting congratulations and hugs, enjoying the enthusiasm for Marybeth. "I want you all to acknowledge that the god on stage is my wife. Can you believe it?" He spent a moment with us and headed backstage.

Louise said nothing until we passed through the lobby, then began her criticism. It was, of course, she said, a terrible production, unbalanced by Marybeth. The other actors couldn't or wouldn't match her intensity, and the director had failed to rein her in. Louise didn't doubt people would be taken in by the off-stage Grand Guignol happenings but it was an over-the-top rendering of Euripides. She blamed Marybeth for distorting the text. Euripides with his dreadful gods should have been just right for Marybeth, who probably couldn't do well in any role that required a show of love or compassion. "She's good at loud. It's quiet that gives her trouble."

I was under the spell of Marybeth and didn't want to hear the criticism, but Louise wouldn't stop. She said the play would have been vastly improved with more nuanced acting, better direction, and less fireworks.

I heard jealousy masquerading as academic judgment and I tried not to be baited into responding. When she insisted that I give my opinion, I said, *"Chacun à son goût."*

What a dumb cliché. You really loved her narcissistic overacting, admit it.

Hunneke intervened. "You have never suffered from the gods, my dear Louise. You have not experienced the devils they are." To him the performance was no Grand Guignol exaggeration but a true rendering of the terrible powers that bedeviled the world he had survived.

She would only concede that Marybeth did narcissism well, which should have been no surprise to anyone who had watched her dance under the naked portrait of herself.

I couldn't hold back. "Louise, you have made yourself crystal clear. Now, please, shut up."

It was a reaction she had tried to provoke, but which she couldn't handle, and she burst into tears.

"Louise, for godsakes!"

The old man glared at me, put his arm around her—Shush, Shush, Shush—and led her from the lobby.

I was enthralled with Marybeth. If she had called for volunteers—male or female—to join her bacchantes and do her bidding, I would have enlisted.

I offered to shepherd her through Detroit in search of a house. She wasn't sure that now was the time; the theater was using all her energy, "But, okay," she said, "let's have a look."

I picked her up at the theater in my newly mastered, ancient Plymouth. Her hair was still a tawny lion color, a vestige of the god she would become again in a few hours. Right now she was Marybeth, dressed for the weather in slacks, tennis shoes, a World Theater T-shirt imprinted with a striped red globe logo. She wore no makeup. She put on almost opaque aviator glasses and settled a wide-brimmed straw hat on her mane of curls.

I apologized for the miserable clunker I was driving and assured her I'd soon be able to afford something more impressive.

"The car is irrelevant. Just so it gets me back to the theater by five."

I'd been to three performances, each time with increasing awe, and now felt shy in her presence, not sure how to deal with her transition from the apparently uncomplicated woman sitting beside me to the divinity on stage. I asked—pompously, I know— "How should I relate to the god in you, Marybeth?"

"Don't waste time getting down on your knees—just find me a house."

We traveled the length of Chicago Boulevard, looking at mansions for sale. Nothing appealed to her. Nothing came close. "Too big," she said of a two-acre estate. "I'm going to have a single kid, not a platoon." We checked a formal Greek Revival with pillared front, set far back in an enormous lot. "What dancing do we do there? Minuets?" We saw a place with a meticulously choreographed rose garden. "A great place for old ladies," she said. Of another, she hated poplars and wanted unconstrained trees that spread and climbed and weren't severely shaped.

I said she could plant her own trees and give them any shape she wanted.

"And wait twenty years before I have what I'm looking for?"

I was no longer sure what she was looking for.

"I'll tell you one thing I'm not looking for. I'm not looking to enlist in the bourgeoisie. I dropped out of that scene when I left Marlboro High."

The next day was the same. Nothing interested her. She had already lost her enthusiasm for house hunting. We stopped at a La Salle Avenue house and she said, "If we go in there I'll smother," and we drove off even though I'd made an appointment and the agent was waiting. "Why do you waste my time with unhappy places like that?"

Unhappy? I told her to consider the array of leaded windows in stone frames, the house encircled by flowers and greenery. There was light everywhere. That wasn't an unhappy place.

She'd had enough and wanted to get back to the theater.

In a last effort to change her mood I told her I'd show her something that would open her eyes, an amazing house—very old—not for sale, but a real surprise.

"If it's not for sale, why bother?"

"It's on our way; we'll just drive by. You'll be amused," and I took her to Gordon Pickering's Queen Anne on nearby Elmwood, ready to make a fool of myself with the story of how Gordon dumped me in compost, anything to keep her interested.

When she saw the house she commanded, "Stop!"

We parked in front.

"What have we got here, Eugene?"

I gave her the history of the Pickering estate of which this home was a remnant. It was almost a hundred years old on a half-acre lot, with a huge yard, in surprisingly good shape for a relic of a long-gone Detroit. Four generations of Pickerings had lived there.

"Who owns it now?"

"Gordon Pickering, a descendant of the original owner."

The house had no right being there, a defiant vestige of a Detroit that no longer existed, exactly what she wanted. "Eugene, I dreamed this house."

It was my pleasure to please her.

"What's the garden like?"

A huge garden, very private, its own world, though I couldn't give her particulars since my view had been obstructed the one time I'd been there.

"Let's check it out."

We wouldn't be welcome. I'd had serious disagreements with Gordon, who was no friend of mine.

She got out of the car. "I'm checking it out now."

"You can't do that, Marybeth. Gordon is not a man you just

drop in on," but she was already on her way up the porch. She rang the bell and to my relief there was no answer.

She said she was going to look at the garden.

I said absolutely not; we'd be trespassing. Gordon had an invalid wife and could be ferocious to intruders. She shrugged and passed through the gate. I followed where I didn't want to go.

She loved the garden. She loved the rim of mature trees, the espaliered roses, the rosemary bushes, the caged tomatoes—overripe and done for—the red chard gone to seed, the squash, the fruit trees—apple and cherry and plum, the apples beginning to come into their own, what was left of the other fruit brown and withered or burst by the assault of yellowjackets—the intricately bricked patio, the looping flagstone paths, the fringe of wildflowers against the back fence, the shingled tool shed, the compost, and—looking back—the faded painted-lady rear façade. It was an overgrown, overripe fairy-tale garden, a blurred elegance. She said again, "I dreamed this place."

I told her it wasn't on the market and never would be. "You've had your look, now let's get out of here."

"How can you know 'never'?"

She climbed to the deck and rapped hard on the back door, peered through the beveled glass port. I saw a window curtain flutter. I warned her again that we were trespassing.

"Don't be so damned uptight."

I had every reason to be uptight. I told how Gordon had dumped me in the compost.

"Well, he isn't going to dump me."

"Marybeth, on stage you're god. Here you're just a trespasser."

I took off and she reluctantly followed. Out front she climbed the stairs again, pumped the bell, peered through the stained-glass door and the stained-glass sidelights. She motioned me to come look.

I saw a broad oak stairway with glistening oak wainscoting from floor to beamed ceiling, a crystal chandelier beyond the vestibule, a portrait of what I supposed was a grim Pickering ancestor with flourishing sideburns on the wall near the entrance.

"You've had your look. Let's go," and I led the way back to the car.

"Eugene, I want you to arrange a meeting with Gordon."

No chance. I wouldn't even try.

"Don't fail me, Eugene."

I told her I respected her, I admired her, but I couldn't work with her. She needed someone able to deal with Dionysus off stage and I wasn't the man.

She laughed, a noisy theatrical laugh, head bent back, perfect teeth. "Eugene, I'm giving you a hard time, I know. Can you recommend someone who's able and willing to handle Dionysus off stage?"

I was no longer in the business. I no longer had contact with that world. She was on her own.

"Thanks anyway for leading me to the house I dreamed."

"It isn't on the market, Marybeth. It was dumb showing it to you."

"It's no longer your problem. I'll take over from here."

I dropped her at the theater, and didn't return to witness her transformation into god.

He called that night. I didn't recognize the eroded, whispery voice until he said, "It's Gordon." He asked what we had been doing in his yard.

I was in the neighborhood and wanted my actress friend to see his amazing home, so we rang and no one answered.

He asked who the woman was.

Marybeth Fuller, a marvelous actress, appearing in *The Bacchae* at the World Theater.

There was a long silence.

"How is she doing?"

It was Kate Wyman he asked about and I told him the Margaret Tessler Home had been razed, one hundred and fifty units going up in its place, and I had no idea where Kate was located.

"Tell her Sarah is gone. She needs to know that."

His wife dead? I apologized for intruding on his grief. Though I didn't know Sarah, I knew their lives were tightly interwoven and I could guess how devastated he was. I had myself suffered a terrible loss when I was a kid and could imagine what he was feeling.

"You got no idea."

I promised I'd find Kate and let her know.

Again a long silence before he said, "Next time call."

Katherine Wyman wasn't listed. I tried Sermon's office. The receptionist wouldn't give me Andy Sermon's private number and only reluctantly agreed to take a message.

"Would you please inform Katherine Wyman that Eugene Victor Smith has news of Gordon Pickering—" I spelled out the names. "It's news she'll want to hear."

EIGHT

View from a Rat Hole

For more than seven years I lived in a shabby room on the third floor of Mrs. Tuchler's rooming house, a room long exhausted of unexplored niches, no mysteries, every inch overworked. Elton Kramer had called it "a rat hole, a dump, a jail cell, an embarrassment." He complained that while I was able to lure timid buyers into risking long-term commitments to three-bedroom homes in new subdivisions, I myself refused to take any risk. Here was a man—a boy, he said—stained, perhaps indelibly, by the orphan blues, cowering in his hole, without the nerve to stand up and claim a decent place in the world. If it didn't trouble an Arkie redneck to plunk down everything he had on a thirty-year commitment he could barely afford, what was my problem? Elton didn't expect me to go overboard on a Grosse Point mansion—I'd never get past the gates anyway—but at least a place whose steam heat wasn't controlled by a miserly "kraut" landlady.

I didn't quarrel. I didn't explain to him—he had no patience for what he considered to be alibis and excuses—what I later tried explaining to Louise—that I clung to memory as tenaciously as a man sliding off a cliff might hang onto a crack in the smooth rock face. How could I let go when there was no net between me and the abyss? I wanted to let go and would let go, once Ponchartrain paid off and I had a plush safety net to drop into.

Louise came to my place only once. She hated it. She said it had the odor of obsession, the musty odor, she imagined, of a monk's cell. Yet after the brief visit she was better able to describe my room than I was. She recited a catalogue of defects I no longer noticed, the unfurling braided rug, the worn cushions of the Morris chair, the mismatched dishes and flatware, the noisy, small Kelvinator, the squealing single bed with cast iron frame and martyr's mattress, everything out of date, unfashionable even when new.

She spotted the mildewed Bible on my bureau top that I had long put out of mind. "A Bible? You with a Bible?" It was tucked under a box of odds and ends on the back edge of the bureau. She opened it and found the photo of my dad and mom, taken on their honeymoon trip.

"These are your folks?"

I replaced the photo, returned the Bible to the top of my bureau, and hustled her out.

If I didn't keep the details of my room in mind it wasn't because I was oblivious. I knew my room the way I knew the unseen parts of my body, the small of my back, the place between my shoulders that I could only see if I twisted and looked in a mirror.

I didn't have to be aware of them, they were mine and I took care of them, even if they were not closely inspected or kept in mind.

When she opened the warped, neglected Bible, she released a fog of recollection that had been reduced to a smudge. To abandon that room I'd lose even that smudge and fall into a here and now without any bearings. Perhaps it was self-deception, but that's how I felt about my room.

One dismal day—the weather uncertain, the season still unclear—Frau Tuchler tramped upstairs, leading Kate Wyman to my room. I heard them coming, Tuchler in a loud voice, "You must not blame me for his room, Missus. I keep the house clean. The rooms I leave to them."

There was no time to get ready. The room was in as bad shape as Tuchler predicted it would be. She put on a show for Kate, loudly bawling me out for the mess. "You give the lady a bad impression of my house, Mr. Schmidt. There is a vacuum cleaner, a mop, a broom, a dust pan, everything for cleanup, and you do not clean up."

I told her once more I was Smith, not Schmidt, and not to enter my room without my permission. I shooed her out and shut the door.

I apologized to Kate for the mess. My room wasn't usually like this. The professor I worked for had suffered a stroke and, with my extra duties, everything had piled up.

She told me she'd seen worse. She was sorry she hadn't warned me she was coming. She hadn't planned to come. She was on her way out of town and had stopped—just for a moment—to say goodbye and get news of Gordon.

She wasn't in her fancy Andy Sermon mode. She wore her simple, familiar tweed outfit, wool coat, and beret. At first she refused to sit—she said she was really in a rush—then, seeing how off-center I was, agreed to perch on the edge of the Morris chair, ready to launch into flight, her strong, erect bearing a model of how to be straight. She refused to take off her coat, but removed her beret, releasing her hair and her scent, and for a moment, I was again within the aura of my orphanage mother.

She was headed northwest to be with her old dad who was infirm and in need.

"How long will you be gone? "

"I have no definite plans, Eugene."

"For a week, a month, a year?"

"Perhaps much longer."

"And the Katherine Wyman Home for Boys?"

"There's no such place and never will be."

"What's happened, Kate?"

"It's too complicated and I don't have the time. You left a message that you had news about Gordon, yes?"

"Gordon's wife passed away. He wanted me to tell you."

"When did this happen?"

"I'm not sure. I think a few weeks ago."

"How did he seem?"

"He sounded isolated and depressed. Probably like your father."

"Did he ask to see me?"

"I guess that was the point."

"Gordon must be devastated. Sarah was his consolation."

"I thought you were his consolation."

She got up, fastened her coat, put on her beret. She refused to explain the urgency of her leaving. Then at the door she unexpectedly turned, smiled, opened her arms for a farewell hug, and we embraced.

"You were difficult, but I always considered you very special. I won't forget you, Eugene."

"I won't let you, Kate."

She told me not to bother coming downstairs but I followed her to her car.

"You won't tell me where you're going?"

"It wouldn't mean anything to you. It's a tiny village on Lake Michigan you've never heard of."

"What about your plans for the Katherine Wyman Home?"

She said bitterly, "Fantasy. Only fantasy," her last words before driving off.

I immediately called Elton and this time got through. He asked if I'd heard from Kate.

"I just saw her."

"Where is she?

"I couldn't tell you."

"What do you mean, 'you couldn't tell me'? You just saw her. What did she say?"

Instead of answering I asked what had happened to the plans for the Katherine Wyman Home for Boys.

"She talked to you about that, did she, and gave you her version of the blow-up, and told you what sons-of-bitches we are, right? I bet she didn't say she jumped ship for no goddamn reason. We tried to tell her it was a glitch, nothing serious, just a glitch, the

Katherine Wyman Home is still on the books, but she refused to hear a goddamn word, just dived overboard."

"What glitch are you talking about?"

"The glitch in the economy. We made it very clear, in language simple enough for a kid, that all we had to do was hang on and ride it out and everything would be okay."

I asked what had happened to the economy.

"Don't you read the news? Are you totally out of it?"

I told him it was timeless stuff that interested me, rarely the news.

He blasted my hypocritical unworldliness. How could I not be concerned about my investment? I'd been an almost slavish observer of demolition and construction. How could I not be aware that Gloomy Gus analysts were hyping the downturn as if it were 1929 all over again, scaring the crap out of the market? He explained with exaggerated simplicity, as if talking to a simpleton, that the auto market had weakened when new car models appeared with big inventories still on the lots. Factories had cut production and workers were furloughed. It was big news in Detroit even if only background noise to me. Periodic downturns were only glitches in an expanding economy, part of Detroit's rhythm, there was no reason for panic. Even after the downturn gathered pace and surged through auto parts, tires, rubber, steel, affecting all of Detroit and spreading country-wide, there was no excuse for jumping ship. It was a matter of a few months—a turn in the cycle—and the excess inventory would be drained off and the market would resume its climb. As always, the only losers would be the gutless and the panic-stricken. It was banker panic that had brought his McNichols Gardens project to a temporary halt. McNichols Gardens was the name he had given to the location I once knew as the Margaret Tessler Home for Boys. And, yes, they also had to back off from the Katherine Wyman Home. It was on hold, not abandoned. Nothing was coming in, a lot going out, a temporary condition. The fundamentals were still there, still terrific—a continued housing shortage, expanding families needing to upgrade, a fear of riot and crime evacuating neighborhoods in the inner city. By next fall the glitch would be smoothed out, employment on the rise again, factories ready to huff and puff after the breather. He had no long-term worries. Banks had assured him his credit was A-one. The riverfront project—our biggest hope for big returns—was moving ahead without problems, and—again his cherished metaphor—"as sure as gold." Andy Sermon was negotiating leases as we spoke. If Sermon hadn't refused to knuckle under to the bullshit argument that the downturn justified lower bids, we'd already have a deal. In a few months—maybe a little longer—we'd get our price and be swamped with sales and the banks would open their purses. Sermon had promised Kate that when we again started rolling, the Katherine Wyman Home for Boys would be a first priority. She refused to hear. She wouldn't listen. They couldn't shake her conviction that she'd lost everything—the Home, the boys, her savings. He and Sermon were ready, for godsakes, to give her whatever she needed, and there was no reason to panic. Nothing Sermon could say had any effect and, with his short fuse consumed, he blew his stack—called her an "idiot" as she put on her coat and hat, then, enraged as she headed for the elevator, upped the rhetoric, called her a "stupid bitch." No one had a right to say that to Kate, and Sermon was practically on his knees begging forgiveness, but couldn't stop her from taking off. When she was gone, he again exploded, and damned Elton for bringing her into his life. "Next time try introducing me to cardiac arrest." A moment later he commanded, "Find her, talk to her, tell her I love her, bring her home."

"He called her a 'stupid bitch' and that was okay with you?"

"He wants her back."

"There's not a chance. She's left Detroit."

"I know she left Detroit. Where is she headed?"

I told him to save what was left of his soul and quit his slavish service to a megalomaniac developer.

"I'll take care of my soul and, by the way, I'm the one who takes care of your investment, and the last thing I need is your advice. So where the hell is she?"

"Elton, even if I knew I wouldn't tell you."

"What the fuck's your problem?"

"You sold Margaret Tessler from under her, promised her a new Home that will probably never happen, stripped her of everything she had, and you wonder what my problem is?"

"Watch it, kid. I don't like your tone."

"What tone do you recommend for a backstabbing hustler?"

"A tone you can afford. I could make a pauper out of you and fast."

"You can't pauperize me, Elton. I'm there already."

Of course I wasn't a pauper. In fact I'd become more firmly established. Old Hunneke had suffered a stroke in mid-semester and Louise tended his classes until he could return. She was almost alone in hoping the old man would be back. His performance had increasingly faltered—it wasn't simply old age, though that might have been at the root of the problem—it was his drinking and his physical distress. His rambling digressions used up class time and he often didn't make it back to the lesson he was supposedly offering. Louise gave the students better service. She was sharp and disciplined and full of energy. She wouldn't tolerate any talk of replacing the old man. She intended to hold the fort until he returned and she wanted my help. "I have money for a teaching assistant. I asked for you and it's approved."

I told her I was essentially Huston Fuller's man, only into reading German for the extra money, less competent than most language graduate students, and she had better choices to make. She said not to worry; together we'd manage whatever problems came up. She was sure I could use the added salary.

I accepted the new position, but warned her that if there were any issues I couldn't handle I'd reconsider. That suited her fine because there were no issues I couldn't handle.

I was elevated from reader to teaching assistant, my salary almost doubled. It was the doubling of a small base, my income still barely adequate, but I was no pauper.

Trying to catch up and stay ahead of the old man's classes, we met in the evening to deal with spillover German language business. She refused to come to my room even though it was close to the campus—"Not that moldy monk's cell"—so I went to her place, far more comfortable, shaped by a will for order characteristically Louise, almost everything spotless and simple, unembellished Danish furniture, a few Orientals placed on glistening parquet floors, a quality kitchen. There were a couple of luxuries: an oversize, plump bed with expensive linen, and a bathroom spa. Everything was in place, everything except me, and it was obvious she meant to put me in order, too. I made it clear I had no intention of abandoning my room, despite its moldiness and lack of amenities. She said not to worry, we were meeting for business and nothing else. It should only concern me that Professor Hunneke, our dear friend, was in dire need.

I was, at first, irritated with Hunneke. I blamed our "dear friend" for his dying. He had refused to stop smoking or drinking. He seduced us with a ruddy, silvery Teutonic imitation of health, but behind the façade was a midnight glutton. The issue was very simple to Louise. Talk of blame was irrelevant. She couldn't understand my stepping away from Hunneke. "He helped you. Now he's alone and needs your help."

She was right. I tried to be more charitable. I went to the hospital with her and saw what I didn't want to see, the liquid, red-rimmed, imploring blue eyes, the immobile left side, the frozen face, the right hand flopping helplessly to show he was still alive. I braced against a flood of pity that would have washed me overboard if I'd allowed it. I stood by frozen while she remained at ease, offering a no-nonsense summary of his classes that affirmed the relevance of his work. She left messages with his son in Venezuela that went unanswered. She went to the hospital daily. I accompanied her a few times and then visited without her. I brought flowers, but no hope. I tried saying what she'd said—the students asked for him and hoped for his return, the Detroit weather hadn't settled on a course, a dull sun one day, drizzly the next, gray and cold the norm, and he missed nothing in his hospital room. His eyes didn't move. His hand remained at his side. It ended with both of us mute. I doubt he noticed when I eased away. I didn't have her gift for sympathy and regretted it, and returned in the evening. I brought *Faust* with me, read from the "Prologue in Heaven," and read to him the timeworn but, to me, still amazing compact he offers the devil in exchange for his soul, *"Werd ich zum Augenblicke sagen: Verweile doch! du bist so schön"* and so on. A flicker of a smile. Was it my accent, or what must have seemed to him my corny and inappropriate selection? Or was he moved by my effort? "Should I say to a moment, tarry awhile, thou art so beautiful, then you can bind me in chains and I'll gladly go to hell." I held his hand when I left and felt the shadow of a return squeeze. My heart opened to him and to Louise.

From then until his death I came twice a week and read to him.

We were in her parlor, working on exams, when the first big storm of the season headed our way. We smelled its coming. She opened windows and we breathed the charged air and watched clouds pile into the pale late afternoon sky, dark, baleful, blossoming upward and downward. The stalled season had finally reached its end; something cold and new and fresh was about to happen. It depressed her to think of me stuck by myself in my awful room with a terrible storm on the way and urged me to hang out at her place until it was over. I told her I appreciated her generosity, enjoyed her home, but—stupid as it sounded—I might have left a window open and felt an obligation to my room. Obligation to my room? She had no idea what that meant, but, no problem, we could finish the work the following day. She led me to the door, and that's as far as we got. The embrace I intended to be a *pro forma* goodnight hug, lingered, became ardent. Perhaps it was the change in weather or her letting go of the reins that revealed her loveliness, but it was really, I think, seeing again how she was with the old man that led me to repeat the night of her pink dress, this time sober and with no regrets.

The storm broke while we were in bed. She shouted to close the upstairs windows, and ran downstairs to crank shut the parlor windows. The park was wild, trees thrashing, the bedroom strobed by lightning. I yelled, "Deluge! Haul in the gangplank! The ark's afloat!" We were on board, breathing the storm. I felt awake and joyful. She was a great friend, an intelligent, generous, loving friend. Why had I resisted her?

"You're stubborn," she said. "It's hard getting through to you."

Huston once said to me, not entirely seriously, light and teasing, "You've got a lot to learn, Eugene, and it's nothing I can teach you. Find a good woman and listen to her and maybe you'll be relieved of the need to run scared."

I didn't get what he was talking about. "I'm not scared. And how do I know when I've found a good woman?"

"You've got a problem, Eugene. Your intelligence works against you. Let your guard down and become available."

That seemed to me a prescription for disaster until that unguarded moment when Louise reached me.

By morning the weather had eased to a steady rain and I took off for campus to audit Huston's class. I detoured past the river-front development. The site was buttoned down, bulldozers hunkered, blades tucked in, cranes cleared of their chains and buckets, elevator hoists stalled at ground level, loaded truck beds covered with tarps. The only worker I saw was a man in a blue hard hat, yellow slicker, and rubber boots, gingerly walking a plank path that wound through mud between drenched foundations. I felt mild sympathy for the unlucky supervisor who should have been warming up inside with the others instead of trudging through mud.

I drove by a few days later when the weather had subsided to cold, steady drizzle. There still was no sound of construction— no wrecker balls, no jackhammers, no generators, no motors, no pounding, no riveting, no pouring of concrete, no bells ringing, no laughter, no warning shouts, in fact, no workers, none. It had been the noisiest place in the city. The silence was unsettling. I parked and walked around the site, looking through fence windows for a sign of life. I came across a segment of warehouse wall that had somehow survived demolition, the upper tiers of brick bitten off. A bulldozer crouched alongside, waiting to be released to finish its meal. The wall was covered with long out-of-date posters. A poster, faded but almost intact, advertised Lola at the Paradise, Sat-Sun, no other date, a buxom woman with glistening black hair, in gypsy dress, an arm raised above her head, castanets at the ready. Farther on I saw a man peering through a plywood slot into the muddy site. He was someone I recalled from the corridors of Old Main, a professor of sociology, a little man with owlish spectacles, under a large umbrella, in head-to-foot yellow rain gear, galoshes buckled over his shoes. Sitting behind him, on leash, was a glum-looking basset hound, a Detroit Tigers plastic wrap around his torso, a roaring tiger logo at the midriff.

The professor thought I looked familiar.

I introduced myself, Eugene Smith, Professor Fuller's assistant, and he said, "Of course. The Negro humanities professor. Exactly," confirming my answer, as pompous as his name, Winston Marx. He lived in nearby Indian Village. The morning walk was his usual round with his dog. He'd become a fan of the hustle and bustle, fascinated by the steel and iron and concrete rising from holes in the ground. "At first I complained about the noise. Now it's the quiet that bothers me. It can't be the weather."

I said of course it was the weather.

"Weather shouldn't close down an operation as big as this. They must have calculated for the weather. Is it the recession? It must be the recession. Everyone's affected. It started in Detroit and now," he said proudly, as if Detroit's spreading misery confirmed the city's importance, "it's reached world-wide."

I didn't know why the work had stopped, but I knew the developers and assured him the project had solid financing. I told him not to be bothered by the quiet. Soon enough he'd again be relieved by noise. It was weather, not the economy, that had slowed operations.

I drove by a week later and the cranes and generators and bulldozers were gone; the only sound, other than the steady rain and my windshield wipers, was the flapping of billowing tarps.

The site was abandoned. It was the economy, not the weather.

A registered letter from Elton's attorney notified me my debt was being called. I was required to deliver six thousand dollars within thirty days of notification.

I told Louise I'd go to jail before giving satisfaction to the traitor orphan with his fake claims of common origins. I'd been stupidly lured by his promise to relieve us from the shame of our beginnings. He'd promised to raise us into the world as proper citizens, and like the easily conned naïf I was, I took the bait, hook, line, and sinker.

She asked what he could get from me when I had nothing to give.

We'd been as close as brothers. I felt betrayed.

"Doesn't that registered letter register, Eugene? He's not your friend and not your brother. Keep him out of your life."

Frucht no longer had any interest in my share of Ponchartrain Associates. He was surprised I hadn't already tried to sell. He himself had bailed out before total loss. He thanked me for turning down his offer. "You saved me a bundle and I commiserate with you on your loss."

"What have I lost?"

"I suppose whatever you owned."

Not lost, I said. We only had to hang on and it would come back.

"Smith, hang on and you could lose another fortune."

I returned from my night class and found Elton in my room, slumped in the Morris chair, his coat off, tie loosened.

"Who let you in?"

"The kraut landlady. How do you turn off the goddamned heat? I'm boiling in here. The radiator handle won't budge."

Mrs. Tuchler controlled the heat. The old woman steamed us between six and ten, then froze us the rest of the time. I'd complained that I was first boiling and then freezing and couldn't get any work done. She shrugged. "Go to bed, Mr. Schmidt. It's not good for you to be up so late."

I asked what he was doing in my room. I wasn't expecting a visit. I would have told him he wasn't welcome to my rat hole.

"Did you get the registered letter?"

"Is that why you're here, to see if I read your mail? I opened it and the smell of betrayal stunk up the place."

"It has legal force, kid, so don't shrug it off."

"What will you do after I shrug it off?"

"For starters I could have your wages garnisheed."

"A few bucks extra will get you out of hock, won't it Elton?"

"It's not so much what I'll get, it's what you'll lose."

"What have I got to lose?"

"Your Wayne reputation as 'Saint Eugene, No Flies on Me.'"

I told him he was in my room uninvited and if he was only here to make threats he could get out now.

"I'm not here to make threats. I've come to offer you a way out."

"I don't need a way out. I'm not in."

"I want you back at Elkram."

I told him I'd sooner go to hell.

"You owe me, you owe the banks, you owe your landlady; for

all I know you owe your girlfriend. The debt gets bigger every time you breathe. It won't go away; you can't run from it. You got to face it and handle it."

I told him I didn't care about my debt. I didn't care about money I'd never had. I wanted to be freed from my dream of wealth. I had no interest in an obligation that offered no reward other than being rid of it. Yes, I grieved for the project. I had watched it being conceived, watched it growing, and it was a blow to see it stillborn, but I'd get over it and be done with fantasy.

He nodded as if considering the merit of what I'd said. "Okay. Forget the letter. I know you got nothing and I'll collect nothing." Then in a shockingly tearful voice, he said, "Gene, this is hard to say, but I'm fucked up and I need your help." I couldn't reply. He continued, almost sobbing, his climb was over and maybe his life. His long odyssey toward fortune had reversed. It had taken him ten years to reach the top and almost overnight he'd plunged to the bottom. "Can you believe it, Gene? I got nothing left." He'd put everything into the riverfront development and the McNichols Gardens project, encouraged by Sermon, who told him, "It's your project, son, my gift to you. Have fun and run with it." When the project faltered, Sermon told him to keep the faith, hold tight, promising they'd soon be back in business full strength. Sermon didn't reveal that no one was bidding for the riverfront leases and that those who'd signed were trying to pull out. The banks, instead of extending loans, were clamping down to cut their losses. The contractors, subcontractors, and suppliers refused any more delays in payment. The morning newspaper publicly confirmed that the project was in trouble. He was named with Andy Sermon as an official in charge, as though the two were equally complicit in the financial over-reach. He had the clipping with him and handed it to me to read.

I told him the item appeared in a dull section of the newspaper. Whom did he know, other than interested parties already in the know, who would see it? And what could they see? The article didn't speak of malfeasance or debacle, only of delay.

"I don't want anyone naming me a loser. 'Elton Kramer, Loser.' How does that sound?"

"Terrible. Awful. Bearer of the plague. Avoid the man. He'll afflict you with dread 'Losingitis.'"

"You think you got nothing to worry about, stuck forever in your rat hole trying to pay off your debt?"

Rat holes, I said, might not be glorious places, but they were at least affordable and safe.

He said he could accept the losses. They were part of the business. It was Andy Sermon's abandonment—every man for himself—that brought him down. "He called me, 'son,' and I hitched my wagon to his star. Considering what he promised, who wouldn't have hitched up?" Sermon had guarded his own assets, keeping Sermon, Inc. apart from Ponchartrain Associates. "He led us to the cliff edge, waved us over, then jumped out of the way." Sermon now made himself unreachable. Elton couldn't get through to him even though they were in adjoining office suites. He couldn't get past Miss Evans, the suddenly aloof secretary. She told him Sermon was never in, always on the move, looking for ways to rescue the riverfront development.

"I'm his son. Get him on the line."

She said Sermon was unavailable and he blew his stack. He called her, "a long-nosed brownnoser," warned her that the "Arkie fat boy" had better become available if he didn't want to be dragged into court. He shocked everyone in the office and he was probably finished at Sermon, Inc., but wasn't his blow-up understandable? Sermon had failed his fiduciary responsibilities to the partners. He hadn't disclosed the financial mess until it was too late to get out. Elton had grounds to sue, but he'd lost his nerve and couldn't act. Could I believe it? Elton Kramer shrinking from a fight? "This isn't me, Gene. You know that." He admitted he was bowled over by his loss, worth more than two million only a few weeks ago and suddenly worthless, his money down the drain, carrying his self-esteem with it, no longer man enough to stand up to Sermon. "I know we had our differences, but we always cared for each other. Isn't that so, Gene?"

Yes, despite our differences we cared for each other.

"I need you to come back."

"Why?"

I'd been with him on the long journey, knew what he'd aimed for and what he'd lost. If I abandoned him he'd have no one. "We'll move from Sermon's office. The two of us will operate like we used to even if we have to start from the bottom. Stick with me, Gene."

I'd spare what time I could—not much—to help him out, but I didn't want him to think I could forget or forgive the vicious way he'd rubbed my face in the demolition of our Home.

"I was crazy. That wasn't me."

"Who was it?"

"I believed in Sermon. He invented the game, made the rules, had all the chips. I don't own enough anymore to even ante up."

I told him to take credit for his own sins and not pass them on to Sermon.

"Sins? If the price I have to pay for your help is I got to listen to your goddamn preaching, I'd sooner cut my throat."

I worried about him, and the next day called him at home and invited him to join me at our old Vesuvius stomping grounds. He thanked me for calling. He thanked me for sticking by him when I had every reason to gloat at his failure and stay away from the stink of his collapse.

We met at Vesuvius and it was a forlorn Elton Kramer before me, as hang-dog as Winston Marx's basset hound. He ordered big and ate nothing of his steak or salad. He ignored my pasta. He couldn't get over what he called Andy Sermon's abandonment. He was orphaned again, and had fallen into the role of supplicant. Sermon had no time for him, merely a note transmitted by Miss Evans, "Where is she? Let me know and we'll talk," as if that were the precondition for Elton's return to favor.

He had no idea where Kate was. Did I? "Are you hiding something from me, Gene?"

"Of course not."

"Would you hide it from me if you heard?"

I called him paranoid.

He felt overwhelmed, unable to work, more than depressed, in despair.

I told him he'd come out of it. Nothing could keep him down.

He had more potential energy than a pinned grenade. Once his anger was released he would explode into action. He was too intelligent to remain stuck; he'd find a way out. In the end he'd be grateful he was freed of bondage to Sermon.

"I sometimes think of giving it all up."

"What does that mean?

"Ending it all."

I refused to listen to that corny melodrama, completely out of character. In a few days he'd be embarrassed by what he'd said. I invited him to have dinner with me and Louise. Did he know she lived only a few blocks from him, on the other side of the Park? He'd be impressed by her intelligence and good sense.

Louise went out of her way to make him feel at home. Cooking wasn't her strong point, but she took pains with a dinner that cost her time she didn't have. Perhaps she imagined she could diagnose and prescribe and cure whatever afflicted Elton, but Elton wasn't about to be advised by a dark, skinny academic type. He either pretended not to hear or really didn't hear. I afterward tried to excuse his behavior. He had no sense of propriety in the best of times and now he was almost suicidal. I'd made a stupid mistake inviting him over.

She found my sympathy inexplicable. He was a nasty, self-absorbed man. He'd made her feel insignificant. "His interests aren't yours. You aren't part of his world."

But I was. I was still invested in Ponchartrain Associates. The development was in small part my doing. His loss was my loss. And in his odd fashion he cared for me, and, the truth is, I cared for him.

In the elevator, rising to the 45th floor, Elton swore he wouldn't be taken in by the father-son bullshit. He was recovered from his funk and ready to do battle. Sermon could no longer snow him. We approached the office, Miss Evans nodding us in. He waited for us beyond the lounge, with a big welcoming smile for his protégé, a hand extended to draw Elton into his private office, and I followed.

Sermon's office was pure kitsch, his own Nuremburg, everything Elton imagined for himself, an enormous room framed by arches, twenty-foot ceilings, a kitchen alcove behind a bar, an elaborate bathroom, gathered drapes bracketing the arched windows, the river and Canada sprawled out beyond, a great view even when dimmed by rain. The walls were placarded with evidence of Sermon's importance. Along with his own degrees he had honorary doctorates from the universities of Arkansas and Detroit. There were photos of him with everyone from President Truman and John Foster Dulles to Hollywood stars Adolphe Menjou and John Wayne. The Arkansan stood facing John Wayne, ear-to-ear grins from the two pals, both in Western garb. It was an office designed to impress whoever shared the occupant's point of view as Elton did. His grievances lost their power as soon as he crossed the threshold.

Sermon led us to a leather sofa away from his desk, for the moment abdicating his throne. He pulled over a captain's chair for himself, his pant legs pulled up, his ruddy boots exposed.

"Are you ready for fun and games, my boy?"

"Andy, I can't afford fun and games. I'm wiped out."

Sermon frowned. "What you can't afford is the whine of defeat.

It's not what I expect from Elton Kramer."

"What do you expect? 'Happy Days Are Here Again?'"

"How about a good fight song, like 'Victors Valiant'?"

He plunged into the fired-up spiel that Elton had promised he would be immune to but that almost immediately re-enlisted him.

It was our luck to be swept into a roiling, dangerous time, almost word for word a description of time I once heard from Elton. Everything was on the table at bargain prices for investors with nerve.

"I got the nerve. I don't have the money."

"I'll tell you what you got. You got imagination, intelligence, ambition, and my support. That's capital enough. Do you think I'd let my boy hang out there by himself? Before we're done I'm going to see you standing four-square and solid." If necessary, he was prepared to cover Elton's initial expenses, a promise of assistance he'd never made before, never. "You'll come out of this a winner. I guarantee you." He wanted Elton to look through the clouds and see the bright future ahead. The development would be rescued. More capital would come on board. He was working on that now. Collapse? Only for the timid and weak of heart. He stood by his original assessment, the slump wouldn't last long and the downtown project would take off. He hadn't abandoned his holdings in Ponchartrain Associates. On the contrary, he'd been scooping up partner shares for almost nothing, acquiring as much as he could get. "Right now we'll let the construction rest and pay our debt with other business." He had projects lined up beyond the city limits, apartment complexes sprouting all the way to Ann Arbor and beyond to accommodate a white flight from the city, a flight that had barely started and would only intensify. "That's where the action is." He leaned over, gripped Elton's knee. "I believe in you, son. And I owe you. You brought Kate into my life." For the first time he looked at me. "I want her found and brought home."

I said that if she didn't want to be found I didn't want her found.

"She wants to be found all right. We're on her trail and I expect everyone to cooperate."

I said that was a project I wanted no part of and not to count on me.

He indicated to Elton with a toss of his head he wanted me out of the office. He had a project in mind he could only reveal in private,

Elton escorted me out. "I'm sorry, Gene. The two of you don't mesh. It's the wrong chemistry. I'll call you later."

"I'll be at work."

"I'll catch you there."

"Not if I can help it."

Once again he pleaded with me to stay on board and see him through this hard time. I was the only family he had other than Kate. "I took over your note. There's no pressure on you anymore. Trust me like you once did."

I admitted to Louise that I had agreed to stick by him until he had his legs under him.

She couldn't understand me. Why wasn't I outraged as she was? The man meant me no good. In witnessing his breakdown, I had done him an insult he wouldn't tolerate. "Appearance is everything to people like Elton. He'll do you in just because you witnessed his blubbering."

He'd been a lousy, disrespectful guest and she was right to be pissed off, but she made him out to be worse than he was.

"You're at a disadvantage with Elton Kramer."

"What disadvantage?"

"He can be ruthless, and you can't," this said as if the absence of ruthlessness was a defect.

My problem with Louise was that she offered her judgments without nuance or qualification. Even when she was right she irritated me.

She said, "I don't know what I see in you, and it makes me furious. I should tell you to clear out and go back to your cell."

"Say the word and I'll go gladly."

"I don't want you to be glad. I want you to stay here and be miserable."

I often stayed and wasn't miserable, but didn't give up my room.

NINE

White Flight

Elton reclaimed our office on Eight Mile Road and stripped it of any show, not masking its money-making design, no celebrities on the wall other than the small Eisenhower photo between crossed flags, hung there to pretend a mainstream loyalty.

He was at work for two weeks before he called me to join him.

I found the old Elton back in form, unapologetic and unremorseful. He declared the other Elton, the one who seemed humiliated and collapsed, a one-time aberration. "I'm on the rise again, kid."

I stayed just long enough to see him rise on the backs of clients, and then I quit for the last time.

We began by scouting what he called 'the field of battle.' We toured along Twelfth Street and saw stores with new identities, a kosher deli's Hebrew still dimly visible above a newly painted liquor store sign, a Star of David still engraved on a Baptist church façade, once a synagogue's. For a few blocks there were only black faces, for another few blocks an intermingling of black and white, then an all-white neighborhood.

He drove with the top down even though it was close to freezing. He kept working his horn, sounding the bugle mess call—*"Come and get your chow, boys, come and get your chow"*—no reason for it except to draw attention. I told him it was ironic that the man who dreamed of a real estate empire drove down streets like an ice cream vendor broadcasting a jingle to attract the kiddies, a way of selling ice cream, not houses.

"I broadcast Elkram Real Estate. If you're worried about being embarrassed you don't belong in the game."

"I don't belong, Elton. That shouldn't surprise you."

In the office, he asked, "What did we just see?" then answered his own question. We had seen the merging of black and white, the boundaries down, everything up for grabs. It was said as if everyone had a proprietary right to whatever could be grabbed. He was planting stakes, not this time in the countryside, but in a fully occupied city, a million and a half people elbowing for space.

He told me to pull up a chair and listen as he sat at his desk and combed through a list of homeowners in the Dexter-Linwood area. He found the man he wanted, S. Bernstein, on Cortland Street. Before dialing he asked if I knew the definition of integration he'd heard from his partner, John Murray.

I didn't know he had a partner.

He was working in collaboration with John Murray, a Negro real estate agent recommended to him by Andy Sermon. Murray provided him with names of possible Negro homebuyers.

"John Murray says, 'Integration is the time between when the first black moves in and the last white moves out.' Be proud of me, kid. I'm helping break down barriers, like you wanted."

"When did I say that's what I wanted?"

"Didn't you tell me you wanted the world opened up for your professor? That's what you asked me to do, right? Well, I'm opening it up."

He put the office phone on loudspeaker so I could listen to his *modus operandi,* which turned out to be his old hustle, updated to reflect the new real estate market. "This guy Bernstein is a power on the block. Get him moving and he'll lead the way."

"What way?"

"The way out, the way to the future."

He started with his usual announcement, "Elton Kramer, Elkram Real Estate here," and began his spiel.

Had Bernstein ever heard the expression 'white flight'?

Bernstein knew the expression, hated it, was tired of being pestered by real estate agents who'd been calling everyone on the block. "You called the wrong man this time, Mr. Kramer." He had no intention of taking flight. "I am here in this house on Cortland Street until they wrap me in my shroud. When I'm a corpse then you can move me, it will make no difference. While I am still breathing, we have nothing to discuss."

Elton told him not to hang up. It would be a big mistake. He had important information about Cortland Street that Bernstein needed to hear whether he moved or stayed.

"Do you offer me news out of the goodness of your heart, Mr. Kramer?"

"I have something to say that's for your advantage as well as mine."

Bernstein said two minutes, no more.

"Mr. Bernstein, you live in a great neighborhood, friends all around. I know the neighborhood. You couldn't ask for a better place to live. I've met the people you do business with on Dexter Avenue—Manny, the kosher butcher, Louie, the barber, the pharmacist at the George V drugstore, the nice woman at the Dexter Theater box office, the kids behind the counter at the ice cream parlor. I've met them all; good, friendly people. It's a terrific neighborhood. Kids roam free and you got no worries. Why should you even consider moving?"

Bernstein said that was right and Elton didn't know the half of it. "I have lived in the same house on the same street for twenty-five years. I tiled the kitchen counter, I put in the cabinets, I put on a new roof, I built the garage, I paved the driveway, all by myself. I put in a vegetable garden, I have beautiful fruit trees—plums and apples, even two persimmons. My boys always walked to school, rain or shine. Even when they were little ones, six years old, we didn't think twice letting them go everywhere by themselves. I have close friends all around me, and when I say 'close' I mean from when we were kids to when we are old men. I don't think of selling. For me to sell is to sell out and I am not a man who betrays his friends."

Elton denied he meant to push Bernstein to do what he didn't want to do. "Why should you move? You live where it's absolutely safe. I'd like to live on your street myself."

"I didn't say absolutely safe. It's only in paradise you are absolutely safe and I'm not yet ready for paradise."

"We don't get there until it's all over, right, Mr. Bernstein?"

"It used to be I didn't even lock my doors."

"You're a very lucky man. If you lived a few blocks away on Twelfth Street you couldn't make that claim. But you say you're now locking up?"

"I see changes, not so much here on Cortland, but not so far away."

"Does that worry you?"

"It bothers me a little, I admit."

"You have good reason to be bothered, Mr. Bernstein."

"It's not so serious but, yes, I see changes."

"A bigger change is coming that you are maybe not ready to admit." Elton then made him ready. He drew a picture of a neighborhood on the verge of radical change. It was happening fast. Homeowners a few blocks away were already in flight. Bernstein knew what they were flying from, didn't he? Otherwise why was he locking his doors, something he never used to do? "Let's be frank. Negroes are on Twelfth and Clairmont and aren't stopping there. We're not bigots, Mr. Bernstein. We know Negroes—don't we—good people, hoping just like you and me for a better life for their families? I have a Negro business partner who feels the same way I do. The trouble is, along with the good guys, there's a mob of not-so-good guys who make life hell on earth for everyone." It didn't matter how welcoming and big-hearted Bernstein was. If he remained on Cortland he would soon be alone among strangers, his family in jeopardy. "Your street is already leaking friends. It's happening as we speak. In a short time—I'm speaking of a very short time—no more than a few months—your home will lose its value. It will be almost worthless. Believe me, the best price you can get is right now. Right now you could sell and join your friends and neighbors on Seven Mile Road, or, to be really safe, even farther out, on the other side of Eight Mile Road, in Southfield, in Farmington, Bloomfield Hills, in a brand new home, on a brand new street, with brand new shopping, brand new cultural facilities, open spaces, parks, swimming pools, away from the race wars. Your friends will be there with you, believe me." Elton told Bernstein that with the sale of his Cortland Street house he'd be able to afford an upgrade to a completely secure neighborhood. "I'll tell you what you can get for your house today—not tomorrow—tomorrow's another story." He shocked Bernstein with his low estimate of the current value of his Cortland Street home.

"I don't believe it. It's worth maybe two times as much."

"It was worth two times as much and not so long ago, but the market for homes on your block has plunged and keeps going down fast. It's hard to admit, Mr. Bernstein. I know you put your heart and soul into your home, all that work—the tiling, the new roof, the garage—and you're still thinking what it was once worth. You got to face that there's not going to be a happy ending for Cortland Street. Your synagogue is moving to Southfield. And you heard, didn't you, that Boesky's Delicatessen is leaving Twelfth Street and another Boesky's is opening in Southfield? If a successful landmark like Boesky's decides to relocate, it's a warning you had better put on your walking shoes. I hate to tell you—I know it hurts—but your property is going down the drain. Who wants to buy into a battlefield? The fact is you don't have a choice. You're going to be moved one way or the other. Let it be your way, Mr. Bernstein, not someone else's. The time has come for tough decisions."

Bernstein said, enough, he didn't want to be pushed, but Elton didn't relent until Bernstein—his resistance eroding—was willing to consider what a half hour before he had refused to consider. He said he'd talk to his family and neighbors.

"That's what you need to do. Consult your family and neighbors. Talk it over. Open their eyes to what's happening. Look at it as an opportunity to begin a new and even better life together."

"I'll talk to them."

"That would be great. But it's urgent you get back to me before the market takes another dive. I'll send along papers so we can move fast after you decide. Then I'll show you and your friends great homes, Sermon three-bedrooms in a new development on the other side of Eight Mile Road, a swimming pool, a community center, a mall close by, a place where you'll be absolutely safe, even closer to paradise than you are now. Leaving Dexter is not the end of the world. You'll learn to love your new address as much as you loved Cortland Street."

It took Elton a little more than half an hour to make Bernstein question the neighborhood he had expected to be his final stopping place.

Elton said to me, "Once you get them talking—and Bernstein is a talker—they'll give you an opening. He tells me he's now locking his doors. That's all I needed to hear. Bernstein doesn't realize it but I got him."

"You're supposed to serve him, not 'get him.' "

"Are you pissed off, friend? You'll be even more pissed off when you hear me finish the deal. If Wayne hasn't made you entirely stupid, you'll come around."

He called Dr. Jackman, a Negro dentist, referred to him by John Murray. He told Jackman there was a house on Cortland Street, not yet on the market, but soon available, in move-in condition, three bedrooms, two baths, an oil furnace, a two-car garage, a deep yard, a new roof, an upgraded kitchen, a mature garden with fruit trees—plums, pears, apples, even persimmons—in walking distance of the best schools in the city and terrific Dexter Avenue shopping. Now was the time to make a bid before the house was put on the market and the price soared out of reach. He gave an estimate far beyond what he'd given Bernstein. He told Jackman he knew it was a stretch, but he would help with the financing. He reminded him that John Murray, an upstanding member of the Negro community, was his associate and would help carry the mortgage.

Dr. Jackman was interested and in little more than an hour, with no investment other than time, Elton had the prospect of as much as a four thousand dollar profit.

"You should applaud me, old pal. We're opening up Detroit like you wanted." Whites in flight would be transplanted to havens on the Detroit outskirts provided by Sermon and other developers.

Why did he want me to hear this?

"Tell me what you heard."

I heard him pry Bernstein from his home as if he were no more than a mussel, pulled from its rock, set in garlic, a little thyme, cooked in wine, the meat gouged from the opened shell, devoured, the shell cast aside. His appetite still unslaked, he then gouged the black dentist. What I heard was Elton Kramer fully recovered, his own heartless, ruthless self. He didn't need my help to do his dirty business.

"Kid, you got no ear. Every word of my pitch is true. I'm knocking down ghetto walls and liberating the oppressed. I'm informing Bernstein what the future of Detroit will be. It may not be the future he wants. It may not be the future you dream about. It's the future that's going to happen."

He came to the point of my being there. He was representing Professor Fuller and his wife. She wanted Gordon Pickering's house on Elmwood.

"She can't have Gordon's house. I told her that."

"She can have anything she can pay for."

"You're teasing her and tormenting him."

"Everything moves. Even the wrestler can be moved. And when his Queen Anne goes, the whole block opens up. And by the way, it will be my pleasure to torment that son-of-a-bitch."

I said it would be my pleasure to watch Gordon dump him into the compost when he dropped by to torment him.

"I'm not going to just drop by. Professor Fuller is your pal, isn't he? Didn't I hear you say Gordon told you to call?

"Asked me to call."

"Whatever. The guy likes you for some goddamn reason. Maybe he enjoyed tossing you into shit. Call him. Tell him I represent clients ready to make an offer. You don't have to tell him the guy's a Negro. Better not. Just tell him the buyer will go sky high. That's all you need to do. I'll take care of the rest."

"The man just lost his wife. Does he need more punishment? Haven't you done him enough damage?"

"What damage have I done him?"

"You conspired to take Kate from him. That's something he'll never forgive."

"I meant to bring up the subject of Kate. Ask him about Kate. That's a good subject. That'll open him up. Ask him, for instance, how she's doing."

"He doesn't know how she's doing. He has no idea where she is."

"He'd have to be blind and deaf and very, very dumb. She's in his kitchen, in his garden, in his bed."

"She's with her dad on Lake Michigan."

"She's with Gordon Pickering on Elmwood Street. Check it out then call the bastard. Tell him I'm coming with an offer. Let's move his big ass out of there."

I didn't call him, but I checked with the school and learned that Gordon was on bereavement leave. Then I watched them walking on Elmwood, loaded with groceries, and he looked hot and alive, out in the frigid damp with his EMU athletic jacket wide open, only a white cotton T-shirt beneath. There was a feel of quarrel in their distance from each other, he, two steps in front, turning to see that she was still on track, she, staring ahead. She gave nothing away, aloof and regal, no sign she was living a lie. They didn't look contented, but neither of them looked bereaved.

I warned Huston that Elton was focused on his own interest,

not his client's. His game was blockbusting.

Huston said he didn't need to be warned because he had no intention of buying the Pickering house or settling in Detroit. He'd made that clear to Marybeth. She was a little crazy; in fact, more than a little. "When she doesn't have any stage work she's prone to over-the-top goofiness." Without giving him a chance to say, "Don't do it," she'd presented him with the *fait accompli* of her pregnancy. "I have the prospect of a professorship in New York, exactly where I want to be, and where she needs to be if she has any real ambition to do something in the theater. Nesting is absolutely not in our interest. She wants a kid and she wants that damned Pickering house, even though I made it clear I will in no way be stuck in Detroit." He asked me to persuade her that buying Gordon's house was insane.

"Why should I persuade her?"

"You're my friend and you're in the business."

"No more."

I tried to dissuade her but she was absolutely determined. She said Elton's character was irrelevant. All she asked was that he get her the Queen Anne on Elmwood. As for Huston, she was sure he would come around. "I dream of my kid in that garden." The one-time Dionysus seemed to believe her dreams could make real life conform.

I told her there were gardens that conformed to her dreams, gardens elsewhere, no hassle gardens, in better neighborhoods, better for her kid, maybe not in Detroit, maybe somewhere outside New York City. To obsess about the Pickering garden was crazy.

"I'm crazy—didn't Huston tell you?"

TEN

Kate Going Home

Marybeth said she had made an offer Gordon couldn't refuse.

I said there was no offer Gordon couldn't refuse. The Pickering house was a Detroit original and Gordon was the caretaker of an important family history. I couldn't believe he'd sell the house, whatever he was offered.

"We told Gordon he could name his price, the sky's the limit. We'll take his house, warts and all, without inspection."

I didn't know the size of her inheritance, but I did know she wasn't rich enough to make a down payment on a limitless sky. The house was a decrepit, probably termite-ridden antique, not worth a sky-high offer.

She was ready to go sky high. "I told Elton Kramer to get me that house whatever it costs."

"A million, A billion? No limit?"

"Come on, Eugene. It has to be within reason."

Huston who had been listening, his eyes closed, his lips pursed, said, "Ay, there's the rub." The qualification, "within reason," made her offer meaningless. She had lost her reason. She was outside reason, not within. "No inspection?" She was absolutely nuts. She had dreamed up the innards of a home she had never entered, already redesigning the turret rooms, elaborating the garden, imagining her unborn child cavorting between rows of flowers. She was crazy about Gordon's house and Huston meant "crazy" literally. "Being reasonable" wasn't her stock in trade. She had been great as Dionysus because she had Dionysus inside her. "You can't bridle Dionysius." He usually loved that in Marybeth. She refused to be reined in by accepted custom and he usually didn't get in her way, but on this he wasn't going to yield. He had accepted the City College position. He was heading for New York. Nothing was going to change his direction. He had warned Marybeth that if she bought Gordon's house he wouldn't be there to live in it.

She asked him mockingly if he was threatening to abandon her.

"I'm leaving Detroit. I've accepted the New York job. I intend you to be there with me."

She had found the house of her dreams and was going to have it whatever the cost.

"The trouble with you, Marybeth, is that unlike normal folks you don't let your dreams dissipate when you wake up."

She couldn't be budged and he finally relented and agreed to accompany her to Gordon's house, but only to look over the property, not to support an offer.

He asked me to represent them. He knew that Elton was playing a devious game of blockbusting. "You know the game. Maybe you can keep us from getting screwed."

I knew Elton's game and the best advice I could give Huston was not to play it. "Stay away from Elmwood Street. Go on to New York."

He was my mentor, my academic father, and when he insisted that I represent them I said, yes, I would.

I was on Dexter Avenue, in the Elmwood neighborhood, a week or so before Hanukah and Christmas. The weather was miserable. A cold drizzle had been going on all day with something more severe threatening. Despite the weather there was a holiday feel to the neighborhood. The street was alive with shoppers; music was being pumped from stores. I was absorbed by the sights and sounds and didn't notice Gordon until it was too late to avoid him. I ducked into the Cunningham Drugstore and he followed me in. He was wearing his EMU jacket over a white T-shirt. His hair was soaked; also his tennis sneakers and his jean bottoms. I was weather-protected—a flannel-lined raincoat, a wool sweater, a scarf, a rain hat—but still I shivered. He saw the shivers and grinned.

"Enjoying the neighborhood, Smith? You got to love it. I've seen you hanging around. Think I didn't notice? Or are you spying on us, Smith?"

I said I knew the neighborhood from my real estate days and I often wandered around Dexter. It was an interesting neighborhood.

He didn't care what I was doing on Dexter Avenue. The streets were free, no toll charges. "Maybe you'll hit the jackpot and run into Kate. That's what you really love about the neighborhood, isn't it, Smith, that you might run into Kate?"

I said, not at all. I wasn't spying.

He knew I was obsessed with Kate. He didn't fault me for it. It was an obsession we shared. "It's your tough luck that she's mine. Anyway, she's too old for you, Smith." It was stated as simple fact, meant to provoke, but he softened it with a laugh as if he were kidding.

I said I had a claim on Kate myself. "I was part of her family for eight years."

"One of her boys," he said, and laughed, "Well, lucky you."

He invited me into the nearby ice cream parlor to talk. "It'll get us out of the wet. We'll pretend it's summer and I'll buy you a soda." I told him it wasn't summer weather, no ice cream for me. Eggnog would be more appropriate.

"You're in luck. They got eggnog."

"With a jigger of cognac?"

"Not in this ice cream parlor. Don't press your luck, Smith."

I couldn't decipher his mood. He was an affable, joking Gordon, someone I hadn't experienced before, his ebullience out of character. I was reluctant to go with him but I felt trapped and we entered the ice cream parlor in the afternoon of a winter day, and sat on ice cream chairs, our knees almost joining under the small faux-marble circular table, and ordered eggnogs. The place was almost empty. There were four high-school students at the counter, evidently friends of the cute, white-uniformed server.

He asked what I liked about the Dexter neighborhood.

I told him it had the feel of a village community, an important quality for a one-time orphan.

"Right. Dexter is a village for orphans. They gather the dispossessed, pile them in and call it a village. I got no problem with that. It's not a Pickering village but it used to be. A generation ago we owned Elmwood. Now the only Pickerings left are ghosts. I live in a haunted house, Smith. We agree, don't we, that that's no way to live? I've had it with ghosts, Smith, and I'm saying bye-bye to all the fucking dead Pickerings."

The kids at the counter turned to stare.

He was very high, and didn't need prodding to talk about Marybeth's offer. He was selling the ancestral home. He needed the money. He was quitting Central High, quitting teaching, and relocating with Kate. They would dump the baggage of the past—all the misery and despair—and live together in rural Michigan, refurbished Adams and Eves, "sinless in Eden"—that's how he put it, "sinless in Eden," a lyrical flourish I didn't expect from Gordon, followed by gleeful laughter. He was dumping history, he said. The Pickerings were founders of a stove company, North American-Windsor Stoves, once a major Detroit manufacturer. They passed themselves off as old Detroit but there was nothing old in Detroit, only an accumulation of beginnings. A few small wars expropriated the Indians, the rest ordinary stuff. When Henry Ford and his crowd thrust the city into the future they made the Pickerings irrelevant but that didn't stop the Pickerings from claiming an undeserved aristocracy. "The pretentious snobs built a house for snobs." He was done with that bullshit. He was cutting loose from the Pickering line and hooking up with Kate's people. There were no snobs among the Wymans. They were farmers and fishermen whose recorded history was no more than a list of names in the back of a family Bible. He bellowed, "Better farmers and fishermen than us. Fuck the Pickerings!" startling the high school kids who had seemed amused by Gordon, giggling quick looks, before he showed he was explosive. Now they hunched over their ice cream and avoided looking.

He said he and Kate would move near her father and settle on undeveloped land. Her father had once made do with a few hundred acres, a pair of mules, a cow, chickens, and, later in the game, an ancient tractor and a Model A Ford pickup. Gordon would learn from the old man how to build an unblemished, sinless beginning.

I interrupted his flow with a slower tempo, hoping to calm him down. I'd considered a new beginning myself but I was a cautious man and played it safe, tightly perched on my roost. I didn't need to be high in the roost. I could be low and safe and content.

He grabbed my arm and squeezed. "Get off your perch, Smith. Jump. Take the risk. I guarantee, you'll feel terrific." His grip was powerful and I was hurting when he released me.

I got up to leave. I said I was glad we'd talked. We'd see each other again in two days. Did he know I was representing the Fullers who were making an offer on his house?

"They're Elton Kramer's people?"

"And mine."

"I'll be waiting for you, Smith. You'll be a spectator at the Pickering demolition. You, me, and Kate."

When I left, he was finishing our eggnogs and seemed a joyful man. I heard my father's voice in his jazzy turbulence and hoped Kate wouldn't be around when he jumped from his perch.

I finished teaching my last German class in early afternoon. I met Louise in the corridor of Old Main and told her I might be home late. The Fullers were making an offer for Gordon Pickering's house and I had agreed to be their informal agent. There might be paperwork, but I hoped not. It would be fine with me if the deal fell through and I came home early.

She couldn't understand why anyone would be involved in real estate at Christmas, a time for families to cozy up. A snowstorm was forecast and she wanted me home to get cozy with her.

I promised I'd be home before the storm. "Keep the soup on simmer."

I arrived a half hour early and parked a block from Gordon's house. I wanted to see Kate before the others arrived. The sky was heavy, on the verge of snow, but snow didn't trouble me. I welcomed snow. It would complete the holiday presence. There were lighted candelabra in windows. Trees were strung with lights. There were garlands of holly on doors, holiday messages in windows. Families were out on benign Elmwood Street, parents arriving home loaded with packages. Kids were gathered on corners after their last school day before the vacation. Elton was assured of a large audience for the show he meant to put on, a show featuring Huston Fuller, a black man, coming to Elmwood Street with a real estate agent in tow.

I thought I was in luck when I saw Kate emerge from Gordon's house, very Christmassy herself, in a dark blue overcoat and a red beret, a green scarf tucked into her coat, secured around her throat, and flipped over her shoulder. I imagined the wonderful smell of her. She was dragging a large suitcase to the edge of the porch, ready for takeoff. I shouted from across the street, "Kate! Hold on. Let me help you."

Gordon burst from the house, naked to the waist, in his jeans. He grabbed her suitcase, wrenched it from her. He raised the suitcase as effortlessly as he once raised me, and threw it and it burst open on the sidewalk. He was weeping all out, a recently joyful big man, broken down to something almost child size, "Damn you, Kate! Damn you and damn your father!" He tore back into the house. She had started downstairs for the spilled stuff, she stopped and twisted to show him her grief and lost her balance. She caught at the railing, and staggered down the stairs and flopped. She lay face down on the sidewalk.

I knelt to lift her, but she struggled to rise on her own, first on her knees, then braced on the porch steps. She looked clumsy and old and injured and pitiable. I gave her a tissue for her tears and held her steady until she recovered her balance. Her right cheek was scraped. Blood oozed from a cut near her left temple.

A worried schoolboy and his mother brought over stuff that had spilled.

"Thank you," she said, accepting a hairbrush and lipstick and other toilet articles they placed in the suitcase. "You're very kind." She glanced at the door, perhaps expecting Gordon to reappear. "I need to go," she told me.

The neighbors helped gather the clothes and load the suitcase. I couldn't get it closed and she told me not to bother. "Put it in my trunk. Let's just leave." She accepted another tissue, wiped her eyes, blew her nose, and in a firmer voice said, "Let's leave now. Please, Eugene." She was parked in front and I wrestled the open suitcase into the car trunk.

The bruise on the side of her forehead, near her temple, was turning purple. She asked me to drive. "I can't right now manage." I found the key in her purse. I helped her into the passenger seat.

As we left I heard Elton's horn, blocks away, bugling the mess call, summoning the neighborhood. "Come and get your chow, boys, come and get your chow."

She told me to drive toward Grand River. When we reached Grand River I pulled over and asked where she wanted to go.

She lay back against the headrest, her eyes closed. She murmured, "I'm dizzy. Give me a minute, Eugene."

I wanted to take her to the nearby Grace Hospital emergency room.

"That's not necessary. I'm just very tired. Let me rest a moment, and I'll be fine."

We stayed parked for fifteen minutes, the engine running, the heater on, sleet hitting the windshield.

She said, now calm, that her father was dying. "He called for me to be with him for our last Christmas."

I told her she had to see a doctor. The injury near her temple might need stitches.

She repeated that it wasn't necessary. "I've suffered worse. I don't have time for a doctor." Her father was on an island in Lake Michigan, near Traverse City, staying at a cottage, near where their old farm used to be. Only the barn remained, leaning on one side, slats missing, the roof caved in. She had to be in Traverse City by early morning.

"That's impossible. Traverse City is six hours from here."

She had tried to leave hours ago but Gordon wouldn't let her go. He said she was leaving him and she said, "Yes, Gordon, I am," and he exploded with rage and grief, bitter and heartbroken. He begged, he wept; he threatened to hit her, threatened to kill himself. Her dying father had implored her, "Come to me," and she had to go.

I told her to drive there in the morning. She wasn't fit to drive tonight.

She said tomorrow would be too late. The island mail boat, the only transport, left in the early morning.

"Take a later boat."

"That's the last one for two weeks."

"Call your dad. Tell him you'll be delayed."

"The only phone is in the lodge a mile away and doesn't work in weather like this. I tried but he can't be reached."

"Why is an old, sick man so isolated?"

"He lives on the mainland. He wanted to end where the farm used to be and is on the island."

She said she was dizzy and her vision blurred. She said she'd stop at a pharmacy and get aspirin and ice and Band-Aids and she'd be fine.

I warned her not to drive. "What good will you do your father if you crash?"

She said she was going to rest a minute until her mind cleared. She closed her eyes and didn't move for several minutes, then opened her eyes and spoke calmly. She had a great favor to ask. It was an enormous imposition and if I turned her down she would understand. "I can't bear the thought of him dying alone. It means everything to be with my father for our last Christmas. I'm still fuzzy and driving would be very difficult. I need your help, Eugene."

"How can I help?"

"Drive me to Traverse City."

A five- to six-hour trip at night in bad weather? Impossible. I was a novice driver, without any experience night driving.

She said she understood and would drop me at a bus stop and go on by herself.

"You'll kill yourself."

"I don't have a choice."

As always, her agenda became my agenda. I said I'd drive her. I said it at first glumly. I had no idea what I was getting myself into. Then I jumped off my roost and told her I'd love driving her. I was excited by the idea. It wasn't an imposition. I'd finally have her to myself. I wanted to discover this new Kate Wyman—hurt, vulnerable, less a guide, more in need of guidance. I'd stay overnight in a hotel and bring her to the boat in the morning and return home by bus. What did I have to lose? "It's settled. I'm driving." Later I'd call Louise and beg to be forgiven. I would have to do penance but I'd be forgiven, and if not I could bear the loss.

She said I wouldn't have to stay in a hotel. She'd put me up in her father's vacant cabin outside Traverse City.

I felt wide awake, everything possible, even what was impossible.

We stopped at a convenience store where she had me buy a

large bag of ice cubes, an ice bag, aspirin, antiseptic ointment, Band-Aids, and small bottles of seltzer water. She washed down the aspirin and applied ice to the left side of her face. I patched her forehead with Band-Aids. She directed me to the road that aimed us past Flint, Saginaw, Bay City, and Midland toward Traverse City. She said she'd try to keep me company as long as she could. She was very tired. She'd had little sleep these past days. We'd put Gordon and Elmwood Street out of mind. We'd put aside everything that had happened this day. We'd talk about happier times. She'd tell me a little about her life on the island, before the orphanage.

We began the night driving in cold, drizzly weather. The drizzle changed to flurries of snow. By the time we reached the countryside we were in a full-scale snowstorm. The weather that alarmed me didn't worry her. She said winter on her family's farm had always been a magical time. She loved the pervasive sweet-sour smell of wood smoke, the snowy fields bounded by pine and cedar and beech and hemlock, ice-skating on the pond. She even loved the chores that took her to the barn after dark. She loved the sound and smell and feel of animals. Her dad lost the farm in the Great Depression. She had already left with her mother two years before when she was fourteen years old. Life on the island, she said, was heaven.

I concentrated on the road and barely noticed when she started to fade.

"Forgive me. I can't stay awake. I have to sleep." She curled into her seat, the ice bag to her cheek, and was instantly asleep. I touched her throat and she was unresponsive. The intensity of her sleep worried me. I thought of turning back to Grace Hospital, but I kept driving.

Traffic flared into view, igniting falling snow, and at first I drove cautiously. Cars came fast behind, flicked brights, honked, veered sharply in front of me. There was no relief from traffic until the night deepened. The snowfall became heavier, wipers swinging full speed. Two hours from the city we were almost alone on the road, among the few travelers who hadn't reached shelter. She slept, the ice bag fallen away. I prodded her and she sighed but didn't wake up. I was alone in unfamiliar, barely visible country. At a forking intersection, signs blanked by snow, I bore to the right, unsure I'd chosen the Traverse City route until we approached town lights and a sign pointed me to Bay City. I stopped for gas, shook her, asked if she needed to use the restroom. She groaned and twisted, but couldn't be roused.

I called Louise from an outside phone booth.

She'd been on the verge of reporting me as missing. What had happened to me? Where was I?

"Near Lake Michigan."

She was infuriated and had a right to be. Her intuition led her directly to Kate. "Are you with her?"

"I'll explain when I get back."

It was Louise who told me about Gordon Pickering. All Detroit had news of Gordon Pickering. She had watched the Pickering house burn on the late news. It would have been consumed but for the snowstorm. As it was, most of the damage was confined to the rear façade. It was a historic house, a Detroit original. The Pickerings, in the stove business, were identified as a once-prom-

inent Detroit family, diminished by hard times. The house blazed
in falling snow, the street jammed with fire equipment, the fire
brought under control after a spectacular show. There was no sign
of Gordon Pickering.

She wanted to know why I was with Kate.

"I need to be."

"You don't need to be."

"I want to be."

"Then stay with her and don't bother coming back."

I returned from the restroom. Kate still slept and I drove on,
caught in the rhythm of driving, more driven than driving, towns
shutting down as we passed through, gas stations and restaurants
going dim, motel welcome signs turned off. Tunnels of forest
sucked up our light. I drove fast and didn't slow down until, past
the Midland cut-off, our light froze a deer in the road. I swerved
and braked, the car whipped around and skidded to a stop. She
woke up and we watched the stag with massive antlers strut
through falling snow and vanish into the forest.

She said, "He's beautiful."

"He almost killed us."

She asked where we were.

We had passed Midland half an hour before.

"What time is it?"

It was past midnight. I asked how she felt.

"Much better."

It was a relief to have her awake.

We stayed at the side of the road, motor running, lights on,
snow falling, wiper blades swiveling fast. I didn't know how to tell

her about Gordon's house and so didn't.

She asked how I was holding up.

I was beyond tired. My eyes were tired, my arms were tired, my back was tired. I could barely remember the start of the day, yet, despite the fatigue, I was eager to keep going. I was with her and that was enough.

She took more aspirin, refilled the ice bag, pressed it to her face. Her headache had eased. Her vision was almost restored. She promised not to fade. She'd stay awake and guide me to her father's house. We started again for Traverse City.

She said the appearance of the stag brought back memories of the island and her father. She associated the island with animals. They had a milk cow, a heifer, two mules, geese and chickens and cats and a dog. The only wild animals were deer and raccoons. These were all ordinary animals, not the exotic animals her father summoned up for her. He was usually unexpressive, met the grind and tedium of working an increasingly unproductive farm with uncomplaining stoicism; but at night, especially in winter when he had more time, he showed another side. After dinner, the chores done, he went to a porch that he'd insulated and heated with a Franklin wood stove. He sat at a plank table under an intense fluorescent lamp. He worked with packets of drawing pens and sharp, pastel pencils, copying *National Geographic* photos of tropical animals—blazing mandrills, mouths gaping, fangs exposed; sprawled lions whose golden brown manes he penned hair by hair; silverback gorillas, buzzards with fire-red wattles and white collars, leopards, tigers, macaws, jaguars. His drawings were vibrant and alive, not mere reproductions. He sold a few to small-town journals. He was paid enough to replenish his art supplies. She could imagine his animals roaring and shrieking and howling. She was his exclusive witness. It was a powerful, unspoken connection between father and daughter. She sat close by doing schoolwork, looking up to see a mere line of color extend and amplify into a screaming mandrill. She didn't know where the tropical interest came from. He had huge, callused hands that seemed unfit for delicate work, and yet he managed the minute detailing of tropical animals, and, to amaze her, animals and half-humans that never existed, dragons and griffins and centaurs and satyrs. When she read of the god Vulcan in her *Child's Book of Greek and Roman Myths*, it was her father she imagined, inarticulate but with god-gifted hands and an unreliable wife. Their communion on the winter porch ended when she was fourteen years old. She left for the mainland with her mother. He stayed on the island two years longer until the farm was lost, then followed them, but too late. Now he was dying, no more tropics in him, and he wanted her and she wouldn't disappoint him again.

"How did you disappoint him?"

"I left with Mother. He begged me not to go. He said there would be no coming back."

I asked why her mother left.

"She wasn't meant for island life."

"What life was she meant for?"

"My mother committed suicide when I was sixteen years old. Enough," she said and stopped talking.

The snow ended and the freeze intensified. The side windows iced up and I kept the wipers going to clear pie sections of the windshield. We passed the Traverse City exits and continued up the Leelanau Peninsula through snow-carpeted dune country that glittered in occasional moonlight. We stayed on the edge of the vast lake and it was almost two in the morning when we entered Leland, a cluster of cottages and smokehouses and fish shanties at the juncture of Lake Michigan and the Leland River. I could hear the lake icing up in the aftermath of the storm.

It could have been a town of the dead. There was no evidence of life. The storm had cancelled the electricity. The only light was from our headlights, drab, weathered shanties coming briefly into view, then blanked out. We maneuvered through a jumble of dark, irregular streets, unable to read addresses. We moved at a crawl, staying within the limits of our light, while she tried to find her father's house. She didn't know the house, but had its description and that turned out to be enough.

At a cul-de-sac near the river, we lit up a cottage elaborately shingled in ovals and crescents, painted in circus colors—blues, reds, and yellows—spectral in car light, vivid and garish when I later saw the house in frozen sunlight. I aimed our headlights at the door while she fumbled with the key. She asked me to take over and gave me the key. I opened to a pitch-black interior. I found a kerosene lamp and matches on a bedside table. I lit the lamp, lit a wood stove already prepared with paper and kindling and a few wedges of split cordwood. I went back to the car and turned off the headlights. She'd asked if I'd get her nightgown and a few toilet articles from the suitcase—they were on top—but she didn't need the suitcase. It was open, a mess. "Leave it in the trunk."

When I returned, I found her staring at a thick, yellow and black-banded serpent that girdled the rooms and bound them together. I held the lantern high and followed the snake around doors and windows until its gaping mouth almost joined the tail above the entrance.

She said it was too much, she couldn't take it all in, she had to lie down. She barely made it to the bed. She lay on the thick feather comforter still in her coat and beret. I helped her sit up. I helped her out of her coat. I pulled off her shoes. I helped her stand while I turned back the comforter. She wanted to put on her nightgown. I could see only the ghost of her in the flickering lamplight, the ghost as lovely as I'd imagined.

She apologized for not washing but she didn't have the strength.

I said there was no hot water anyway.

She was instantly asleep.

I lay down on the other edge, under the comforter, coat and shoes off. I thought it would be impossible to sleep until abruptly I slept and when I awoke the lamp was out, the stove almost out, and it was freezing and we were together. I held her in a haze of fatigue and ardor. It was nothing I intended, nothing I was prepared for, nothing I could keep from doing. She slept through my silent, choked effort at control and when I whispered, "I love you," and lost control she sighed and still slept and I've spent a lifetime trying to decipher her sigh.

I left the bed, put on my coat and shoes, huddled in an arm-chair. I'd changed what had needed to be unchangeable; everything had shifted, the world no longer familiar. I wanted to be rid of myself. It was five in the morning; there would be no traffic. I wouldn't be able to find a ride. I couldn't take her car. I'd walk in icy sludge in my street shoes. A few turns in the dark and I'd be lost, unable to find my way back. I returned to bed on my edge, a ridiculous, out-of-control fool, not expecting to sleep, but again I slept and woke up shivering in a cloud of color, the sun pouring through the east-facing window. Kate wasn't there. I saw what the farmer saw every morning when he awoke and every night when he went to bed. The snake held a lady in its mouth, not the entire lady, only her head. There was either clumsiness in the portrait or deliberate ambiguity and I couldn't tell if she was being devoured or was herself the face of the snake. She resembled Kate but couldn't have been Kate, who had been fourteen when he last saw her—this was not the face of a fourteen-year-old. I guessed I was looking at Kate's mother, who had been placed in the mouth of the serpent. The grief and venom in that portrait was impossible to be with.

Kate was gone and so was her car.

She'd left a note on the table addressed to "Dear Eugene." She said I'd been wonderful and she'd never be able to thank me enough. She told me a shuttle bus stopped at a diner a block away. It would take me to the Greyhound in Traverse City. She wrote, "I don't have the strength to say what I want to say. I love you, thank you. I'll be in touch."

I parsed every word of her note to find signs of my future. "I love you," was a way of ending a letter. And the "Thank you" stripped the love claim of any force. Could she be aware of what happened in the night and yet still say, "Thank you?" She wrote, "Dear Eugene," a motherly expression, not a lover's. She said, "I'll be in touch," and that was vague and uncommitted. And what would she have said if she'd had the strength?

I learned at the diner that the boat for North Manitou was to have left a half hour before. The dock was nearby. I saw her car in the parking lot. The boat was still in sight, a small barge, backed from the dock, maneuvering to turn, leaving a trail of splintered thin ice. She was at the railing, waiting for the boat to complete its swing; she would then be in position to search the horizon for the island. She wore a full-length tan parka she must have found in the cottage, the hood up, a scarf wrapped over the gaps, her face almost covered. I waved and yelled but she didn't respond. The boat completed its swing and aimed for the invisible island.

The schedule and rates were posted next to the ticket-booth window. The boat was on a changed schedule after Thanksgiving. It made the round trip every two weeks.

I kept watch until the boat diminished to a tiny wedge on the horizon and then melded with the water. My coat and shoes were inadequate to the weather. I didn't have a scarf, hat, or gloves. I wasn't wearing a tie. I gripped the coat, shivering, while I watched the boat disappear. Thin ice reformed behind the boat. It was the earliest freeze anyone in Leland could recall; so I was told at the diner. I was told that, in the past, severe winters had made ice thick enough to support a car on the twelve-mile drive to the island, but no one could remember a freeze so early in the year.

I ordered eggs and bacon, hash browns and toast. I ate a mouthful, then barely made it to the john, where I threw up. The illness came on full blown.

I took the shuttle to Traverse City and spent seven fevered

hours on a Greyhound bus. Louise picked me up at the station and brought me to her home and tended me there. When I emerged from sickness a week later I found Bernstein had sold, Jackman had bought. ELKRAM REAL ESTATE placards were staked everywhere. Elton's fortune was on the way to being restored.

AFTERWORD

I followed Louise to New York, almost rootless, almost free floating, tethered only by Louise, and later by the job I got through
Huston. It was years before I saw Detroit again. I returned to an
unfamiliar city, gripped in a spiderweb of freeways, neighborhoods
blotted out by fire. Tuchler's rooming house and my rat hole were
absorbed into the Wayne campus. A riverfront development had
incorporated what had been our own riverfront project. The Fullers' apartment, where Marybeth and I once danced, had disappeared. Only the building's foundation remained, half-hidden in
a weed-choked field.

Detroit itself seemed to me devolved, its population almost
halved and still declining, a hint of something both retrograde
and original in its composition.

I saw Elton on my last day in Detroit. He insisted we meet for
lunch at the London Chop House. "1:00," he said. Too late, I said.

I was driving to San Francisco to meet Louise in our new home. I had to rent a trailer and pick up furniture Louise had put in storage, big pieces too large for our New York apartment. I faced a long solo drive and had another stop to make. Then 12:30, he said. I said 11:00 at the latest and he said, "Make sure the restaurant is open that early and I'll meet you there." I waited in the restaurant until almost noon and was about to leave when the maitre d' gave me a message that Elton was on his way. He arrived closer to his time than mine.

No knobs on him now. He was sleek and classy, from the manicured nails, rings, French cuffs, and tailored suit, to the marvelous hair that topped him.

"You know the note you turned over to me? Know what you'd be worth if you'd hung on to that note? Another quarter of a million."

I told him to enjoy it. I didn't want it.

Elton was clearly developed. He wanted me to understand that. The one-time orphan had succeeded the retired god as chairman of Elkram-Sermon, Inc. and was now himself god, or so he wanted me to believe. His projects took him out of Detroit, to the Middle East, the Far East, and South America. In the face of his vast demolition and construction, moral questions were pointless. He was the developer of worlds. Whatever world you could pay for, Elton was ready to create. If you wanted a world erased he'd rub out any trace of what had been, and provide a new-minted past. Yet, he still clung to a remnant of his own past. He had traced Kate to the island. It was to become a national park, stripped of residents, reduced to what was presumed to be an approximation of its original state, before deer or deer hunters had crossed over, before even the Pottawatomies and Ottawas had found the island and made their fires and planted their potatoes. Kate was long gone.

He asked, "Where is she?"

I received an annual card with no return address, only Hallmark information and an added, "Love, Kate." It let me know I wasn't forgotten.

He wanted the card. He had the means to decipher it. He'd locate her even without an address.

"Not if I can help it." She was where she wanted to be, out of touch, out of sight, beyond demolition.

My last stop was Elmwood Street. I knew that the fire-damaged house had been restored by Marybeth and that she didn't have to go sky high to buy it from Gordon. According to Elton it took less than an hour for Gordon to agree to everything. Gordon was desperate to get away, and it was an easy and important sale. Gordon took the cash and ran for the backwoods. A copy of the closing papers was sent to an address somewhere in North Michigan.

Marybeth converted the Queen Anne turret into a child's space, a playroom connected to a second-floor bedroom. She imposed her vision on the garden, a labyrinth of flowers and bushes and fruit trees. Then, three years later, everyone settled in the house of her dreams, she abandoned her house and family. She told Huston motherhood wasn't enough. It was a defiant, unalterable decision; she left her husband and her child for minor stardom in Cleveland, Ohio. She told Huston she'd be back. Huston said, "Not if I can help it."

"Abandoned," that's how Huston described it. "Anchored me and then took off."

I phoned when I heard they'd split. Huston was terse and bitter. She'd joined a Cleveland repertory theater. He called her a sick woman, a monster. He had no forgiveness. A sick woman. The bitch. No return for her. He was adamant. At first he didn't allow her to visit the child. Eventually she took up house in Cleveland with a playhouse director. She made no apologies; she didn't beg to be allowed home. Huston grudgingly gave me a few details. When I pressed for information, he said, "I can't talk anymore."

"Can't?"

"Won't," and hung up.

I gave him time to simmer down and phoned again a couple of weeks later. I told him I didn't want us to drift apart. He was important to me. I had the New York job because of him. I was shaped by his ideas. He had given me the direction I needed and I was forever grateful. "Forever," I said, not yet experienced enough to know that "forever" didn't last very long.

He said his ideas had changed and we were no longer headed in the same direction. I asked why the coldness and he blew up, "I don't need to answer goddamn questions about the past. It's gone, for Christ sake." I told him he didn't sound like the Huston I knew. He said, "I am not the Huston you knew," and cut me off again. I stopped calling and we remained out of touch until I showed up in Detroit almost eight years later.

I called to tell him I was in town. After a long pause he said,

"Come on over." I drove through the city, passing through sad, devastated neighborhoods on my way to Huston. I saw boarded-up buildings and burned-out buildings and gaps where there was no longer evidence of buildings and was prepared for disaster when I rounded the corner onto Elmwood Street. The block was intact. There were no empty lots with overgrown weeds and alien, snake-like trees. The lawns and gardens were neatly tended, the sidewalks swept. At the center, standing alone and anchoring the block, was the Pickering Queen Anne, luminous in vivid, joyful colors. The gazebo looked ready to pump out calliope music.

The angel of death had passed over this part of Elmwood. I met a smiling Huston, waiting on the porch. He looped his cane over his forearm, spread his arms, and with a boisterous laugh, said "Come to Papa," teasing me for once having called him "my academic father," and welcomed me into his embrace.

He had aged. He still seemed unbent, but needed a cane for balance. He was retired from Wayne State, had never managed to get away, and no longer had any academic ambition or resentment. That was a life he had discarded. There was no sign of bitterness. He loved his house on Elmwood Street. It was alive with music and dancing. The entirely black neighborhood was secured by his house. He was the unofficial King of Elmwood, and this was his only office. He pointed to his white hair. "I have become an *Emeritus Gris.*"

He could now speak easily about Marybeth. His great living room, with fifteen-foot high ceilings, included, in one corner, somewhat obscured by an armchair, the nude painting of Marybeth. "For our kid," he said. Marybeth visited every few weeks, stayed with them. There was no rancor or desire on his part, no resentment. He was temperamentally unsuited for resentment. Her stays had become more prolonged. He didn't entirely rule out her coming back. Whatever grievances he had were trivial compared to the gift she had left him. He was grateful to Marybeth, could I believe it? She had brought Nora into his life. Nora was now eight years old, a slender, olive-colored kid with a bushel of jet-black curls and a butterfly agility. "And her eyes..." Huston rolled his eyes. "You get lost in Nora's eyes." He said he was transformed by his feeling for his daughter, a feeling he could never have anticipated. She was his love. She was his joy. She was his hope for the future. He corrected himself. "She is my belief in the future," and roared, "Nora! Come meet my son, Eugene." She flitted down from her tower into the room, delayed for a moment, studied me, said, not so much mocking as teasing, "Are you his son? You don't look like him."

"I only wish," I said, "because if I were his son that would make me your brother. You are beautiful. Will you adopt me?"

"I don't have time. Bye," she said, smiled, waved and flitted away.

I left my city with a U-Haul trailer hitched behind. I rented the U-Haul near the storage place on Plymouth Road. The major piece we had in storage was the bed Louise had inherited from her grandparents. It was enormous. The mahogany headboard was topped by a pineapple finial. The boards were broad, solid mahogany. The footboard, curving into the sideboards, was shaped like the stern of a ship; when we were aboard that ship